FINDING A HERO

MORE TALES OF SWORD AND SORCERY: BOOK 2

JOHN RICKS

FINDING A HERO
MORE TALES OF SWORD AND SORCERY: BOOK 2

iUniverse books may be ordered through booksellers or by contacting:

iUniverse
1663 Liberty Drive
Bloomington, IN 47403
www.iuniverse.com
1-800-Authors (1-800-288-4677)

ISBN: 978-1-5320-9508-5 (sc)
ISBN: 978-1-5320-9507-8 (e)

Library of Congress Control Number: 2020905458

Print information available on the last page.

iUniverse rev. date: 03/20/2020

Foreword

Book 2 of Fantasy Short Stories

In the days of Dragons and Magic, Demons and Undead, Elves and Pixies there were times when man was not the best of creatures. Sometimes the good did not outnumber the bad and nothing was as it seemed. Then again, is this not true of every age on every planet?

Book two describes some of the issues. In most stories, there is good and evil. Only you can determine which is which. It depends on which way your tendencies lean.

Bio

John Ricks was born in Longview Washington and moved thirteen times before he finished middle school. After graduating high school he joined the Navy where he spent twenty more years traveling the world meeting new and astonishing people. His degrees, extensive reading, and travel have helped him see all life in a wonderfully different way. He developed a great sense of fantasy and loves to tell tall stories.

Acknowledgments

This book is dedicated to bacon, good on everything.
- John B. Ricks
Fremont, California
Dec. 2019

CONTENTS

PALADIN

THEY STOOD UPON THE LITTLE HILL LOOKING OUT ON the battlefield wearing blood-stained armor that made them look nearly demonic. Yet one was stained more than all the rest. The dents and cuts in his armor and body bespoke of recent action in the middle of combat surrounded by the enemy, yet he stood there tall and straight with a look that demanded all stay the battle as he surely would. His presence gives strength to our arms and gives us the will to carry on when any sane man would have given up. Defiant against evil, concerned for his men, but clear of eye, he scanned the battlefield checking every knot of fighters for something. Then his entire stance changed and he yelled, "To the KING! He still lives!" He ran straight down the hill at breakneck speed and two hundred worn, tired, bloodied, and broken men followed him into battle with renewed hope and vigor. They ran down the hill and onto the battlefield never slowing but constantly yelling, "To the king! To the King!"

The cry drew the attention of another hundred or more men and they joined the run. Nothing could stand in the way of the Paladin as he led his men into the battle once again. He ran right through groups that were fighting and cut the enemy down like wheat. The three hundred men that quickly became four hundred, finished killing the rest of the enemy and picked up anyone that could move. "To the King!" Soon the numbers were five and then six hundred. The Paladin drew men to him like hungry dogs smelling victory in the hunt.

He reached the King and took up the front of the line forcing the enemy back and telling the Clerics to heal the badly wounded King and remove him from battle. Then he drove into the enemy with a courage born of his God and a will to not disappoint the God he loved more than life itself. He prayed out loud as he burst through the enemy and ran at their King. "Valoris, grant me this victory. Let me taste the blood of evil with the edge of blade once again. Guide my arm to strike true and strong. You own my soul, you have my heart, my spirit is yours, and if I die on this field today I die a happy man to know that I died in the service of your love."

The men cheered and ran ahead of the Paladin with renewed stamina as if the God himself were in them giving them strength. They tore into the evil King's protectors and cleared then out of the path of the Paladin.

Running full on with sword in both hands the Paladin came at the King standing there without concern. Knowing he was protected by his Witch. Knowing nothing could harm him. As the Paladin's blade came down the Paladin and blade turned into pure energy and cut through the King's blade, his mighty armor, the Witch's protections, and down into the earth. The evil King was dead and the Paladin disappeared.

He reappeared at the edge of another battle on the same field and he instantly cut through the backs of the enemy yelling so that they would know to turn and fight him face to face. When he finally cut through to the center he found the Prince badly wounded and picked him up and carried him running through the battle to the Clerics and gently set him down. Then he disappeared.

He reappeared in front of the enemy's champion; a supernaturally large giant that had laid to waste most of the King's army. Many of the men fled in fear of the creature. The Paladin yelled up to the Giant as it started to move toward another knot of combatants, "Stand and fight creature of evil."

The giant rose a foot to stomp the Paladin and the Paladin stood his ground. He quickly picked up two iron pikes, dropped on the ground by fallen comrades, and stood them up. As the foot came down it impaled itself on the pikes. The Paladin rolled out of the way as the Giant screamed in anger. It pulled out the pikes but took several cuts from the Paladins sword while doing so. The Paladin's sword was the only one to cut him in this battle. Nothing else could penetrate his thick hide and that enraged the Giant even more. He tried to grab the Paladin to crush him in his devastating grasp but the Paladin would not be grabbed. It was like he was fluid and the Giant's hand could not pick him up. The Giant tried to eat the Paladin but the Paladin stuck another pike up the giant's mouth and down his throat. He could not close his mouth fast enough to bite him without great pain and every attack by the Giant gave the Paladin the chance to cut him more. Soon the giant was staggering from loss of blood and that gave the men courage enough to return and destroy the creature. Again, the Paladin disappeared.

He reappeared in a room, in a tower, overlooking the battlefield. In the room was a Witch and she was casting curses on the invading army. The Paladin was not silent in his full plate armor; yet, as he ran toward the Witch she did not turn. She was in the middle of a spell to summon a Devil among the fight below. To lose the spell would be devastating. The Paladin's blade cut at the Witch and her contingency spell went off at the same time her other spell went off. She summoned a Pit Fiend inside her own 'Orb of Protection'. She could not get out and no one could get in and she was stuck with a creature she could not control. The Pit Fiend looked at the Paladin outside the Orb and the cowering Witch inside and ate the Witch before it disappeared from the Orb, something thought to be impossible. The Paladin disappeared.

He reappeared where the Pit Fiend transferred to. The Pit Fiend saw that the Paladin was being protected by something more powerful than he. It spit out the words, "Faith protects you, Paladin. We will meet again." The Fiend plane shifted to his home.

The battle was over and the Paladin walked among the wounded showing care and goodness to both friend and enemy. These men were not responsible for their Evil King's actions, or the actions of his Witch. The Paladin used all his abilities to ensure as many men as possible would be going home to their loved ones this night. Of course, he had them swear allegiance to his King and they gladly did so. They knew their King was dead and soon their land would belong to another King. This Paladin was showing that being part of his kingdom would be a good thing.

When all was taken care of and all his men were accounted for, alive or dead, he went to his knees in prayer. "Thank you great Valoris. As it was, is, and will always be, my life and all that I have is yours." His prayers went on throughout the night and deep into the next day. Even the King did not disturb him until he stood. And, when he stood cheers from a thousand men, both friend and new friend, raised through the valley.

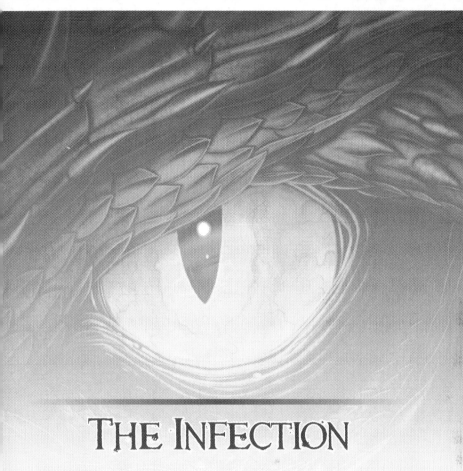

THE INFECTION

"OH LOOK WILLI, ANOTHER HUMAN CHILD."

"That one looks to be only four of five, Filli. When are the humans going to learn to keep a better eye on their little ones?"

"Little ones! That child is eight times bigger than us and weighs more than the two of us can carry. Humans are giants and cannot be trusted. What do you think we should do?"

"Nothing."

"The child will surely die."

"Your point, my friend?"

Willi looked over at his pen mate with tears and said, "She'll die."

Filli placed a tiny hand on her friend's shoulder. "I know. Remember the last time we saved a human child. We led it back to the village and the humans tried to arrest us. They claimed that we led the child into the forest and they said that the child would not have gone off on its own if we didn't lead it off. They blamed their bad parenting on us!"

Willi felt his head and the bump that was still very evident. "They tried to kill us by throwing boulders at us."

"I know what to do. Let's go tell the Queen!" The two pixies took off flying through the woods so fast they startled dozens of slower creatures and got chewed out by several others.

An old bear yelled, "Slow down, fool Pixies. You'll run into a tree. Mark my growl."

A Dadorus with its eight tentacles tried to grab them for a snack but missed as they were far to fast for the lumbering beast.

They slowed-up only when they reached the nest. Willi exclaimed, "My Queen, my Queen."

An older pixie dressed in shinny sparkly cloth looked up while counting the treasure before her. A cracked jewel fallen out of a ring, several copper pieces, a shiny silver piece, and the greatest treasure of all was three brass buttons that shined brightly in the sun. She looked at the two pixies coming forward and asked, "Now what's got the two of you so excited?"

Both said at the same time. "Another human child is entering the forest."

Willi added, "This one is very young, Majesty."

The Queen flew up a few feet, picked up her crown of shinny silver-thorn leaves, and placed it on her head while saying, "Lead me to this child."

Willi and Filli took off in the direction of the child. The Queen and twenty others took off after them. As they approached the human child the party stopped back far enough that the child did not see them. The Queen said, "This presents a problem. If we try to save the child by leading it back to the village they will surely blame us for it getting lost."

All the pixies bobbed up and down in the air in agreement.

The Queen continued, "If we allow it to stay in the forest we will be blamed for leading it into danger. If the child dies we will be called murderers and hunted down and killed."

All the pixies bobbed up and down in agreement again. Some cried, "Not fair!"

The Queen said, "I know my subjects. The monster humans are not a good species. They are evil to the core. I have thought long and hard on this matter. Should we move again or should we stay here where the food is plentiful? Every day the humans cut further into our woods while destroying our food source. Soon they will reach our home and destroy everything. But, if we move they will find us and do the same all over again."

Willi asked in reverent tones. "War, my Queen?"

The Queen did not answer. She ordered, "Willi, go tell the Wizard I want to see him."

"Yes, my Queen." Willi took off flying faster than ever before and reached the Wizard in his tree quickly. Still, he had to take time to catch his breath before exclaiming, "The Queen is at the edge of the forest by the village. She is thinking of war with humans and told me to tell you she wants to see you."

The old pixie Wizard took his time gathering some items and then touched Willi and instantly they were at the eastern edge of the forest. The Queen was only a few hundred pixie feet away or twenty-three human feet. The wizard flew over.

"Hello, Queen Dilli. Do we have a problem?"

She pointed to the child and said, "We cannot save the child as they will blame us for the child leaving its home. We cannot constantly protect the child as I do not have the resources and the humans will say we kidnapped it. If it dies the humans will destroy us. I refuse to move again and the humans are cutting into the forest very close to our home. We planted thorn sword brambles around the edge of the forest and that did not stop them. My next move is war unless you have another option."

The old Wizard thought for a moment out loud so the Queen would know his mind. "I talked to their leader and he laughed at me. I tried to tell the farmers not to cut certain areas and they said they would not but they did the next day. I talked to their Cleric and he said that his God does not recognize us as sentient beings and therefore not to be taken seriously. I spent many moons trying to persuade the humans not to infringe on our lands and they have taken eighty percent and will take it all if not stopped. I am tired of this issue. Sad as it is. War it must be."

The Queen started flying back to her tree while giving orders to gather all resources. "Send messengers throughout the forest. Tell the dryads, fairies, wolves, dark elves, fierners, gallwids, dire bears, imps, and all manner of forest creatures that we are having a war council about the humans. Contact the old druid Wizard and let him know." She thought for a moment before saying the last, "Contact the Gormera."

Shock reverberated throughout the party and the old pixie Wizard flinched. "The Gormera, my Queen? Is that necessary?"

She turned her head just a little and he could see the tears being held back at great effort. "Yes, I am afraid so. This is war, my friend. There will be a lot of deaths on both sides. I will do what is necessary to ensure that the cost in lives is worth the price."

Filli flew up and said, "Willi and I will go tell the Gormera, though it be our lives, my Queen."

She turned to the little pixie and patted her head. "You are an exceptionally brave pixie. I will sing a song for you."

Willi and Filli flew off in the direction of the Gormera's cave.

It took nearly a day to find it but in front of them was a massive cave opening. The opening was so massive you could see it from as far off as three hours flying. All kinds of fools have entered the cave including great human adventurers. None have ever come out except one. A small pixie wandered into the cave entrance to get out of the pouring rain and went insane from fear. An old Cleric helped her and she told the story of how she met the

Gormera. It is told as a fireside fright story to keep children from wondering. It works too.

Willi said, "Your grandmother went into the cave and you know what happened to her."

Filli said, "You don't have to go in with me. I will take all the blame if we are not successful. You just make sure that I get back to the Cleric. I do not want to wander around the forest until someone finds me and drags me in, or eats me."

"They will have to find us both as I will not let you go in by yourself. I love you, Filli."

They hugged each other and hand in hand they slowly flew into the cave. It was very dark and instead of using their innate ability to create light, which is said to attract predators, they waited for their eyes to adjust. They continued in a little further. Willi got brave at one point and said in the tiniest quiet voice, "Gormera?"

"WHAT!"

The heat from its breath was almost enough to fry their wings and it knocked them back a hundred feet and right out of the cave. Laughter filled the cave and then stopped. It was totally quiet.

Willi and Filli were hugging each other and shaking with fear. Still, they flew back into the entrance. Filli said, "Great Gormera, the Queen wants us to tell you that we are having a war council about the humans." Then they flew out and away as quickly as possible. Their speed was incredible as their wings were betting faster than a hummingbird.

The Gormera exited the cave and its shadow covered the forest. With one beat of its massive wings, it passed the two pixies and landed in a clearing near the pixie trees three leagues away. Twenty trees fell from the impact of its landing.

The Queen flew out of her fallen tree in a rage and quickly backed up when she saw what the cause was. The Gormera was standing on six long legs with claws longer than a human and sharper than the Wizard's wit, four massive arms holding weapons that glowed and sputtered in the daylight, a head as big as the entire pixie city, and each fang longer than a three-year sapling. Legend says it was created by the Gods as a hunting dog. What it hunted was only hinted at. No one knows how old it is but they know it predates the Elves and Druids and that is very old.

Gormera snorted at the Queen and fire shot out nearly blasting her. "What do you want little pixie Queen? It is not wise to waken me."

She went to the grown, and on shaking knees said, "Oh great Gormera, I want my forest protected and the humans off this continent and kept off."

"And, what will you pay me for such a service?"

She brightened and said, "I have three brass buttons?"

Laughter filled the forest and even in the human capital city two hundred leagues away people trembled from the sound. "I will take that and the sole of every creature I kill to make this happen. And, Willi and Filli soles are forfeit the moment the humans are off this land."

With tears streaming down her tiny face she said to the shock of all her people, "Done."

The Gormera raised its head and yelled in triumph. Natura, Goddess, I have made a pact with the lowliest of sentient life. When I am done fulfilling it the term of guardianship will be over. I am coming home."

In the forest came the most beautiful sound imaginable, the voice of the Goddess of Nature. "My pet, remove the humans and then I will set you up as the God of this land."

"It shall be done as you request, Grand Goddess," said Gormera. With one flap of his wings, he took to the air and the war was on.

The humans fought hard and though Gormera destroyed most of them they were eventually successful in defeating the Demi-God. When the pixie Queen flew up with eight hundred followers – all that was left of the humans were standing around the central fountain in the only city still partially standing.

The leader of the humans turned to this new issue and said, "Welcome, Pixie Queen."

"Welcome? That is a great change of attitude from only two years ago when you tried to stone to death my people for saving your child. It is much different than the way you treated me when I came asking you to leave our forest alone. It is interesting how kind-hearted you are with those that are stronger than you."

The human knew not what she was talking about but the tone told him she was mad. "Dear Queen, it is not our fault what others did to you before."

"Yes, it is. Kill them!" The attack was over in minutes. Every human was killed. The Queen gave one last order before Gormera rose from the ashes and looked down on her. "Find every human and kill them. Let no human no matter the talk, the reason, or the type. Let no human step foot on this continent again. If they try, do not believe their words, their pleading, do not trade, kill them before they can get a foothold. We have stopped this infestation on our lands but the other lands have lost and the human infestation is going to multiply to a point where they will need to spread out or die. I say they die! Become strong, learn, work together, build grand armies, build fortresses, make traps to destroy the unwary. I have united all races together. Work together and grow strong. Strong enough to keep the human virus from taking hold on our lands again."

Gormera said, "Willi and Filli, have them come forth."

The Queen gave a sign and two frightened pixies came forward. Gormera picked them up and took their lives. Their soles entered his body and his sole left. Every creature watched as a God of great beauty was born and a new Gormera was created.

Willi and Filli, in their new body, flew back to the cave to wait the time when Gormera would be needed again.

The old pixie stood and closed the book. A child called out. "What about Willi and Filli?"

The Pen Master said to the children, "The guardian lies asleep to this day." He pointed to the mountain, "He is in the cave on the higher hill. Two brave pixies who saved our world. Now, get some sleep. Tomorrow I will tell you about King Silli the brave."

BARBARIANS!

ONE SITS WONDERING HOW LONG ONE HAS TO SIT AND wonder. I have heard many grand statements about patience; patience is a virtue, all things come to those that wait, there is no remedy but patience. What about sayings like; patience overtaxed turns to rage, and patience loses the race. One of my favorites is "Don't keep the King waiting!" Yet, here I am. I came on time and have been waiting for three hours. I'd leave if they hadn't taken all my weapons. I need those weapons and if I leave without permission I may have to leave them behind.

A page came into the long main hall looking at all the attendees waiting and called for the next in line. Great! I heard them talking and I am sure it will take the rest of the day to settle their argument. Now I've moved up to twenty-fifth in line and I need to go to the privy!

"Page? Would you be so kind as to tell me where the privy is?"

He laughed and in a snide tone said, "Two doors down on your right, Fool. You can count to two, can't you? There is a sign if you could read."

My hand was around his scrawny neck in an instant. Guards pulled weapons and waited to see if they needed to use them. I pulled him close to my face and said, "One, two. Am I correct?"

He tried to stammer out, "Yes, my Lord." but without air flowing into his lungs he was having a difficult time. I tossed him against the wall thirty feet away and walked down to the privy. The guards sheaved their weapons after I let him go. When I returned to my place it was waiting for me. I had seen others get up and go someplace, probably the privy, and when they returned they were at the end of the line again. That was not going to happen to me. I don't know what the King wants but I am not going to continuously start over trying to see him.

Some of the others were intelligent enough to bring other family members to hold their place in line. I have no family here and no friends in this town that I know of. I did not do anything wrong that I know of. What did the King want with me?

Lunch was brought around and everyone was given a good size platter of food and drink except me. That page I tossed around to spread the word and I was left until last. When the food eventually made it to me it was cold, stringy meat, mostly fat, and tasteless unseasoned greens that look old and wilted. The water was dirty, which would normally be no problem as that is the way most taverns serve water, but that and the food set me off. I stood up and waited for the next servant to pass through.

Shortly one did and I grabbed her. I held her up and said in a tone deep and angered, "If a hot plate of good food and a tankard of good wine are not in front of me shortly then I will break things on servants coming through until there is."

I let her drop to the ground. She scampered out and just before she was out of earshot I heard her say, "Tell the Mistress, it is hostile. Don't let anyone pass that way."

In only a few minutes a stern-looking woman came through and stopped in front of me. "Are you the fool threatening the King's servants?"

I stood up and she had to look way up to see my face. Being eight feet tall and as strong as a dragon I make an impressive appearance. She stood up on the bench and looked up at me saying, "Do not try to intimidate me you, stupid creature."

I picked her up and slapped her only once. Then I dropped her on the ground and kicked her across the floor. I took the dirty water and dumped it on her face. Then I picked her up again and tossed her into a guard. "Here, take this woman out of my sight."

The guards were looking worried. One said, "Do you have any idea who you just beat?"

I said, "The woman in charge of the castle and the servants. The Castle Mistress. If she teaches her servants to be rude to people the King requested to see, then she is in the wrong position. Next time she forfeits her life."

A human, in grand armor, stepped out from the throne room and whispered, "What's going on out here?"

The woman stood up and her fear went away with the protection of the Captain of the Royal Army. "That creature is threatening the servants and now he has attacked me. I want him arrested and taught a lesson."

I started toward the woman and she ran behind the Captain. He asked me, "And, your side of the story?"

I looked at him as if to say I need no story but out of politeness, I said, "A servant belittled me and I threatened him. Because of that, they brought me cold scraps for food that I wouldn't give the dog and dirty water. Everyone else received good food and wine." I pointed to the plate. "I became angry that a little servant was treating me this way and I grabbed the next servant and told her that I wanted the good food and wine or I would start breaking things on any servant coming through. Then this woman came in all steamed up and acting above me. I took offense at this on top of what the others did."

The Captain looked at the plate and touched the food and felt the grease. He turned back to me and asked, "Who are you and why are you here?"

"I am the fighter Lennar. I have no idea why I am here. Your soldiers came and told me the King wants to see me. They would not even let me eat my breakfast first – saying I can't keep the King waiting. I was escorted to this room and told to wait in this line. I have been waiting five hours now, treated with rudeness several times, and I don't think the King and I are going to have a very good conversation as I am now very hungry and extremely upset."

The woman yelled at me, "You are in the wrong line!"

I yelled back, "Your stupid servants put me here, wench!"

The Captain said, "Stop!" Then he slapped the Mistress of the castle. "We will have words later, Mistress Akee." He turned to me and said, "I am sorry Lord Lennar. The King has been wondering where you are. He is most interested in seeing you. You will be staying here the night." You will likely be here for several days."

"No, I won't. Give me my weapons and I will stay at the local tavern. I am not liked here and I don't stay where I am not wanted."

The Captain said, "The King will insist. He has said that he wants you found and kept here until he can talk to you."

I picked up my pack and said, "Tell your King I am at the Toad's Breath Inn. I will be there two days and no longer unless I hear from him before then."

I headed back to the entrance with the Captain staring at my back. Before I turned the corner I heard the Captain say, "The King may have your head for this, Mistress Akee."

I made it to the front gate and asked for my weapons. They wanted to know if I made my appointment. "I showed up on time. Don't worry." That satisfied then and they turned over my weapons. I checked to ensure they were my weapons. Magical weapons like mine are worth more than most make in a lifetime and I did not want them being swapped out for look-a-likes. However, these were mine and I headed across the street to the Inn.

At the Inn, I waited for the proprietor to come out. The servant at the counter was reluctant to give me rooms and sent for the owner. I don't suppose my frame of mind had anything to do with his cowering. The owner looked at me with only a little interest and asked, "One large room, my Lord?"

I smiled, which never goes over well with four top fangs showing and three rows of needle-sharp teeth. "My good man. I will have a large room, a large bed, a large bath, but first – a large lunch."

"Two gold a night for the room and bed, a gold for the bath, and depending on the type of food and amount?"

"Same food you eat and cooked the same way but three times more."

"Three silver. How long will you be staying, my lord?"

"Two nights are planned at this time."

"Two nights it is. That's three gold and three silver for the first night. I will add three meals for five silver a day?"

"I may be waiting at the castle through breakfast, lunch, and dinner so I need to pay at the time of use."

He frowned a little from his own experience, "It can be a long wait."

I counted out the gold and silver and his face lit up when I let him see that I could afford to stay a lot longer. The food was hot and very tasty, the bathtub short but wide enough for my frame, and the water was hot. The room was converted while I was eating and bathing. They took a double and changed it into a single. The room looked out the front so I would be able to see when the King's men were coming for me. Everyone was very friendly. I went down to the market section and purchased some items for adventuring. I was planning out my next job and it was going to take some extra work to get in and out with my thick hide intact.

They came for me right after breakfast the next day. The owner had been watching and came over to me to let me know soldiers were on their way.

I said, "Thank you." Then I put a marker in the book and placed it in a pocket. I went over to the door and opened it just as a little guard was trying to open it. I pulled him through and caught him before he fell. "Sorry about that."

The guard looked up and said, "My fault and my apologies."

I thought to myself, "Well, that was a different attitude."

The guard said, "I take it you are Lord Lennar?"

"That's me. Though, I don't normally use titles."

The guard looked surprised. "Then, you are a Lord?"

I smiled, "Not difficult to be a Lord where I come from. The stronger and meaner you are the higher you become in rank. Only the King outranks me and that is because I lost the fight. You lose the fight with anyone other than the King and you have no right to challenge for five years. Keeps the challenges down to something manageable. If you lose a fight with the King then you leave for at least five years. I'm just starting my second year."

The guard looked worried. "You do know it's not that way in the human lands?"

I smiled and shook my head, "Little man. I am highly educated by your standards. I have held peaceful and violent negotiations with Elves, Dragons, and Dwarves and won. I can read and write eight languages, do some very minor spells, and I am considered ignorant by my people's standards. Do not let the size fool you. I am a master of battle strategies and will return to my lands as the royal General."

The guard started walking toward the castle. "In this land, if you threaten the King they will kill you. I am surprised that it is not the same as your people. Do you hate your King?"

"No, my friend. I love my King and would gladly give my life for him."

"Then why fight him?"

"We disagreed on how to achieve something our people needed. I lost the fight but won the battle. The King saw my point before I was knocked unconscious. My plan worked and my people benefit from what I achieved. The King told all that it was my idea and that he cannot wait until I come home to the land I love."

The guard looked confused and asked, "You knew you would lose and have to leave but fought anyway?"

"There are simple things that prove you are sophisticated, young human. When you love your people enough to give them up, when the populace is educated and not just the ones in charge, when you have laws that are based on good morals that are written and enforced according to those morals and not to the ideas of someone that was not at the writing, and when there is a good working structure for who is in charge that keeps a strong body and mind in the seat of power. Those are but a few of the things that tell us apart from the barbarians."

The Guard look confused even more. "Then, how do you view humans?"

"Few of your people can read or write, you have laws that are enforced differently depending on the view of the person prosecuting, and your order of structure allows for the weak-minded and weak-bodied to be in charge. In fact, the only legal requirement to be responsible for the lives of every person in the kingdom is blood." I bent down and looked him right in the eyes. "And blood goes bad, Boy. Human history has shown us many times where human Kings were allowed to rule when known to be insane." I straightened back up and said, "To answer your question. We consider you to be barbarians."

We headed into the castle and I had to give up my weapons again. Hard doing that. Then we went directly into the thrown room and before the King.

King Kline was sitting in the big chair talking to his Captain. There were several people on the side. One group of five were standing by themselves. I recognized two of them. I bowed to the Fighter and he returned the courtesy. His name was Dramil from the barbarians of the north. Human Fighter of some renown. Near my level but not so close it would be worth challenging him. There would be nothing to learn from the fight. Next was a Cleric of some human God called Solbelli. After he was a Wizard. He looked frail, but his equipment said powerful. Then came Rul, a tiny thief from the Hinder lands. Caught him once and tanned his hide before laughingly letting the little creature go. He is a good Thief but made a bad mistake. I place spells of protection on my equipment including my money belt. Last came a Sorceress that looked strong of the body but the expression said weak of mind. That's the problem with magic users that don't need to study daily. The King finished with the Captain and motioned us forward.

"So, you are Lord Lennar. The one that destroyed the ghost of Tiber, the one that cut the head off of the King of Mosfall, the one that bested the reigning champion of the Hostore gladiators, and the one that led the battle for Pacor against the Demon Horde and turned a losing battle into a route?"

I said, "Actually Majesty, the Tiber ghost was easy with a little research and planning, King Mosfell was insane and his people let me in wishing an end to his rain of terror, but the fight with Maxgor the Hostore's champion was a challenge and I learned a lot. That was a good time. I could hear the Pacor battle for miles off. I ran over to see what was happening. There was one of our ladies holding her ground but she was being cut up badly as her human allies were running instead of fighting. I was enraged and ran in to help the lady and in so doing the rest followed my battle cry. They thought their King had ordered a charge. I saved the lady and continued to fight alongside her. Few demons can stand against two of my kind. We know how to maximize and mirror our skills making two fight as one. It was a glorious battle. I just happen to be in the right place at the right time."

The King leaned forward, "The Tiber ghost killed hundreds of adventures and many innocent people. He was thought impossible to destroy. At Mosfell, I am told, you killed eighty-six royal guards to get to the King because he ordered your death. Hostore's champion rained for nine years and you were the only one to cut him. And, I am friends with the King of Pacor. He told me about the near-death rush, the bloody battle, the fighting that turned the tide, and the amount of devastation you and your lady friend left behind. Where is your lady friend? I could use her also."

"Her time was up so she went home."

The King sat back, "To bad. I hear she is a living terror when it comes to battle. I called you here to ask you to join a group I put together to destroy a certain pest."

I looked over at the five adventures standing on the side. I turned back to the King with my hand going to my empty scabbard in anticipation of a good battle. "Must be a big pest, Majesty. What's the reward?"

"The pest is very strong and thought impossible to destroy. The payment is one hundred thousand gold in rubies for any survivors."

I looked at him with a little concern. "Either you are not expecting any survivors or you are expecting to find some way to not pay. I cannot see how this kingdom has that kind of financial backing."

He smiled, raised a hand, and snapped his fingers. A servant came out with seven guards and a large chest. They opened the chest and in it were rubies. I walked over to the container, reached in, and pulled out a ruby from the middle. I held it to the window light and it was a good ruby. I took it back and dropped it in the chest. They closed it and left.

"Very well, you have the funding. As you know my people are warriors, but contrary to popular belief we are not murderers. Why do you want this 'Pest' destroyed? What did it do to this kingdom that warrants its destruction?"

The King became upset, "It defies my order to vacate the valley so that I can place a much-needed road through there. Every time I send anyone into the valley it sends them running back with messages threatening me. It has killed over a hundred of my soldiers."

Keeping my calm I asked, "How long has it lived in this valley?"

The King could see where I was going and said, "Longer than humans have been on this part of the continent."

"Then what gives you the right to displace it?"

"Being the King and owning the land gives me the right."

"How can you claim ownership of the land if you have never possessed it?"

"Because no one else is using it."

"Not true, Majesty. The creature is using it."

"The creature is just a dumb animal and does not count. Would you state that a bear has the right to own land?"

This conversation went on for most of the day. The King was enjoying himself. He may not be strong in body but he has a great mind. It came down to sentient beings are sacred and can own land, all others are food.

I finally said, "I will go see this creature and determine for myself if it is sentient."

The King's eyes went wide. "That will get you killed, Lord Lennar. However, if you insist on this folly then I will start looking for another to add to this group. If you travel to this valley by yourself you will not be coming back."

"Start looking then, Majesty. I will find out if the creature is sentient to the point we agreed upon. If it is I will not help you murder it. If it is not then I will accept the price if I get to keep any treasure found."

The King smiled, "You are the only one that bargained. The others were satisfied with the rubies. I will split any treasure with the survivors."

"Equal shares?"

He laughed, "Equal shares and I will give you the first choice."

I put out my hand. He looked at it and then shook. He had a good firm handshake.

The six of us gathered our equipment, researched the creature we were going to see, and then traveled to its valley.

At the top of the pass, there was a sign. "Stay Out!"

A little further was another sign, "I said STAY OUT!"

A little further was another sign, "FOOLS!"

We continued our approach and about a third of the way into the valley, there was an immense raised hill with a very large hole in the side. I called out, "Creature! I would have words with you."

An answer came back instantly, "A horned Lorger. A rare sight. It has been many years since I conversed with a Lorger, and that one was a lesser Lorger. A horned Lorger is top of the breed." It crawled out. Instantly the Thief pulled his bow and so I back slapped him. The Cleric revived him and I said, "I told you, no fighting until I determine if it is sentient."

The creature stood about eighty feet high, nearly a hundred feet long, had four legs and four arms, her entire hide was plate armor, and her eyes burned red. The body coloring was dark brown with bits of golden areas that dotted her sides and back. There was a ridge of spikes running from the back of her head to the tip of her very long tail.

"So, you come to try to destroy me, little Lorger?"

"I come creature, and I call you that as I have nothing else to call you at this time, to determine if you are a sentient being or not. Do you have a name?"

"I have been called many things, Lorger. But the truth is I am the last of my kind. I call myself Crash."

"Well Crash, can you read and write?"

"You saw the signs."

"You wrote them, Crash?"

"That is my handwriting. I read a lot and have a large library. Would you like to see?"

The others were saying, "No, don't go in there." They were trying to hold me back.

After shaking them off I said, "I would be delighted."

I walked forward and into its cave. It followed me in and pointed to where I need to go. The cave was massive and had many different areas. We made it to the library and there was a light by a desk and thousands of very old books.

"Crash, how do you read such little books?"

She said, "Watch." She changed into a female Horned Lorger. A very nice looking female Lorger. Then she walked over to the desk and picked up a book. She read out loud several passages and then closed the book. "Satisfied?"

I smiled and said, "Good enough for me. How long have you been living in this valley, Crash?"

"About three thousand years. When the humans came to this land they pushed my entire race out of our old home. We traveled to the far coast to get away from their foolishness. But, they have spread out and now they want this place also. I have nowhere else to run. I am getting very old for my race. I expect that I will be killed someday soon to make room for a road."

"Not going to happen."

She looked at me with a look that said, "I don't believe you."

I told her, "I came here to find out if you are sentient. You are; therefore, killing you would be murder. You have not harmed anyone except those trying to take your home away or infringe on your home. You are innocent of any crime and I will tell the local King that you are to be left alone. He simply needs to find another route for his road."

We talked on the way out and I told her I would be back to let her know what the King decided. As I approached the five they spread out which gave me caution.

The human Fighter asked, "What did you find out?"

"She is sentient, my friend. The King will need to reroute."

They attacked. I was prepared. For two years I have been around humans. They are such irrational creatures. I killed four quickly and kept the fighter for last.

"Why, Dramil? Why attack me?"

"The King knew you would find out that the creature is sentient. He doubled the offer if you turned against him and we brought him your head."

I snapped the fighter's neck and dropped him. Barbarians! After taking enough healing potions to keep me alive as I was bleeding a good bit, I rested.

Crash came over and asked, "Are you alright. I watched the fight and I am shocked that they attacked you. Why?

"It was my understanding that the King would leave off if I could prove you were sentient. I was wrong. Instead, he paid the others to kill me if I turned against his plans."

"What will you do, Lorger?"

"Kill the King."

In shock, she took a step back. "That will be very dangerous."

I smiled, "Not really. A simple thing to do."

The next day I walked back toward the city and the castle. I was beaten up, bloody, my armor was cut to shreds, and I looked like I had been in the fight of my life. The guard at the city gate let me in and the word was passed. When I reached the castle the Captain was waiting for me. His hand was on his sword and his knuckles were turning white with tension. "Well, Lord Lennar, you look like you've been in a grand battle."

I sat down on the bench. I knew what he was doing. He was trying to find out who the battle was with. "Hello, Captain. It attacked from a direction we were not prepared for. It cut us to shreds before we could mount a defensive position. Did the Sorceress show up here?"

His hand left his sword but not far, "No, she did not."

"That coward teleported away without fighting at all. I would have sworn she would come here."

"If the King found out she ran he would have ordered her death, Lord Lennar. Running out on the party is the same as killing the members yourself."

"I agree. If she had stayed to fight most of us would still be alive and the creature would be dead. I nearly had it, Captain. I know how to defeat it now."

His hand strayed closer to his sword. "Did you find out if it is sentient?"

"It is but that makes no difference now. It attacked and killed without warning or provocation. It has forfeited its life. I need to talk to the King. I will need a written document giving me the authorization to kill it for the crime of murder."

The Captain helped me up and led me toward the castle throne room. They didn't even take my weapons. I was taken in front of the King immediately. I said, "Majesty."

Word of what happened had passed the guardhouse and preceded me inside. The King immediately called for his top Cleric. "Cleric! Heal this champion."

I was instantly healed by his Cleric. As soon as I was fully well – I drew my sword and killed the King, Captain, his two War Wizards, and his Cleric. I dropped a note. Then Crash teleported in and teleported me out. She had been scrying on the castle throne room.

I stayed in the valley for the next three years taking care of Crash and she taking care of me. No one visited. No one tried to attack us. I suppose it was the note:

"Human Barbarians;

I am appalled at the act of your King and Captain. They paid several adventurers to attack me if I did not help them murder a sentient being. To protect myself, I had to kill the adventurers and remove your King and Captain. I do not like barbarian traitors. I have researched the land and you had better bypass the intended valley. There is a better pass on the left side, two valleys over. It will be harder to make a road through there but it will be impossible to clear a road through my valley. I am taking up residence with the creature in mutual protecting. Anyone trying to come into our valley and harm us will find themselves dead and their King also.

Good Day,
Lord Lennar

Temporarily Absent General of the Lorger Armies."
They built that road through the other valley and the humans had no reason to travel through this one anymore. I even helped then by destroying many non-sentient creatures that were killing their workers.
"It was sad parting. Crash was a good partner. Still, I needed to return home. I received word that my King had died and that my brother Gormon was now King. Gormon is physically strong but weak-minded. I can't have that. When I beat the snot out of him I will tell him of this valley and the good creature in it. He will need the rest.

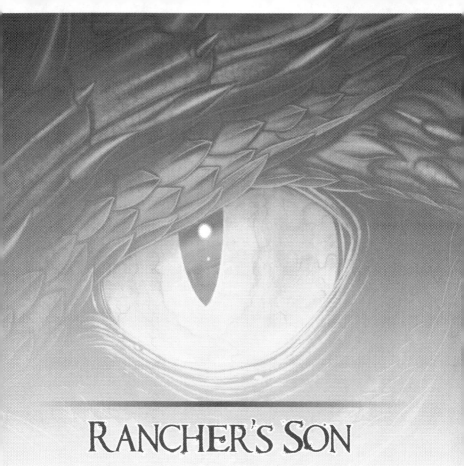

RANCHER'S SON

THAT WAS A GREAT MEAL; YOUNG FEMALE HUMAN, basted in spicy adrenalin, with just a hint of sweet sweat. I roasted her alive over a slow fire. I used a golden ball to stuff her mouth so her screams would not wake the neighbors. I do love a midnight snack.

It is nice being the son of a rich rancher. We breed the best humans. We have nearly six thousand of them kept in the cages. They are constantly trying to get away but we've put a stop to most of that. Father figured out that shoving a red hot barbed needle through one ear and out the other does something to their tiny brains. They become very docile if they live. Though they lose a lot of water weight from crying. That cuts down on poundage and makes them worthless at auction so father doesn't do it to very many. When he does do it he ensures that many see him so they get the idea that escaping is not good for them. It is difficult to teach the dumb creatures anything but they do learn from pain, even the pain of others.

They used to talk and some of the new ones can talk so father cuts their tongue out as soon as we get them. The newborn are not cut until they reach the age of five. With no parents that can talk they do not learn early and can wait until branding time before the tongue cutting.

Humans bread quickly but it takes a long time for the pups to grow up. Still, many consider it a delicacy to eat them young and sweet. Father keeps them caged so they cannot exercise and feeds them constantly. They grow nice and plump and demand a great price. We just made a bargain with one of the bigger chain stores here in the abyss. They are going to buy most of our humans, butcher them, and freeze the meat until time to sell. There is a grand demand for fresh human but most cannot afford the fresh and have to buy from the stores.

Cleaning out the cages with humans is easy. You simply turn on the water and spray the crap out. It is good to spray the animals also as they tend to catch disease easily. Most will allow the spray and even seem to enjoy it if the water is warmed first. Some fight it and so we chain them to the wall before spraying.

The little ones are fun to pet. They like affection, being scratched up and down the back, and having their filthy hair petted. We normally cut the hair off once it reaches several feet. Father sales the hair to a clothing chain for sweaters, and hair lined mittens and coats. The hides of the humans are used for lots of items; the covers of magical books, hats, curtains, sheets and pillowcases, and anything that does not have to take much punishment. Human skin is very frail and does not wear very well. Some of the upper crust, or royalty, have dresses made of baby human skin. Just the butts as they are the softest part. They dye the skin different colors and add frills. I once saw one that had tiny fingers hanging from the neckline, the hem, and the sleeves.

It was beautiful and expensive. They used only the little finger of the newborn.

You can use the intestines for bowstrings. Most braid the testicular threads as they make a better bowstring. You can use every part of a human. Pickled eyeballs are always a treat on salad. Heart and liver are good to eat, the bladder is considered an aphrodisiac, and salted roasted ears are crispy and a fun snack. Finger and toenails are used to decorate pouches and once I saw a cloak made of them all polished so that it shone and sparkled with each movement. I think the only thing not editable or usable in any way is the, the, nope, can't think of anything we don't use.

I had better get back to bed now. Father gets angry if he catches me snacking. Good night.

ROGUE

MY QUEEN SENT ME OUT HERE TO FIND OUT WHAT'S going on, so why did she send someone else? I don't mind normally, but this guy is about to get eaten and I don't like him enough to help him. Besides, if I help then I'm desert.

When I first arrived, a three week trip through the deepest part of the forest, I had to kill an eye sunder, a nasty creature that blinds you and then kills you slowly while playing with you. That was difficult enough but after a day of resting, I wondered around the site and was accosted by a stupid dragon. Not a normal dragon either. A treasure hungry Dragon that would not allow me to hunt the site unless I promised him half of everything I find. I hid out trying to figure out how to kill the dragon and came up with several ways to damage it but not enough to destroy it.

The dragon and Wizard were quarreling over the same thing now. It was easy to see that they would not agree. Question is...is the Wizard smart enough to walk away and figure out a plan? If he does I can help him and then we could do this together. Or, is he going to be stupid enough to become dinner?

The Wizard backed up and started casting. He got off two good spells that did a lot of damage to the dragon before he was swallowed whole.

My turn! I took to the sky and used my bow. I put five arrows into the dragon before he could finish swallowing. That gave me time to put five more arrows into his hide. He took to the air and came after me. His flight was not so good and when he missed me he had to take time to bank around to come at me again. I put twenty arrows into his head and he died. It was an easy battle thanks to the Wizard, but now I was out of adamantine tipped arrows. Darn, those are expensive.

Using a wand I summoned a wolf and asked him to find the dragon's lair. He started me in the right direction and, after eleven more wolves, I found it. Not part of the plan I told the Queen about but you have to be flexible. I opened my Magical Baggage Pit and filled it with treasure, then I filled my large magical bag and then filled my magical deep pocket haversack and I only had about half the treasure. I was rich, or the person I was leaving it all too.

I walked out of the cave and back to the ruins. As I did I heard something and instantly went into a sneaky mode. I snuck up onto the site and there was a group of adventurers. Before this adventure started, I saw them leaving the Queen's chambers just the day before I left. Now they were waiting for something and talking.

The Ranger was looking around and said, "There was a caster standing his ground and he got eaten. Something else took to the air from over there and shot arrows into the dragon. The arrows killed the dragon. The same style of arrows we found in the eye sunder. The feet are tiny. I would say a Halfling. A wolf magically appeared at this point and sniffed the dragon and then it took off in that direction." He pointed toward my treasure.

I went back and summoned an air elemental to wipe out my tracks. When I came back the woman was talking.

The Sorceress asked, "What would a Halfling and a magic-user be doing out here together?"

The Cleric asked, "Did we not see a Halfling rogue near the Queen's chambers before we left? I know we saw many Halflings, but this one was remarkable in that we almost did not see him and he was standing right in front of us."

The Ranger said, "They were not together. They came at separate times. The Halfling was here first, backed away, and ran from the dragon. He hid over in that area waiting on something. Probably trying to figure out a way around the dragon. The Wizard came and by the looks of the tracks, the Halfling was surprised and tried to warn the Wizard. The Wizard was not as smart as the Halfling and attacked the dragon. The Halfling took a potion, probably for flying, and dropped the vial here. Then he simply finished the wounded dragon off. He is very good. Every arrow is in a critical area. The wounded dragon had no chance."

This Ranger was good. It's the bow. An artifact I picked up fighting pirates off the coast of Lamburg. Every hit is in a killing spot and any fool could hit with this bow. Still, I am very good with the bow and two of my shots drove other arrows deeper into the dragon. Try that when flying and dodging.

The Cleric asked, "Watch for the Halfling. I don't need an unknown at my back. What's taking the Rogue so long? Simon? Simon?!"

I stepped out and walked up to them a little. "Simon, of the Circle of Nine Fingers? You need to watch your back for more than just me."

The Barbarian drew his sword slowly.

I said, "Put that away you big ox. I am not here to hurt you."

The Ranger asked, "Who are you and what are you doing here?"

"I am Tiptoe. I am here because my Queen asked me to come here and find out what is going on inside that ruin. Now, who are you and what are you doing here?"

The Ranger laughed, "So, the Queen does not trust us to figure this out and has sent another. I am surprised you are alone."

"Nice way to see if anyone is with me. You did not answer my question."

The Sorceress tried to impress me, "I am Whitefire, a Sorceress of the Flame of Gildensal, Mistress of the True Sun, and Daughter of the Huntress."

"Impressive titles, Whitefire. I suppose the rest of you are equally as impressive with stupid titles?"

The Ranger said, "I am Didlong. I am but a humble ranger of the Forest of Pentera."

"Humble my backside. Any Ranger from Pentera is probably the greatest ranger alive. I've been there. I know."

The Barbarian said, "I am a Fighter from Colesmire."

I started to tear up a little. "I knew a Barbarian from Colesmire. Her name was Dorshine. I loved her like a mother."

The Barbarian sheaved his sword, "You are my sister's Tiptoe?"

My eyes narrowed. "If you are Formore, what did your sister nickname you?"

He smiled, "Spider."

I walked over to him and hugged him. He patted me on the back. I looked up at him, and that means way up, and said, "I miss her."

"So do I, Tiptoe, so do I. Our King sent us. I think we saw you at the Halfling's castle when we stopped to get permission to investigate this ruin."

I stepped back and said, "You did as I allowed it." I looked over at the ruin entrance. "Simon is a fool. He goes around with adventures, and when he is on watch and the adventurers are asleep his eight friends come in and cut their throats. Simon and eight friends, 'The Nine Fingers.' They have become very rich killing adventurers. I am surprised that he actually went into the ruin. He must know that no one has ever passed the front door."

The Ranger said, "So that was what that was about. We killed the other eight fingers when they attacked us the first night."

I smiled, "And, now Simon is trying to be a rogue. Pardon me." I walked down into the ruin and slowly made my way forward. Simon was there alright, missing his head. I found the head after disabling the first trap. I then pulled the body away and reset the trap. I took the body and head out. "Here's your friend. Do not go into that trap-laden place without a great rogue. You would not live to see the front door. Go home and find another and then come back."

While they were arguing, I walked over to the dragon and took out my sword. I cut the creature open and pulled out the Wizard. Most of his belongings were chewed up or destroyed by stomach acid. There was an artifact key and I took that expecting that it would fit the impossible door. I turned to the others and said, "I will be back to go through the ruins. Be of good cheer. I may leave you some scraps. Right now I need to report to the Queen. Goodbye."

Using my Twist Ring of Shifting I teleported to the travel room and checked in with the guard. Then, I went directly to the Queen's small meeting room and knocked.

A servant answered the door. His eyes widened. "Just a moment, Prince Tiptoe. I will see if she can attend you." He closed the door.

It was only a moment before it reopened and the servant beckoned me in with a sign to be quiet. As I passed he whispered, "You may need your weapons."

I entered and stood in the corner about twenty feet from my Queen and ten feet from the two men she was talking with. They seemed to be envoys of some sort. They both saw me enter and then dismissed me like some bloody popper in trouble. I have to admit, I did look the part. Cutting the Wizard out of the dragon's body was a little messy.

"Diana. We are not here to mince words with you."

My hand edged toward my dagger. Calling my Queen by her first name was not proper and I could see the anger in her face.

"Our leader sent us here to let you know that we are going to take over one of your seaside towns. The Brotherhood of Buccaneers needs a place to repair ships and pick up supplies. He did not send us here to ask permission. We are here to warn you to stay away. Move your men out and your ships away or we will kill and sink."

"And, what about the people that are part of the town?"

"They can stay. We will need women to slate our lust and slaves for the markets."

The Queen said, "I will send a message back to your leader. A good strong message." She nodded to me and I killed them both.

Then she said, "And, your heads will accompany the message." She turned to me. "Thank you, my Son."

"Not a problem, Mother. When will people start to understand that the Queen of this land is not some tiny weak fool to be pushed around?"

She laughed, "The leader of these two will find out shortly." She turned to the servant and said, "Send for the Wizard. I have new orders for the fleet."

I shook my head. "It's going to cost you to fight the pirates, Mother."

"They have left me little choice, Son."

The Wizard came in and bowed to the Queen. He smiled at me with a slightly less bow and then addressed Mother. "You have a message you want to be sent to the Admiral, my Queen?"

"Tell the Admiral to hunt down and destroy every pirate he can find. I do not care if he has to cross borders to do so. He knows what ports they are in. I want people to be afraid of being a pirate, being with a pirate, or helping a pirate."

"I will send the message, my Queen, but you know what he will say. There is not enough funding to build the ships he will need to wage war against the pirates."

My turn to smile. I went over to an empty corner and unloaded my magical deep pocket haversack. The eyes from the two of them were identical. Wide and shocked.

Mother asked, "My wonderful child. Where did you gain such wealth?"

While dumping out the Sack of Holding and the Magical Baggage Pit I told her about the eye sunder, dragon, foolish Wizard she hired, and the party from a neighboring country. I ended up with a pile of treasure taller than an Orc and twice as wide as a dwarf. I said, "Mother, I need to teleport back and pick up the other half of the treasure."

Mother looked delighted, "Other half? Oh my."

"Please Mother, don't let anyone mess with my treasure until I can sort through it and pick out any magic I may want."

Mother, now in one of her greedy moods said, "I will have them sort and count for you. How much of this can I have?"

"I get any magic I need, all written knowledge, and ten percent. The rest belongs to the crown."

She laughed, "Written knowledge. How many books do you have now?"

"I have a bigger library than the Wizard's University and there are more magical books in mine. Though, I am not sure what to do with the crazy books that keep trying to manipulate me. They tried to take me over but I put a stop to that."

The Wizard asked, "What are the titles to these books?"

"Let me see. Oh yes; one is 'Enchantment Compendium', another is 'Natura's book of Wonders', then I also have 'Malificus' Guide to the Underworld', and my favorite reading was 'Good and Evil, Two Views on Morality' by Silvestris."

The Wizard nearly fainted. "You own and read those artifact God written books!"

"What are books for?"

Mother asked, "Is there a problem?"

The Wizard looked at me and said, "I sense no change. Amazing! He should have been turned to evil or good yet he remains exactly the way he was. How is this possible?"

I said, "I read a good-aligned book and it tried to persuade me to be good-aligned, so I read an evil-aligned book to see if it would try to change me that direction. I must say that it tried very hard but I just could not buy into what it was saying. Then I read 'Two Views' and I like that book. It pointed out that Good and Evil both have their place and that both are needed. Many things depend on your point of view and everyone's point of view is different. It helped me to see that I should not try to be one or the other. Just be me. I asked our grand and good-aligned Goddess Dimidims to thank Silvestris for letting me find that one. Though, I am not sure she likes me praying to her. We don't see eye to eye on everything."

Mother said, "I have tried to change you for eighteen years and failed. I don't see what a book could do that I did not. If I remember correctly, I used a good thick book on your backside as persuasion once. Ruined a good book for nothing."

I laughed, "I remember. I will be right back." I went to the travel room and teleported to the dragon cave. I collected the rest of the treasure and then used my last teleport to go home. At the travel room, the guard let me know that the adventurers were here and talking about me. I said, "Thanks. Where's Mother?"

"Still in the small meeting room. Last I heard she was counting coin. One of her favorite things to do."

I laughed, "Isn't it the favorite thing of all Halflings?"

He laughed as I headed toward the meeting room. I knocked and was let in immediately. I went right to pouring out the other half of the treasure in the opposite corner.

Mother was delighted and said to the Barbarian, "I told you he would be right back."

I hugged Mother and said, "Happy counting day." She stood up and climbed into her chair.

We Halflings do not put our chairs higher than others to look bigger like some do. Who would we be fooling? We build our castles short so others will have to stoop. It's a lot of fun. All four of the party was stooped over and looking uncomfortable until Mother said, "Please sit."

They gladly did. "Majesty, I did not know that the Halfling we were discussing is your son, the Crown Prince."

Mother looked shocked, "He is not the Crown Prince. For goodness sake no. I have eight sons. He is the youngest and a black sheep of the family. We are so proud of him. The rest are the kind to follow the law. It is almost sickening. But, that is what it takes in this world. Dimidims insists that we be goodly and follow all laws. I, myself, am a grand rogue forced to follow the laws because I am Queen. However, I taught this one," She patted my head, "everything I know and he has learned a lot since then. Best Rogue in our nation."

There were three Wizards at the corners pulling out items. One exclaimed while nearly fainting, "Artifact." They pulled that out and placed it in the pile of magic.

The Cleric asked, "Then you would not mind if we hired him to be our Rogue."

"What?" I turned to Mother. "I don't need these people. I can do this on my own."

Mother asked, "Then why did you leave me a note saying that your sister gets your share when you don't come back? Not if, but 'WHEN' you don't come back."

My answer came stubbornly, "I said I can do it on my own – I did not say I would live through it."

Mother asked, "Are the traps that bad?"

"Worse, but it is not the traps I am worried about."

"Then what?"

"The creatures. While I am finding and disabling traps this complex I must concentrate so much that I leave myself vulnerable."

The Cleric said, "We could protect you. You find and disable all the traps and we will protect you while you're doing it."

"I suppose that would be helpful. I don't know. I could gain a lot more if I did not have to share what I find. Besides, there is something specific I am after. Well, two things but I already found one of them."

They looked worried and the Cleric asked, "What two things? We are after one set of items for the Wizard University."

I must have grinned as they looked uncomfortable now. I exclaimed with just a little hint of laughter, "They want the casting set."

Mother questioned with her eyebrows rising. "Casting set?"

I said, while watching their guilty faces, "It's nothing special, Mother. The ink and pen of casting are artifacts and the parchment of lasting knowledge is also. When used together you can scroll a spell and any fool can cast it. You could create a full heal scroll and a fighter could cast it. The problem is, there is only enough ink and parchment left to make maybe twenty or so scrolls. They are hoping to duplicate the materials. I wish them luck as it took a God to create them."

The Cleric looked relieved, "If not the casting set then what are you looking for?"

"I have a grand library and I am told the people that lived in that ruin had a better library. I am after knowledge. Books, scrolls, bits of knowledge, and all information. Oh, and parts of traps I can find. They were renowned for making deadly traps."

"I will make you this deal. You help us find the casting set and all trap materials and written materials are yours."

I asked, "Equal shares of everything else?"

"Done."

I spit in my hand and put it out. The Ranger took it and we shook. I said, "Done. Get some rest. We leave tomorrow early." I yelled out, "Cleric!"

In only seconds a Cleric was in the room. "Highness?"

"I will need a Protection Banquet for five tomorrow morning just after prayers."

"As you wish, my Prince." He left. I walked over to the Captain and said, "Ensure that my guests get food, drink, and a good night's sleep. Put them in the inn at my expense. They'll need the headroom."

"As you wish, Highness."

They turned to leave, "Barbarian."

He turned to look at me. "Yes, Tiptoe."

I handed him a book. "Read this tonight. It is your sister's diary. We have been planning this trip for years. She will be proud that you have taken up protecting me. There is a lot of information about that ruin in those notes. Read those parts to the rest. She speaks a lot about her love for you. I had planned to go visiting home with her after we finished this trip."

"How did she die, Tiptoe?"

"We were battling pirates near our neighbor's lands. She was eaten by a sea monster that their Cleric conjured up."

Anger filled his face as tears poured down his cheeks.

I said, "I avenged her death on the sea monster, the Cleric, and after this adventure, the pirates will know my sadness as we are now at war."

He straightened as much as he could in our room. "Then after this adventure, you will have company." He turned and left.

The next day we teleported to the ruins. Getting in was difficult but we made it. I collected enough materials to build a home made completely of traps. We found the Casting Set and the Library. The antique books and scrolls filled eighteen rooms in the castle. Every one of the written materials is magically preserved.

I am taking part of the gold we found to build a grand library and hire protections so people do not abscond with my books. I am calling it "Dorshine" in memory of my favorite barbarian. Apparently, the Wizard that was with us told the University about my collection and now I have eighteen Wizards and seven Clerics volunteering to help run the library. Go figure.

WHAT WE DON'T KNOW

NICE DAY I PICKED TO TRAVEL. THIS IS EXTREMELY strange weather. It is the beginning of spring and it's pouring down freezing rain so hard it hurts. My magical cloak is becoming stiff and heavy from accumulated ice and my joints are complaining about every movement. Here I am – a powerful Wizard and I am out in the rain freezing. I need to get out of this weather.

I was just about to teleport when I noticed a light just in front of me. It winked in and out as if the storm was trying to hide it. I headed that direction. Funny, I don't remember anything being out this far. I made my way to the tiny light and to a shuttered window with a crack just big enough to allow the light to escape.

I followed the building to the right looking for a door and found a covered porch. I climbed up out of the rain. I hadn't noticed before but the sound of the rain was deafening. I knocked on the door and waited. Shortly a little woman came to the door and peeked out. I could smell good food and hear the sound of a harp. What was an Inn doing way out here?

The woman said, "Well? You coming in or staying out?"

I entered the main room of the inn and stood there in the lobby as the woman shut the door. The woman called out, "Mac! We have a frozen human."

From the back, I heard, "He can stand there until he drips dry. I am tired of mopping up the mess."

I took off my cloak and stomped my feet while looking around. The room had many guests of every shape and make sleeping on the floor, bent over chairs, hanging upside down from the ceiling, attached to the wall, and floating in mid-air. The sound of their snoring was worse than the rain. A bard was playing light slow music on a harp on a small stage. It looked like he was helping keep some of them asleep. There was no one behind the bar and no serving wenches. I asked, "What is this place?"

The woman looked up at me after putting my cloak away in a small check room on the right. "You are at the Inn of Bereavement, in the City of the Dead, on the Isle of the Damned." She smiled up at me when she saw the shock on my face. "Just kidding."

I said, "That's not funny, Woman."

Her smile widened, "You." She poked me in the ribs. "Are in the Lost Your Way Inn. We travel around picking up lost people and take them home on a roundabout route. Follow me." She moved deeper into the main room and pointed to an empty seat. "Sit, warm yourself by the fire."

I said, "Thank you." and took a seat next to a roaring fire that perfectly warmed my nearly frozen body.

She continued, "We are expecting a long night. That storm you were in is a planner displacement. It is blowing itself out but until it does there will be many lost soles needing rescue. As you can see you are not the first."

"But, I was on the road to the capital. The road was still under my feet."

Her smile was gentle, "No, you were not. You were shifted to another plane of existence. It was close enough to yours that the road seemed the same. Look at the facts. Was it the dead of winter in your world? Were you expecting a blizzard?"

"No. It was early spring and should have been sunny."

"You were lost in the planes and didn't even know it. Oh, you would have noticed the difference when you reached the town." She turned to go into the kitchen. "The plane we found you on is populated mostly by ice demons."

I shuttered as she walked away. She turned and said one more thing before moving out of sight. "Oh, and Wizard, don't do any spells in my Inn."

It wasn't long before she came out with a plate of mush and a cup of water. "I don't suppose you have any gold to pay for your stay here?"

I asked, "What's the cost of rescue?"

She went into a repartee of memorized statements.

1. "Rescue is free. We pick you up and we drop you off at the first plane that is friendly to your kind. That is not likely to be your home plane. Meantime, you get to sleep on the floor here in the main room and eat a full plate of mush once a day.

I looked around. That did not seem like a good or welcomed prospect. She continued.

2. One gold a day for minimal room and board. That gets you three small mush meals a day with a shared room for

eight. Still, you're let off as soon as possible on the first
available friendly plane.

3. Ten gold a day includes a four-person room with others
    of your species, a bath, and three meals a day with meat.
    And, you can stay long enough to pick your plane. Within
    reason.
4. Twenty gold a day gets you a double room and the previous.
5. Fifty gold gets you a single suite with a bath and privy
    built-in, three grand meals a day, snacks, and all the wine
    you can drink. You receive full access to our considerable
    library and you can wait until your plane comes around."

"Any idea how long before my plane will 'come around'?"

"You're from the Prime Material Plane, on the planet called
Slisick." She pulled out a book and started checking schedules.
"The next lost that we pick up on the Prime Material Plane is,"
Her hand went down the page and over to the next. She turned
the pages several times before she found it. "We pick up a Crocker
in thirty-two days and sixteen hours, twenty-seven minutes and
three seconds from now."

I thought for a moment, I am going to be stuck in this Inn
because I do not have my key to plane travel to the Prime Material
Plane. "You wouldn't happen to sell keys to the planes here, would
you? I can do a Planer Travel spell."

"Of course we do, except the Prime Material Plane is not used
very often so we don't carry that key. The Gods normally protect
that plane from planner distortions. You are an abnormality. I see
it is a difficult decision. May I make a suggestion?"

"Of course."

"Get the best you can afford. Being with your kind is helpful.
Sleeping with other races can be disconcerting at best. Having a
place to go when you want to be alone is always good. This Inn
is almost full. It will get very crowded down here in the tavern
very soon."

"It seems crowded now? Why is everyone sleeping?"

"Oh, you're still thinking it's mid day. Not in this place. We picked you up in the middle of the night and our next pick up is in eight minutes."

I pulled out my magical pouch and took out a grand ruby and twenty-three platinum. "Will that pay for the thirty-two days?"

She beamed, "It will indeed." She turned and yelled, "Daphne!"

Instantly a very lovely young girl appeared in front of us. She was rubbing her eyes. "What? It's my sleep time."

The woman said, "This man paid full price. Show him to suite ten."

The girl looked at me as if sizing me up. "Full price. Very nice. Not bad looking either."

The woman said, "Take him now. I need to change into another creature to greet our next lost. If it sees me in this shape it will surly try to eat me. GO!"

As we started to leave she added, "And, tell him the rules."

The girl took my hand and we were instantly in a long hallway with doors lining each side. The doors had writing on them but the numbers were not in a language I understood. We stopped in front of a door and Daphne said, "Place your hand on this door and hold it there." I did and she said something in an old language that I did recognize. "This one paid and is welcome to this room until otherwise stated."

The door opened. Daphne said, "All you need to do is think of this room and you will instantly be inside. This set of rooms is now yours for as long as you paid for. Don't worry about a maid as the room cleans itself. No one will disturb you here except staff and don't count on that happening until your drop off point and time."

"Thank you."

"I'm not finished. The rules are simple. Do what you want. Read and study in the library anything you want. We don't care. But, do not use any spells without direct permission and don't count on that happening. Do not harm another. No physical confrontations and no verbal confrontations. You start it and we will know and we will drop you off at the next plane even if it will not support your life form. If another tries to start something let it go. Let him be the one kicked out. You can protect yourself but the best idea is to think of this room and you will be pulled here without the one that caused the trouble. Then think of me and I will come. I can sort things out." She yawned. "Get some sleep. Breakfast is early. You will hear a chime when it is starting to be served. You can have it here or eat in the dinning room. I would suggest you have it here. The others do not necessarily eat what you do and it can ruin your appetite."

"How do I get the food to come here?"

"Room ten? The man will have his meals in this room unless otherwise stated."

"Understood."

I was looking around for the person to the voice and Daphne started laughing. "Oh, you are going to be fun. Here is something to sleep on. The room is part of the intestines of an enormous creature that sits on the back of a giant bird that is flying through the planes like a pink cloud and smelling out the misplaced before they become lost."

After laughing at the look on my face she kissed my cheek and said, "Goodnight, innocent Child."

She departed and at first, I could not sleep. Finally, I decided that she was just teasing me. I laughed at my foolishness and went to bed.

A chime and the smell of food woke me up in the morning. I got up and had a grand breakfast before getting dressed and going down stairs. The place was buzzing with activity. Creatures were waiting in line to go out the door. Others were looking like they just came in, frightened and unsure. There were creatures with gossamer wings at the bar getting drunk in the morning. Sitting around one table was a group of devils talking about and creating contracts. Near my table, there were three liquid blobs playing games. I saw a Caelum Seraphim in the opposite corner reading. There was every creature imaginable and some I would not have thought of in a thousand nightmares. Some were doing things I did not understand and a few were watching with wide eyes like me. In the corner was a praying mantis the size of a human sucking on the remains of some creature. Breakfast? On the ceiling were creatures walking back and forth as if pacing, and then I noticed that they had holes for taking in air but nothing to suck the air in or out. They were walking to get air into their lungs if they had lungs.

A little girl pulled on my shirt. I looked down at her. She looked normal and very pretty except she had an extra eye on an eyestalk coming out of the top of her head.

"They have lungs, Mister."

I smiled, "Oh, they do?"

"Yes sir. They are called Japperfish. The oldest is only five years. They have very short lives. Their planet is windy and so they developed without the need or ability to intake or exhale air. On their planet, the wind does it for them."

"Thank you. Where are you from?"

"I am an Anroll. My name would translate into your language as Mensy. I come from a plane that is so rare it only shows up every one thousand years. I will have turned to dust and died before my plane shows up again."

"That is sad."

In a pleading voice, she begged, "I could go to your plane. You could take me with you."

I said, "Just a moment." I turned and called, "Daphne."

Instantly Daphne showed up. "What's up?" She looked at the child and put her hands on her hips.

I asked, "May I do a spell to check this one's alignment?"

The child looked shocked and hurt. Daphne said, "No need. It would turn out not evil or good. This creature is an Anroll.

I suggest you look that up in the library before you make any promises."

"Will do. Thank you."

She disappeared and the girl walked away. As Daphne departed the little girl turned into a different creature but still with that eyestalk. She walked up to another being that was looking new. I got directions to the library and headed that way.

As I entered an old man's voice asked, "May I help you?"

I looked around and the voice said, "You will not find me by looking for a body. I am part of the creature's intestines. Oh, and by the way, Daphne was not joking."

It took a minute to calm myself and let the color return to my face. "It seems that I am very ignorant of this place. I need to study where I am and what I can expect. I also need to know about a creature called an Anroll.

The voice said, "There is a book on the shelf nearest you that is a guide to this place. As far as Anrolls are concerned, an Anroll is a creature that feeds off the energy of unborn babies by sucking on the air of the mother while she is sleeping. They can become invisible at will, can cause deep sleep, change shape, read minds, and they have a ferocious hunger. Their limitations are that they always have an eyestalk at the top of their head that they cannot hide as it is their antenna for brainwaves. Also, they cannot normally leave their planet. It is displaced in time so that it shows up only once in a thousand years. Last, they cannot leave this place unless invited. However, once invited you cannot turn them down."

"How are they destroyed?"

"You cannot do that here. This place is protected from allowing harm to others. However, if you did find one on your planet I would suggest you destroy it as quickly as possible. They die as easy as you would and by the same means if you can find them. They teleport and shift at will. They also go ethereal and can walk through walls. They are harmless to those that are already born but if one were loose on your world you would know it. Every creature in the area would have still borne children."

"I am glad I did not invite her."

"Remember this Wizard, always ask Daphne. She will tell you the ins and outs of each situation. Do not make any deals, bargains, agree to anything, play any games, or invite anyone up to your room until you talk to Daphne. After she enlightens you then it is up to you to decide if it is a good idea. Daphne will be interested in seeing if you are intelligent enough to make the right decision. She always gets a kick out of what stupid things creatures do."

"About Daphne?"

"Oh, very good Wizard. You are the first to ask that in a hundred years. Daphne is a Gordomaturwi. She feeds off the soles of those that do stupid things like brake the rules, and there is plenty to keep her full. However, don't tempt fait and invite her to stay in your room. That would be a bad idea. Another issue with her is that she gains energy from being asked questions and giving answers. She likes you because she thinks you will be calling upon her a lot. You have that innocent look that the predators here will flock too. Did you know the entire table of Devils are working on a contract for you as we speak."

I looked worried, "Wonderful. Perhaps I can simply stay in my room."

"That would be a good idea but you are a curious race and I doubt you will be able to stay away from the tavern. There is much to be learned."

I reached over and picked a book from the shelf. The edge said, "Inside the Beast." On the cover was a picture of an enormous creature sitting on the back of a giant pink bird flying through the planes like a cloud grabbing up people that looked lost.

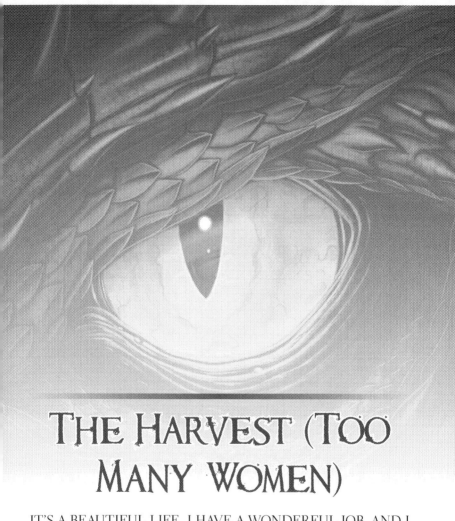

THE HARVEST (TOO MANY WOMEN)

IT'S A BEAUTIFUL LIFE, I HAVE A WONDERFUL JOB, AND I get paid a grand sum. Enough to buy this small house and furnish it, set aside gold for a time of need, and feed and clothe my family in good style.

I am considered a minor noble due to being the sixth cousin to the Crown Prince. Still, the Prince has a lot of cousins so I am way down on the line to succession. Thank the Gods for that. I'm at a position where I don't need to play politics.

I have a wonderful wife given to me by the King himself. She is the best. She greets me when I come home with hugs, love, and a hot bath. Oh, she isn't a "trophy wife" like most of my royal cousins have. In my opinion, she is far better. She may not be the prettiest girl in the kingdom but she is prettier than most. My girl is intelligent, wise, easy to get along with, happy to be married to me, a great mother to our children, and we have been in love for eight years now.

Of course, we didn't start out in love. It was rather a shock to go to a summons in court to find out I am married to a woman from the farm lands, a pig farmer's daughter. Even more of a shock was that she had been married before and that she is not a virgin. In this world of twenty-three females to every man, I grew up dreaming of a wife that was a virgin, the loveliest girl in the kingdom, and the envy of all my pears. It was easily possible. Instead, I got Glenda.

My brother has a trophy wife. Asked the King himself he did. The King tried to warn him, but he wanted her. Said he was in love. As far as looks, on a scale from copper to platinum, his wife is a platinum plus. Even the Princess is jealous. His wife is an eye full and every man is watching especially when Jim is not at home. As a sergeant in the guard, he is surprisingly gone a lot. I think he volunteers for out of city assignments. I think I understand why. His wife has no intelligence, can't cook, can't clean, is a horrible mother, is expensive to maintain, is stuck on herself, and my brother hates her and loves her at the same time.

My wife thinks she is foolish, irritating, and boring. She does not like her around. Not because she is worried about me straying. She ensures I am well taken care of and I return the favor. She does not like her around because she talks only about herself. She is interested in nothing else. I once heard my wife say, "I would love to get that hussy out in the country under my control. She'd learn real fast how to take care of that husband of hers."

While I was laying with Glenda one night she asked me what I thought of the girl. I said, "My brother made a bad mistake there. She is nice to look at but not to live with. There is no warmth to hold onto during the cold nights, no one to talk to about your job, and no one to keep you out of debt. Besides, I don't think she can boil water without finding someway to burn it."

That got Glenda to laughing. Glenda is a grand cook. Each year she wins several prizes at the fair. Her roast pig is to die for and no one, not even the royal cooks, can make peach cobbler better than my sweetheart. I keep teasing her, "If I didn't have such a physical job I would grow fat."

She always teases back, "You could use some weight. You're skinny. I keep trying to fatten you up but you never gain a pound. You should go see the Cleric and find out what's wrong."

Having the job I have and being married to a pig farmers daughter go hand in hand. I doubt anyone else would have me. I love Glenda and would kill to keep her. You see, I am the Sewer Master. It is my position to keep the sewers clean and running smoothly. I have twenty people working for me. One Cleric, one Wizard, three Guards, a Rogue, and the rest are cleaners. We have three dogs we take with us and two cages of small song birds. It's a smelly job but extremely important. We keep the sewers clean of creatures, thieves, dead bodies, trash, explosive fumes, and clogs. We scrub the sewers to ensure smooth flow at all times. The most difficult part of the job is the rats. That is a constant battle. However, a fireball or two normally fries them well. Then it's pick up and dispose of.

On another note, I purchased a lot of worthless land from the King at the insistence of my good wife. The King was happy to sale it off. The entire disposal goes to that land to build more farm lands. Glenda taught me that if you add dead creatures, excrement, and any trash that will rot to a soil that is deprived of minerals for growth, in a few years you have more farm land. Stinks horribly until it turns to soil, but eventually it turns. Glenda said they do it on the pig farm all the time. It's called composting. We have been composting on a grand scale for eight years now.

I hired wagons and men to pick up rotten materials, fruits, meats, vegetables, from the vendors and our entire sewer waste and take it out to my lands. They spread it over my two hundred square leagues of land and the sun and rain does the rest. I have three men that plow the fields constantly to turn the soil and compost and remove rocks.

The Clerics have checked our land and it is not worthless anymore and that makes the King very happy and I got a big pay raise. Our land is considered some of the best top soil in the country. Glenda had trees planted three years ago. Now we own orchards. Imagine that, I am a farmer of apples and oranges. Now she is planting peach and nut trees. She tells me it will be years before they produce but the income from the apples and oranges has made us very wealthy.

When my two boys grow up they will have plenty to do. I was not sure about having so many children. Two boys and two girls just to start. But Glenda wanted as many as possible. I asked her why. "Sweetheart, four children are a lot and you want to have more? Why? I'm not complaining mind you but I would like to know your reasoning."

She looked at me with that 'love you and need you' look that she has that melts me to putty in her hands. She said, "I was married and we were doing very well. He died, and I was sent home without anything. Women cannot own land and as I had no sons to give the land to I lost it all to the local Baron. He put his son in charge. I was sent home. I thought I would never get to marry again. Most people will not have a pig farmer's daughter. You gave me another chance at having a good life, children, land, food, and all I could ever want, and you did it while loving me. I was shocked when father received the summons from the crown. So was father. I am one of the lucky ones. My two sisters were not. Their husbands died in the war. By the way, did I mention that they are coming to stay?"

"No. You did not!"

"Father is not doing so well and is likely to lose the farm. He had no sons and my sisters have no children so they are going to be out on the street. I told them to come to us. You're not upset are you?"

As if I could ever be upset with Glenda. "No sweetheart. I am sure that you will put them to good use." Teasingly I added, "Are any as lovely as you. I may be tempted."

She messed my hair, "Oh you." and we got down to making another child.

When we were relaxing again I asked, "Where are you going to house them?"

"What?"

"Where are you going to house everyone? This place is not big enough."

She answered, "I was thinking of building a home on our land. A good size farm house should do."

I lay in thought for a little. "Let me talk to the King first. I will ask for an audience tomorrow."

The next day I went into work and let them know I needed to see the King. I let them know where I wanted them to clean today and what needed doing there. It was a place away from any possible harm. As I was the lead Fighter it would be bad leadership to send them into harm's way without me there to take the front.

At the castle, my Cousin, the Prince, saw me immediately. As I entered the Prince's counsel chambers I went to one knee.

"Rise Robert and welcome."

I rose and walked forward.

"You want to see father? As you know, it is my position to ensure everything that I can legally take care of is accomplished. It leaves father time to investigate the more important issues."

"I know, Highness. However, this issue may require the King's hand. I do not know for sure so I put in to see the King in the hopes that it would not go that far. I do hate to disturb him if not necessary."

"You have always had a good head cousin. I should promote you to a higher position."

"That is the rub, Highness. I am thinking that this new situation will require me to be removed from my current position."

"How so? Your current position is to protect and please the second cousin to the King of Dormer. Your marriage and willingness to love Glenda have kept us from war. The King of Dormer loves his cousin and was extraordinarily upset when she lost everything. The sewer position is only a cover-up to the first."

"Highness, I am talking about the cover-up. I would not wish to leave Glenda. I love her with all my heart, as I love the King."

"That is good to hear. What is happening that causes you to think the sewer will become a difficult situation?"

"You know about our lands?"

"Yes, the King and I are most happy about the new orchards and now I hear that we will have peaches and nuts in a few short years."

"Yes, Glenda is wonderful at farming. However, her father is not. He has become ill and it is not likely that he will last the year."

"That is sad and unpleasant news. The King of Dormer has no love for his first cousin which is why he is a pig farmer. Still, he will not like to hear about his death. Have Clerics been sent?"

"Yes, Highness. Unbeknown to Glenda I sent Clerics several weeks ago when we first received news. They report that he refuses help. He is tired of farming and not having sons to grant his land to. He is not in a good mood and, with the loss of his wife, has lost all wish for life."

"This will not go over well with Dormer."

"Highness, I have been giving it much thought and have come up with no ideas until last night. Glenda accidently gave me a possibility."

"Continue."

"She wants to build a home on our new land so we can house our growing family and her two sisters. The land the King sold me borders Dormer and us. One week ride from our capital, and one week ride to their capital. It is exactly in the center. If I build a house way out there to house my family and take care of the orchards, Glenda will have the chance to visit Dormer and see the King. Something he has asked for several times. We could split the food shipments so that both sides benefit and their King would see that we are doing well together."

The Prince said, "The problem with that plan is you cannot protect her in your current position. You would always be a week away. Besides, if she travels to see the King of Dormer I want you going with her. I want the King to see how happy the two of you are together."

"Exactly. I need a position that keeps me out on the border between our two lands. Besides, I want to be with my wife and family."

The Prince thought for a moment. "We have a garrison at the border. I could put you in charge of that but then you would not be traveling with your wife if she goes visiting. I could release you from duty so that you could take care of the orchards and the food we so desperately need. That would go well with the King's plan. However, it may be seen through and that could cause issues."

"May I suggest something, Highness?"

"Please."

"Reassign me to protect the King of Dormer's cousins. You know we need too, they know we need too, and if she moves out to the country they would expect that someone is assigned to do exactly that. I will have all three living with me and therefore all would be under my protection. Grant me enough to build a small garrison and man it for that reason. Secondary, the garrison would also be there to protect the orchards. Now that the land is fertile the protection is needed."

"You are saying. Make the prime position public."

I answered, "Yes and no, Highness. Tell everyone that it is for protecting our precious food supply form wilders, the creatures that haunt the night in that region. Let the people know that the King is interested in ensuring that the food makes it back to the city. That should make him very popular. Give good cousin Rodney, the Queen's illegitimate son, the contract for shipment too and from the city. That should keep the Queen in check. However, let word get back to the King of Dormer that it is all a cover-up."

"Cover-up? The protection of our new orchards has been top most on the King's mind."

I was shocked, "It has?"

The Prince smiled, "Yes, and he is close to taking them away from you since you are not protecting them. The only thing stopping him is Glenda. If the King of Dormer found out he took all she owned there would be war."

"Then this should play nicely into the King's hand. Assign me to protect my land but make sure that the King of Dormer hears that all the money going into this project is to protect his three cousins. That the garrison to protect the orchards is just a ruse so that I will have the men in place to guard and protect those that I love. Ensure he knows it is because I love Glenda that I am taking this post. You know he has a spy in the castle. You know who he is."

The Prince sat back thinking and after a while, he stood up. "Follow me."

We walked through the castle and into the King's main audience chamber.

Being with the Prince we walked right passed the guards, the people waiting in line, the legal staff, and right up to the King.

"Hello, Father."

"Good morning, Son. To what do I owe this pleasure?"

"Majesty, regarding that rather delicate topic we discussed last night." He whispered just loud enough for several others close by, including the spy, to hear. "The protection of Glenda."

The King looked around like he did not want others to hear the conversation and called for the room to be cleared. Everyone left and the doors were closed. Everyone was out except the three serving men. The spy being one of them. "Go ahead, Son."

"Father, it seems like the issue has just tripled."

"TRIPLED!"

"Glenda has told her sisters that they can come stay with her. It seems our efforts to help the father have failed."

The King looked sad. "It's difficult to lose one's wife and have no sons. That law should be changed." He looked at me and asked, "Well, you are tasked with her protection. What are you going to do? Stuff the sisters in the attic?"

I went to one knee and returned to my stance, "No, my King. Glenda wants to move out to our lands on the border. I would go with her. I love her dearly and all my children. The problem is I cannot protect my love if she is a week away. Therefore, I must forbid the move unless I can be released from being Sewer Master. I would like to take my crew with me. They are good and trusted men and Glenda knows and loves their families and they love her."

The Prince added, "I would not allow them out of the city without more protection; therefore, I am proposing a cover-up. We need to protect the orchards from the wilders. A garrison out near the border would look good. With Robert, who loves the woman almost as much as he loves you sire, as protection, and a garrison to back him up she should be well protected. Robert is one of our best fighters and strategists. Everyone sees him as a simple Sewer Master but what Sewer Master has worked eight years and never lost a man." The spy's eyes went wide as that is an unbelievable accomplishment. "With Robert protecting his love and her sisters, Glenda can move closer to the border and even visit home. At the same time, the crown looks good because we are protecting the food supply and we look doubly good because we are sharing it with Dormer." Everyone could see the Queen was thinking a mile a minute so the Prince turned to her and added, "Robert thinks Rodney would be the best for moving the food between

JOHN RICKS

the city and orchards. We will have to find someone else for the Dormer side."

The Queen visibly relaxed. "Rodney does have the necessary wagons and men. We may have to repair the roads."

The Prince said. "I have already repaired the roads and bridges so that I could bring in the needed supplies to our border garrison."

I said, "I would expect anyone taking over the Sewer Master position to continue shipping me the waste. I will take it off your hands for free, my King."

The Queen said, "Rodney told me about your wagons and what they were hauling. I am sure he would love to take that over as well. Especially if the crown is paying."

I smiled, "That would be wonderful, Majesty. It would sure take a load off my back. I will also need supplies for the orchard garrison."

The King was taking all this in. "So be it. In truth, we need the orchards and Glenda has done us a big favor creating them. I love that child as if she were my own." He leaned down and looked me right in the face. "You take good care of Glenda, Baron Robert, or you will find yourself before my displeasure." The King called for his legal staff. "Do we have anymore worthless land near the border that this new Baron has not purchased?"

A young man said, "Sire, we still have eight hundred square leagues up there that are exactly the same as the ones he bought."

The King smiled, "As a new Baron, I grant you all the land stated. Find the best place for the garrison and make me more food. That should keep Glenda busy and happy. You have my leave."

The Prince and I talked for a few hours and then I returned to the house and Glenda's arms. "Did you talk with the King?"

The smile on my face got her curiosity up. "Well, what did he say? Can we build a home on our estates?"

"Nope, we have to build a lot of homes and a garrison to put them in. Seems he is worried about the wilders and our new food supply. He wants that food. The country needs it and so does Dormer. We are to split it and send half to their Capital."

She hugged me tight, with happiness, and then she stopped. Looking sad she asked, "And, your position in the sewers?"

"I am no longer the Sewer Master. I will miss that job. You are looking at the newest Baron in the kingdom. We have been granted the entire north-east section of land. Eight hundred square leagues more than we originally purchased.

She nearly fainted. I held her up while I dropped another egg. "We have been granted all our men and their families as well as fifty soldiers that I can hand pick and their families."

She became defensive and asked, "Just how do you think we will pay for all of this, Baron Robert!"

I held up the last surprise. "This is a grant from the crown for one hundred thousand gold. It is free and clear and ours to build the garrison and small castle. For every additional gold we put into the land for the first five years the crown will match it. And, no taxes for the first five years."

It was back to happy hugs and screams of laughter. The children came out looking curious. I said teasingly. "Is that any way for a Baroness to act, and in public?"

She stopped, her entire stance changed, and she asked in a tone of pure evil intent. "Robert dear, does your brother's wife know yet?"

"Daphne? I don't think so. No one knows except Captain Loren. He is my pick to run the garrison and pick the troops and the only order I gave him was not to pick Jim."

She smiled, "Resend that order, please. How long before the proclamation comes out?"

"Any time now. Why would you want Jim to come with us? You know he will have to bring his wife."

"Perfect. When do we leave?"

I looked at her in shock. "In about a week. I am expecting the entire family to come with me. We will be roughing it for a little while. We need to pick out the place where the garrison will go. Then build temporary quarters before working on the main structure."

She thought for a second, "There is plenty of wood for the temporary structures but the main building needs to be built out of rock and as solid as possible. There is an old temple that my people use to use up there. It is how I knew about the land. It would make a grand garrison with a view of the entire central valley. It will take a lot to fix it up but it will be near impregnable. I will show you on a map when you have one. Right now I have tons of planning to do and the children need to be prepared."

I said, "About the children. I do not want them running around unwatched. Who knows what trouble they could get into in the wild?"

She smiled and stroked my cheek. "City folk. You will be surprised by the difference between city life and country life." She turned to say to herself, "I have packing and planning supplies for the entire winter. Goodness, I need to buy everyone new clothes. These silly city clothes are far too flimsy. A good bow for Edward and plenty of arrows. It's a new sword for Richard, he can have Edward's old bow. No sense wasting. Susan will need a sling and a belt knife, and Rebecca will need a new pacifier. My husband will need new armor and he can finally use his father's grand sword and shield." Her voice trailed off as she walked into the house.

Running up nearly out of air came Jim. He was just off watch. As soon as he caught his breath he said, "Robert, brother, take me with you. Please, you need to take me away from her. I can't afford to keep her up. She's killing me."

"Jim, she is cheating on you. Kill her. You know the law. I will be a witness. Kill her and then ask the King for someone you can trust. The new wife won't be pretty but she will make you happy."

"I can't do that. I love her."

"If I tell the Captain to include you in the count will you promise to bring her and keep her with us? No sending her back just because she complains."

"Sure. Why?"

"Glenda has a notion she can teach her to be a better wife."

Jim's eyes nearly turned in their sockets. "Glenda would be a Baroness and can legally order her around."

"Exactly. She would be assigned like everyone else. She would have work to do and if it does not get done you can expect to see her sitting tenderly for a few days. Glenda will not put up with laziness. Nor, is there anyplace to spend money for a weeks travel. Your wife will help prepare meals even if that means hauling water from the creek. She will do laundry, take good care of her children and her husband, or Glenda and the others will be all over her hide."

Jim smiled, "Please brother, tell the Captain I'm coming along as a sergeant. You know I am good."

"What about your wife?"

"Camp help."

"Done. Tell the Captain I said it was agreed. Tell your wife after. Let her know Glenda will be in charge and that she better prepare well or at least see Glenda for preparations. You don't want her and the children going without because she has no clue."

"I have a clue what with all the camping I've done to stay away. We will be ready. When do we leave?"

"One week. Funding will not be available to you. Not with your wife's tendency to spend. Order what supplies you need from Glenda. She will purchase them." Jim took off to find the Captain.

Glenda, Gods bless her, handled everything while I trained my replacement. She sent the Wizard to fetch her two sisters and teleport them back. Between the three of them, we were on our way and on time. Jim's wife, Daphne, was not looking very happy.

Her two children were being very quiet. Jim was riding upfront with his troops.

I heard Jim arguing with his wife as we started, "Look, sweetheart. We either go with my brother, who is being very kind to take us along, or I become the Sewer Master. I won't last two days down there and you will be a widow and out on the street. Two daughters and no sons are not good in this kingdom. What with the ratio of twenty-three women to each man."

"But Glenda is just looking for an excuse to make me work. It will ruin my hands."

I decided to put a stop to it. "Jim, upfront with your troops." He departed. I leaned over and said, "Daphne, you are going to work and work hard. You will do everything the Baroness tells you to do and do it with pride and pleasure. If I find out your lazy hide is not taking care of my brother and my nesses I will take a knife and make it so the only looks you ever receive again are cringes."

I grabbed the rains as she fainted. One of my sisters-in-law saw and hopped up on the wagon. I have it, my Lord. And, we will ensure she learns everything a good wife needs to know and practice it constantly."

I smiled, "Good, because I expect all my men to be loyal to me and their wives, and I expect all my women to be loyal to me and their husbands. My Glenda will be the shinning example of the best wife a man can get, and I will try to be an example of the best husband."

That is how we started. We've lived in the border land valley for twenty years now. I have eight children and nearly twice that many grandchildren and all but three are boys. All the square leagues are planted and harvests have made me the richest Baron in both Kingdoms. We are constantly visited by both sides of the family. From the Kings to cousins we never knew we had. You see, both my sister-in-laws married my soldiers and they had boys. Something about the two races and country cooking I think. But, in this world of twenty-three women to every male. My little piece of paradise has sixty-four unmarried boys and few little girls to marry them to.

The King has said, "The food has been a great harvest for our kingdom, but the sons are a greater harvest."

THE ROSE WIZARD

I STOOD PROUD AT GRADUATION. I WAS SECOND IN MY class, a capable student, untried but moldable, no ties as I do not know who my Father and Mother are, and I was not picked. Again, I was alone.

When I came to the Wizard's University I'd chosen to multi-task. I was first in my class the first year and by the second year was teaching the first year students. I was so good at the simple spells that I choose to learn divine spells in addition to the arcane spells. Everyone said I was being foolish but the rules apply. You must stay in the school for four years and you are capped at third circle spells until graduation. I could do most third circle arcane spells the second year. I am a Sorcerer type of Wizard.

My mentor talked me into becoming a full Wizard. "Your natural ability to use some spells will do you good but you would do better if you learned as many spells as possible so that you

JOHN RICKS

have a greater repartee at graduation. That will gain you the best position. With your talent, you could become an apprentice to a Wizard in the great city, or even to the royal house. You have no ties. They will like that."

So, I took up being a full Wizard. Some spells I can do without memorizing them for the day due to my Sorcerer ability, but most spells I need to study each morning. I have several full books. That cost me but I worked off the cost doing things around the University and town. It was late in my second year that I took sick after taking a bashing from Kam while learning to use a staff. It was supposed to be practice but Kam made it deadly. They called for a Cleric. He did a simple Light Healing on me and I was completely healed. I took to studying the divine spells. I am not much for praying to any God but the simple spells do not require assistance from the Gods. By the end of my fourth year, I knew all third circle arcane and divine spells. Problem is, everyone else knew some of the third circle arcane spells and one young girl passed me up as head of the Wizard's class.

There I stood as they announced our standings. This is the Wizard's School so they don't announce that someone can do divine spells. They announced that I was second in my class of six. It made no difference that the four below us were way below are abilities and could just barely do the third circle, or that the class started with thirty-two students and twenty-six failed. That was not stated as it would be an embarrassment to the others. It was also not stated that Carroll and I are the top two Wizards of the decade as that would be improperly bragging. Carroll was picked by the Grand Master of the Royal House. Just my luck this would be the year he needed a new apprentice. The others were picked by their home towns. I was left standing. People don't come to the Wizard's University unless they have a good reason. Picking up family is a good reason. Teleporting in because you are a Grand Mage and need an apprentice is a good reason. Traveling two weeks across the seas at this time of year in the slim hope that someone will be left standing is not a good reason. I was not picked. The next day I found myself out on the street with my packed belongings.

I had saved up plenty of gold from practicing healing spells on the town populace and students. Just before graduation, I was asked to heal the Master of Potions. I did and was paid seven hundred gold and some potions that I could not do yet. With that, and my other gold, I bought a used magical deep pocket haversack. All my belongings went inside and it weighed only two pounds. I still had enough gold to spend years in the country looking for work. I decided to become a traveling Wizard. There are plenty of little communities that have no magic user and need one. After receiving a letter of introduction from the head of the University, and my graduation papers, I was off. I booked passageway to the main land with all the others. Their passage was paid for by their towns while I was working my way across to save gold.

I spent my days controlling the wind so that everyone had a nice journey, talking with my friends, and generally having a good time. The Captain was happy that he did not need to hire a high-level Wizard for the wind. I saved him a lot of money and got me a good cot and some extra spending cash when we reach port. Several times town folk would ask the others. "Can you control the weather like he is doing?"

Always the answer was, "He is not controlling the weather, Sir. That would be against the laws. He is controlling the wind a little. And, no sir, I can't. He is one of the best the Wizard's University has ever seen. He even knows divine spells."

I had to use divine spells several times. Even in calm weather a ship rocks and rolls. Several had seasickness. The Captain asked if I could do anything about it and so I did. It cost them very little. Just enough to replenish what I used from my spell component pouch plus a gold piece or two. One student noticed that I was wearing a belt with twenty metal vials.

He asked in front of the others, "Hay Joe, what's with the vials?"

"Five are healing potions and the others are an assortment of potions that would be good in an emergency."

"They all your creations?"

"All but two. I can't do Shift Position potions yet."

Janet asked, "You bought two Shift Position potions? That must have been expensive."

I smiled, "I didn't buy them. I traded several healing potions for each. I needed some Shift Position potions and the Master of Potions needed some healing potions. We traded."

Janet asked, "Did you get to bring your staff? You put a lot of work and energy into it. We had to leave ours for the new students."

"I did some work in the town and raised enough money to buy my staff for the first year. It was my staff and that is the only reason I put so much into it. I knew I was going to be allowed to take it with me. I started out buying the best Iron Wood with good grain I could find. It's heavy, but it has an impact that can shatter another's staff and Iron Wood can hold a lot of magic. More so than any other wood. Difficult to carve though, I went through three knives the third year."

Mack asked, "You never told us. Why did you wait until the third year to start carving it?"

Janet said, "Because silly, there is a big difference between what a first-year student can carve and set into the wood, and a third-year student."

I said, "Janet is right. She has a good head on her shoulders and will do well for her town. They should be proud of her. I practiced carving first until I had that down very well. The spells carved into my staff are simple spells but very needed and placed into the staff in such a way that I can pound on the wall with it all day long and the spell carvings will still be there. They only disappear when I use one of the spells. Then I need to sit down and carve it back in. Disappointing that."

Janet laughed, "Even the Staff Master has to carve depleted spells back into his staff. There is no easy way around that issue. What spells did you choose?"

"Some third circle healing, a few minor renewals, heal poison, heal disease, heal blindness and deafness, regeneration, fire ball, and lighting shaft."

They were all shocked. Janet asked, "You mixed arcane and divine spells in one staff!?"

"Sure."

"We were told that was dangerous. Very dangerous."

"It was and I paid the price by nearly blowing myself up several times. However, you know me. When has a little pain ever stopped me from doing what I want?"

Janet said, "If you were not of goodly nature I would be worried about you."

I said, "Interesting, those were the exact words Master Glen said to me just before graduation."

One of the town folk quietly asked their young Wizard, "This Joe, he seems to be very resourceful, very hard working. Why was he not picked? He looked so lonely on the stage by himself. If we could have afforded we would have helped him, but we were afraid there was something wrong with him and that is why he wasn't being picked."

Lyle looked up into the Mayor's eyes and said, "We could not afford him, father. His price was near double that of the top student. He is that much better at near everything. She was only the top because she is better at politics. And, though she is powerful in the arcane, Joe is nearly as powerful in three disciplines."

"Three?"

"Yes, Father, arcane, divine, and bardic. He tells great stories and has used bardic stories and music to put the first years to sleep on stormy nights. That is how we found out. There is nothing wrong with him. He is a good friend. Watch." He turned to Janet and I. We were going over a simple third circle spell that has always eluded her. "Joe, you are always welcome to come visit us in Tyler Town. Father has extra rooms and you can stay as long as you want. I am sure we can find lots of work for you."

Janet broke in, "No, he's going to my town to help out."

Mack said, "Actually, I was talking to the ranger that was sent for me and we could use another good Wizard, especially one with divine abilities also. I was hoping he would come our way."

The only other graduate was quietly talking to his friend in the corner of the ship. He knew that the only reason I would visit his town is to kill him. Some Wizards don't get along well with others and that boy, Kam, is evil. Even Master Cornersmith warned me about him before I left.

I said, "I will visit all of you at one point or another if you will have me. I plan on being a traveling Wizard for my first few years before deciding on settling down to any one place. I may go adventuring. I hear there are some very interesting places up in the spike mountains that hold wondrous treasures."

Everyone was quiet for a second and then Janet said, "You're teasing."

I looked at her and she knew that I was not. She said, "Please Joe, you are needed. There are many towns, villages, and cities that need a good Wizard. You're one of the best. Don't throw your life away."

I said, "There is something up there that I want. It is calling me. I will go and fetch it. I will not tell you what it is; only that I want it. It is wasting away up there and I plan on using it."

Mack asked, "I have seen that look in your eyes before, Joe. You're going. I hope this item is worth it. Is it evil?"

"No, my friend. It is not evil. If it were; then I would be going to destroy it, not use it. I can tell you no more."

Things became quiet after that talk. They believed, and with good reason, that I was going to my death after some item that should be left alone. Their town representatives tried to talk me out of going. One even offered me a good job.

"When I have the item and have tamed it, then I may take you up on that offer, Sir. But, I still think traveling around for a while is best. Make a name for myself as a good kind Wizard. Then getting a job with people I have already learned to love and who love me will be far more enjoyable."

The Elder said, "That is a wise plan but I am not sure the adventure you are planning first is so wise."

"It is not, Sir. It is probably the most unwise thing any fool Wizard can do. Dangerous to the maximum, deadly every step, my chances of being successful are extraordinarily slim. But, while I am not needed, and not missed if I fail, it is the best time possible to try. Have you ever had something stuck inside your head and you could not get it out? Eventually, you just had to do it?"

"Yes, and I have regretted it the rest of my life."

"Still, you knew you would. Somewhere in the back of your mind, you knew you would regret doing it but you did it just the same."

"True."

"I have that problem now. Do it now or latter makes no difference to the way it has to be done. Beginning Wizard or Grand Magi makes no difference. It is not a matter of what you are but a test of what you will become. If you see me again after this trip then you will know I was successful and that I will always be the best Wizard, goodly of nature, kind, and helpful. The kind of Wizard you want for a friend. That, or I will be dead."

I turned away and he departed. But before he left he said, "You're that kind of Wizard now. No reason to test it, Boy."

The trip ended uneventfully. Again, the others offered to take me with them. I told them I would be by to see them soon. I waited until I was sure all were gone, especially Kam. He was the least capable of the four but a backstabbing rat. If he knew my path he would be waiting in ambush for the chance I would return with the item.

When I was sure all were gone I set off in a direction that was not the way I needed to go to reach my goal and near opposite the direction Kam should be going. I traveled several days until I reached the forest and after entering the woods I took to hiding on the side. It was only a few short hours before Kam and eight fighters came through on horseback. The one in the lead was tracking me and looked off in the direction I had originally entered the woods. However, I entered, went two hundred paces following the road, then crossed the road and doubled back on the other side. He was looking the wrong way. I hit them with a grand fire ball followed up with a fast grand fire ball placed where it would not harm their pack horses. True, the University limited us to only third circle spells, but I could learn all the enhancement skills I wanted and as my mentor found out I am powerful even beyond him. Why was I given this kind of power? I do not know, but I was going to find out.

I waited to see movement but they were all dead. I came out and healed the last horse that was wounded. I did fixing spells on his tack and saddle. Then with their two pack horses and this fine mount, I headed out toward my goal.

It was on the fifth day I found the pass. It traveled nearly straight up the mountain. There was nothing to show where it was. The mountain it was on did not stand out as anything special, yet the calling told me that this was the way. I have had the calling for three years now. My mentor knows and he has spoken with the heads of the University. He told me, "It is a lonely path that has been set before you. Something knows your power. It is calling you. We cannot determine what or who it is but we know it will continue until you go to it. We suggest that you do so as soon as possible. After graduation of course."

I took the horses as far as I could and then let them go. They would freeze up here if not protected so I placed a picture in their minds of green pastures down the mountain and sent them on their way.

After doing an Elemental Cold Comfort spell on myself I continued my climb. The calling was getting stronger. At one point I thought I heard a voice. I stopped and listened but I did not hear it again. I continued.

When I reached a point near the top there was a cave. It was hidden and I doubt I would have found it if not for the calling. The cave opening was small but this is where the calling was coming from. I went inside and waited at the front for my eyes to adjust. It was near midnight outside but it was brighter than noon day inside the cave. When I could see properly what I saw was unbelievable. I was standing in a temple, old and crumbling, white as snow, and the light was coming from a book on a raised dais in the center of the cave. There were no other doors. No way in or out except the small cave entrance.

I walked up to the book and felt a goodness wash over me. The love and warmth were amazing and made me cry. Behind the book appeared a beautiful woman. She smiled and said, "Welcome, my Son. I am your Mother."

Tears fell from my face like rain in the forest. She smiled, "I met your Father during a battle over one of my temples. He was a grand Wizard and a good man. I am an old God. Your father and I fell in love. He died in that same battle but left me with child. That was a surprise to me as I was not expecting to become pregnant. It seems your father had dragon blood somewhere down his ancestral line or it could not have happened. Still, there I was with a human child. I could not take you to the place I am going so I placed you into capable hands with instructions to send you to the University at the right age. I have no worshipers anymore and I am dying out. I go to another place of peace and plenty so do not cry for me. I waited until this moment to depart." She motioned to the book. "I created a book of spells that you must read, my Son. Please do so now."

I opened the book and as I read, the spells disappeared. Every spell was permanently etched into my mind. I could easily recite each from memory. When I was done I knew all spells through the ninth circle. Arcane, divine, druidic, bardic, all spells. And, the book disappeared.

I looked puzzled but she said, "I cannot leave such an artifact on this plane. If Kam, or others of his sort, would have managed to read it the world would be in trouble. I have destroyed it."

"I killed Kam, Mother. What is your name? I will worship you."

She smiled, "I will not tell you my name as I do not want you praying to me. I go where I long to go. I have lingered only for this moment. She looked stern for a second. "For goodness sake, Child, pick a God and worship that God. You could be so much more with the help of a good-aligned God."

"Any suggestions, Mother? I find it difficult to pick."

"You will come to know one God above the rest. It will take time but you will learn. I must leave you now, my Son." She raised a hand and said, "I grant you the knowledge to know what is right and wrong, and the wisdom to do the right." We talked for hours, maybe days. She slowly disappeared and I cried. She touched my tears and each tear after her touch that reached the ground created a yellow rose. Her parting words were, "Remember me always, my Son, as you see the yellow rose."

The cave started to crumble so I held it up with my mind as if it were nothing until I departed and then I let it fall. I stood upon the mountain crying out to the wind and in my sadness, the wind answered back. It was a woman's voice. "Go forth child and make your Mother proud."

I left the mountain and called the horses to me. I untied their burdens and removed their harnesses and tack. Then I turned them loose. I reached out and my old staff was in my hand. With a word, I erased all the carving I had so painstakingly dug into the wood. With other words of power, I created symbols and ruins of ancient powerful might. On the top, I placed a crystal embedded with blue star shine and the tip I balanced with the weight and burden of love.

With staff in hand, I started walking this earth, doing good deeds, helping people and creatures wherever I could, destroying evil, and visiting friends. I made a name for myself. It was inevitable that I would shed a tear, if not for sadness, then for joy. It was at the birth and blessing of a child I shed my next tear. I am now known as the Rose Wizard.

THE BEGINNER

WHY IS IT THAT LITTLE PEOPLE ARE NOT TAKEN seriously? I may be little but that does not give my town the right to refuse me and pick another just because he is taller. When the candidates for the Wizard's University entered the stage there were cheers, ohs, and ahs until I entered and then it turned to laughter. The tallest was next in line and he kicked me in the rear creating even more laughter.

The city counsel was looking on and so was the local Wizard. The city counsel was laughing, the Wizard was not. The mayor stood and climbed upon the stage.

The Mayor said, "This year, as in the past and once every ten years, we the people pick their newest Wizard trainee. Our most esteemed Wizard has chosen these five as the most likely to succeed. He has given his opinion on which are the best choices and I must say he was candid about some and less than happy about others. As I place my hand on the head of the child, you are to cheer for the one you want to be your next Wizard." He went behind the first and put his hand on his head and the cheers where loud. He placed his hand on the girl next to him and the cheers were not very loud. Next came the guy beside me. The cheers were near deafening. He did not place a hand on my head. He skipped me and placed it on the head of the guy that kicked me. The cheers were OK but not loud. He returned to me and said, "How many want a Wizard that needs to sit on books to be tall enough to eat at the table?" Then he placed a hand on my head. The Wizard wanted to cheer but he had to live with these people. No one cheered. No one laughed. It was completely quiet. Even the birds and animals were quiet for that very long couple of seconds.

"Then we have our next Wizard." He took the hand of the one that received the most cheers and raised it as the rest of us were escorted off the stage. On the way down the back steps, the one that kicked me pushed me off and then hit me hard. "You got me in trouble up there. I couldn't help but kick you. You're pathetic and that made me look bad. I should kill you now and put you out of our town's misery."

I picked myself up, no one else was going to, and dusted myself off. "You don't have to worry, I'm leaving."

I walked away to the laughs of the others. I didn't walk far before I was home. Mother and father were not there and neither were my sisters. They were all in town celebrating. They cheered for the tall one also. I packed and left. I did not take the road as father would send the Sheriff after me. I took to the forest. No one saw me leave or so I thought.

I stayed in the forest but kept the road in sight whenever possible. The road is where the bridges are and not taking the bridges makes a long walk near impossible. I was gone several days before I set camp well back from the road. I was tired and wanted hot food. I caught a rabbit only that morning and was planning on eating it that night. Cold hard tack is good for sustaining you but it does not warm the belly.

After I set camp and gathered fire wood I made a split and skinned the rabbit. Dinner was good and so was sleep. Something was bothering me though. It was as if I was being watched. I couldn't shake the feeling.

I continued traveling this way for weeks, sneaking around creatures that could eat me, always headed in the same direction, toward the University. You don't have to be sponsored by a town or another Wizard. Any person can walk up to the University and if they show any type of talent toward magic then they are let in. The King decided that trained Wizards are safer than untrained fools.

The entire time I traveled I practiced using the three spells I knew. They were the lowest level of spells. Fire Finger will start a fire for you, Perfect Shot will help in catching dinner, and Illumination helps in the dark places of the forest. Don't want to fall into holes or over a cliff. When using light I stayed way back from the road.

Several times I saw the Sheriff and his men. Twice they combed the forest on both sides of the road. At one point they stopped and the Sheriff said, "Stupid scrawny punk. I get my hands on him and I am going to strangle that fool child." They turned back the next day and I never saw them again. Still, that feeling of being watched never left.

It took me most of the summer to reach the University. It was starting to turn cold and "fire finger" is not for warming the body. I walked up to the main door and entered the University. Two boys were on watch. They looked at me as if I was a vagabond. Spending three months in the woods with only one change of pants will do that. One asked me my purpose and I said, "Training."

A tall boy was on watch and he laughed, "In what? Tying shoes? You won't even need to bend over."

His laughter was cut short when an old man came over and asked, "What is so funny, Child?"

The boy said, "This shrimp wants to be a Wizard, Master."

With all seriousness, the old man asked me, "Can you do any magic, Young Man?"

"Yes, sir." I did "fire finger" and then light for him.

The old man smiled brightly. "Welcome young man. Welcome to the Wizard's University."

The boy was shocked. He was a second year and could barely do what I just did very easily. The old man said, "Check him in and treat him well. If I find out you are treating any more potentials in a bad way, you're out!"

The boy said, "Come with me. You've already gotten me in trouble once. I don't need any more problems."

I followed and asked, "Why is it that tall people who pick on short people and get caught think it's the fault of the short person?"

"Because."

That was his answer, 'Because.' I was most disappointed. I was hoping it would be different here. He showed me to a room and said, "This is the new person's room. Be quiet as two others are waiting. Someone will be by in the morning to escort the three of you to breakfast and then the testing room. Take any empty bunk you want. Good night."

He left and I entered. Figures, two sets of bunk beds and no ladders. The bottom beds were occupied so I curled up on the floor and went to sleep. In the morning I could hear people getting up and getting ready for the day. I was up before the others. I was still dressed in the clothes I wore through the woods. They were dirty and torn but I had made it to the University and didn't care how I looked at this point. Looking out the window I saw Wizards and students and they were all in a hurry. Someone knocked on the door so I went over and opened it. A student looked in and then down. She was very nice looking but I am not a fool anymore. Nice looking girls pay no attention to boys that are half their height.

"Well, who do we have here? I am Tammy and your name is?"

"I am John. It is nice to meet you, Tammy."

The others were getting up. Tammy introduced herself and they responded. Scotty and Mike. She escorted us to breakfast and as we ate she asked the others all kinds of questions. I was ignored. Fine with me, I'm used to it. It was a good breakfast but cleaning up before eating would have been nice.

After breakfast, she escorted us to the testing room. Mike and Scotty talked the entire time and probably missed all the wonders to see. There were lights without fire, torches without heat, and statues where the creatures moved to watch your travel. I waved at one and he licked his lips, scary. I had to smile. At one point we paused before a door and had to wait. There was a baby dragon in the corner. I went over and sat down and petted it. The other two paid no attention as if they didn't even see the dragon. The door finally opened and we entered into a large room. Several Wizards were sitting in a half-circle. Tammy closed the door as she quietly left.

An old man said, "Well, come in. Don't be shy. We are not here to harm you."

Another said, "We are here to test you. To see if you are capable of taking the training or have any magical talent at all."

An old lady said, "Come forward Master Mike Forlong."

Mike walked forward with pride and strength. "I am here…"

He was cut short by the lead old man. "We know why you are here, Child. What magic have you learned?"

Mike was not looking so proud now. "I have not learned any magic yet, Sir. I just got here."

The old man asked, "Then what makes you think you can learn magic?"

Mike said, "My father is a Wizard."

The old lady said, "That does not mean that you can be a Wizard or that you possess the aptitude. Have you ever shown any ability to learn magic? After all, your father is a Wizard. You must have been around magic users all your short insignificant life."

"No, maim. I have never been given the opportunity."

Another old man said, "You mean you have never taken the opportunity. We have watched you for years and are greatly disappointed in your lack of initiative."

A younger Wizard came forward. "Stand still, Mike. As you have not shown any talent I will need to push on your abilities to see if it is possible. I am sure your father did this already." She placed her hand on his forehead. Her hand and his head glowed for only a second and then she stepped back. "He has some minor talent, Masters. Just enough to make him dangerous to himself and others." She looked at Mike and said while shaking her head, "Tiny child."

The Oldest said, "Very well. We will train him just enough to keep him from harming himself and others. Step back child and let Master Scotty Horman come forward."

The Oldest asked, "What magic can you do, Master Scotty Horman?"

Scotty became a little belligerent and said, "If you have been watching me then you know what I can or cannot do."

Fire lit in the eldest's eyes and Master Scotty flew across the room to slam into the wall. In a calm polite tone screaming "Never Upset the Masters!" he said, "We have watched you, fool child. You know one tiny little spell called Illumination. You have not practiced it. The Wizard taught it to you and cautioned you to practice but you did not and now you are not sure if you can remember it correctly. Your entire trip, in your wealthy caravan, you tried and never once duplicated the simplest of spells. You are a great disappointment, Child. Measure him."

The young Wizard came forward. She placed a hand on his head and her hand and his body started to glow. It glowed longer and a little brighter than with Mike. "This one will make a good

Wizard with a lot of work, Masters." She looked at Scotty and said, "Little child."

The Oldest said, "Very well. We will train him to be the best he can be if he can take the training. It is not easy and not for the lazy. Step back child and let Master Jonathan Wiser come forward."

The Oldest asked, "What magic can you do, Master Jonathan Wiser?"

I went to one knee and rose in the best and most humble bow I know. "I can do only three of the simplest of spells, Great Master, Fire Finger, Illumination, and Perfect Shot. I am sorry."

The Grand Master stood and bowed to me. "I have watched you with great interest, Master Wiser. You learned these spells by watching your town Wizard teach others when you thought he was not aware. No one would let such a small child be the Wizard and your wise Wizard knew this. He did not teach you but he moved his position so that you could see and hear. I watched as the selection was made and you were ridiculed. I watched as you took the punishment from that bully and did not strike back, knowing full well that fire finger could have killed him with ease. I watched as you traveled on foot through over a hundred leagues of the dark forest to reach the University. I watched, Master Wiser, and I know. And now, the only child to have the guts to learn on his own and come on his own in years stands before me humbly. No pride, no stubbornness, apologizing that his impressive accomplishments may be so little in a Grand Master's eyes. They are not little, Master Wiser, and I am proud to have you in my school. Lilith, test him, though it be not necessary."

Lilith came forward and placed her hand on my tear-streaked face. And, the strength of the glow blew us both apart. A Cleric was brought in to heal us both as the Masters discussed what just happened. Lilith came forward again and this time said some protections for the both of us. She placed her hand on my head and sunshine radiated throughout the room and the school, lighting every corner for leagues. It lasted for hours before it started to fade. By then a gathering of Wizards and students were standing watching. When Lilith stepped back she said, "I know why he is so small, Masters. His magic is so strong it is taking longer for him to grow. But, he will grow and become even stronger." She looked at me and said, "Welcome, Young Wizard."

Cheers rang out as I was carried to the first year's dorms. I found out later that the tall boy from my town did not show enough magical talent and was sent home. The town found out about me. They came to talk with me but the Royal Grand Master showed up at the gate.

"Wizard Sir. We have a boy from our town that is here at your school. We would like to talk to him."

"No."

"Excuse me, Sir. This is important."

"Let me guess. You had a town meeting fifteen days ago. It was decided that you made a big mistake and that the 'shrimp' should be your Wizard. You traveled all this way to ensure he knows that he is to be your Wizard when Master Tanner moves on."

"How did you know that?"

He pointed to himself and said, "Royal Magi War Master."

The Mayor backed down in fear of his life. "When can we see him?"

"You cannot, Mayor. He is destined to be the Royal War Wizard's Apprentice, and then the Royal War Wizard, and someday my replacement as Grand Magi of the realm. The King already has his Wizard watching the boy. They are very interested and excited. I do not think the King will let such magnificent talent be a Wizard in a worthless little town. Goodness, he has already surpassed the second year students and has just started. Good day to you sir. The gates shut magically and hard."

Many of the students and Wizards said that was the first time they have ever seen the Royal Magi smile.

CRYING WITHOUT TEARS

I WISH I WISH, I WISH I WERE IN A LAND OF MAGIC, WITH dragons, and a handsome prince, and unicorns. Instantly a lovely little creature appeared in my bedchamber. It looked like a china doll.

"You have a request child. You worded it poorly. For instance, what do you want to be in this land of dragons, handsome prince, and unicorns?

"A princess, a beautiful, wealthy, young princess."

"OK, that can be arranged. This place you live in, called the Prime Material Plane, has dragons, princes, and unicorns. I could place you in a family I know that needs a princess. Tell me, what would you give me in payment?"

"What do you want? I don't have anything."

It smiled, "I want you to play a game. I will give you this simple contract and you get as many people to sign it as you can. All your friends, your family, and everyone you can."

"That's all?"

"That's all? Just say, 'I wish' three times and I will return."

"OK."

She took the contract and signed it in front of her brother. Her brother wanted to know what she was doing so he asked. She said, "I will go away forever if I can get enough signatures on this paper."

"I'll sign that." He took the paper and signed it and then handed it back.

She went to her mother and said while holding out the paper, "Field trip."

Her mother signed it without looking. She went to her father and said, "Field trip, needs both parents' signatures."

"I'm late for work. Did your mother read this?"

"Yes."

"He signed it as he was leaving."

She went to her sister, "This is a pledge that I am never going to go into your room again without your permission. I need you to witness it." Her sister stopped kissing her boyfriend long enough to sign the paper.

At school, she caught the teachers at their busiest times and said, "Bathroom pass" while she pretended to need to go and they signed. She even caught the principal at a bad moment and he signed. Eighteen of her friends and other children signed when she told them it was a demand to have more ice cream during lunch. The paper was covered with signatures. She took it home that night.

"I wish, I wish, I wish."

Instantly the little creature appeared. She handed him the contract and said, "Well?"

The devil smiled and raised a hand. Instantly she was turned into a toy. He picked her up and placed her in the little castle she received for Christmas. There were dragons, a handsome prince, and a unicorn. He put her in the arms of the prince and left her there. Fully aware where she was and nothing she could do but cry without tears.

THE BET

THERE IS A PLACE WHERE EVERYONE IS MAGICAL. Everyone can read each other's minds and no one can harm another because everyone would know they were going too and stop it long before it happens. A place where there are no wars, no hunger, and no disease. A mother knows exactly what is bothering her newborn, hunger, wet diaper, discomfort, are instantly known. There is no need for police as there is no crime. There are no fire departments as everyone can control fire and put it out. There are no contracts as all the people do what they say. This place is called Jessnee.

There is a place where no one is magical, no one can read another's mind, and anyone can do harm to another and no one would stop it for fear it will happen to them. A place where there are grand wars, starvation, and deadly disease. A mother has to guess what is bothering her newborn, hunger, messy diaper, discomfort, insanity, sisters, brothers, and seldom gets it right. There is a large police department in every section of every town as there is constant crime. There are few fire departments as most have burned down. Few contracts are fulfilled and the participants never know what the other is planning. This place is called Kessnee.

Jessnee and Kessnee are an experiment by the Gods. An experiment about Law and Goodness compared to Chaos and Evil.

Jessnee has worked hard on fixing social issues and now people live happily for hundreds of years. However, their world is overpopulated so people are working hard to fix the problem by expanding out into other worlds. They are building grand colonizing ships and expanding away from the direction of Kessnee as influenced by the Gods.

Kessnee has found out about Jessnee as the Gods have told them to stay away from that section of the galaxy; therefore, that is the first place they looked. They want what Jessnee has and are planning to take it and enslave their people. At least, the few people that will be left. They also are building ships. The Gods are laying bets on the winner.

Before Jessnee could build their grand ships Kessnee attacked them. Kessnee thought they had the advantage because Jessnee never had to fight another species before. They did not fight among themselves and had no experience. The surprise attack was devastating. Much of Jessnee was reduced to rubble.

Jessnee sent dreams, mind talk, anything they could to calm their neighbors but Kessnee was not interested. They wanted the planet for themselves. Jessnee had no choice and fought back. By using magic they pushed Kessnee back to their planet and destroyed their ships so they could not attack again. Then the good people of Jessnee helped their neighbor Kessnee so that they did not have starvation and disease.

Thirty-two years later Kessnee attacked again and this time they were prepared for magic. They came from several directions and as the people of Jessnee were concentrating on sending one group back, the Kessnees attacked from another direction. The Jessnees won the war but they were left badly hurting. Their planet in complete disorder and most major cities destroyed. They started rebuilding. During the war, the good people had to harm the other race and this saddened them. They did much to rebuild what they destroyed on Kessnee.

About the time they finished rebuilding their planet the Kessnees attacked again. This time Kessnee developed weapons that removed all people from the planet leaving only the ones on the few ships. Kessnee won the war and killed all Jessnees they found. The wars were over.

A God of Good said to his Evil counterpart as he handed over one small copper piece. "You win. You were right. Good, in their compassion, helped evil until evil was strong and smart enough to destroy good completely and without mercy. Therefore, if left alone good will kill itself. There must be a mix so there are morality and someone to hold the morality at bay."

The Evil God smiled, "It is as I said. Evil is relentless and good constantly makes the mistake of feeling sorry for them and helping them. You cannot win if you constantly help revive your enemy and your enemy will not return the favor. It was not a fair playing field as Good has rules and Evil Chaos does not. Eventually Evil must win. Evil only needs to win once while good must win every time. Winning every time is an impossibility."

The Good God said to the Evil God in near shock, "You are saying that Evil must be limited?"

"Severely."

The Good God said, "As you represent Evil I am surprised you would argue this line."

The Evil God laughed, "Do not be surprised. I have foreseen what it would be like if there were only evil. It is not a pretty sight.

The Good Gods would die off as they would have no worshippers. Then evil would destroy itself somehow. It is in their nature. Then there would be no Evil Gods. First I would lose my adversary and then I would die. Where's the fun in that?" Then he reached out and destroyed Jessnee and Kessnee and working together they created Earth.

HELPFUL DRAGON

IT WASN'T LONG AGO THAT I KILLED MY FIRST HUMAN. They are very easy; however, they do tend to stick together, and like bees become upset and swarm. That's the problem now. There are at least twenty adult size humans down at the bottom of my mountain working their way up. I can't eat that many. For goodness sake, I just fed on two of them only yesterday. These seem to be more the human warrior-type class. Their long sticks with sharp little points can be dangerous. Their little bendy sticks that throw other sticks at you tend to stick you hard and penetrate deep into your hide. And those long steel stingers cut and stab. Time to leave.

I spread my wings and flew off the mountain top. It's not like I have any ties to this mountain. I have no ties anywhere. I use to have a grand home filled with gold and platinum that I dug up myself. There was plenty of game in the nearby forest and water from the glacier that ran through my cave. It was wonderful, a good place to raise children, a place of plenty. Then the humans came. I watched as they put a road through the forest. They saw me but I left them alone and they left me alone. Still, more and more came like a blight on the land. They cut down the forest and killed or captured all the food. So, I simply hunted in another valley and let them have their fun.

One day humans came up to my cave while I was out hunting and took all my gold and platinum. I could smell them as they stink very bad. I went down to their hive and yelled for them to return my property. They attacked. I was surprised and angry. I destroyed them and the entire valley looking for my gold and platinum. I never found it.

Humans came to kill me. I had to fight over and over again. I killed many humans. They are like bees that demand to have nests and get angry when someone destroys the nest. Well, they destroyed mine. Fair is fair.

I looked back and the humans were still climbing the mountain I just left. They are so tenacious.

One day, about a moon ago, a single human came to me and asked in a broken form of my language what I was doing there. Why I chose that mountain to live on and why, after getting along with the humans in the valley, did I kill them all? I said, "You took my bed. I worked long and hard on mining the gold and platinum for my bed and you took it. I went down to your nest and demanded it back and they attacked me. So I killed them looking for my bed. I did not find it. I am still looking."

He had the gall to say, "These humans did not take your treasure. Some other humans must have taken it. You can't blame the valley humans for what someone else did."

I said, "They did not tell me that. They attacked. They could have told me that they did not have it and then helped me find the humans that did take it. You all smell the same to me and it would be impossible for me to tell which the right ones are."

"I know who took your 'Bed'. It was adventures hired by the King."

"What is a 'King'?"

"The King is the human in charge of all the rest of the humans."

I asked, "He is the bull human. He owns the rest?"

The tiny human said, "That is about correct."

"You tell the bull human to give me back my bed and I will leave the humans alone."

"I will relay your message. I will return with his answer in a quarter moon."

I waited and in a quarter moon he returned with five others and said, "The King's answer is this." They attacked. I grabbed the messenger and left. When I landed on another mountain I put him down.

"Why did you attack me?"

"The King said he would not return your bed. He needs the gold and platinum to expand his lands. He told me to put together a group and kill you."

"You go back to your king. You tell him I am going to eat every one of the humans in his nests, and then I am going to eat him." I flew off.

I have been gorging myself every day on humans every since. They don't taste that good but they are filling. So I throw up and then eat some more. They try to kill me but I move around a lot and they don't fly all that fast. One tried using a funny means of travel and became like a cloud. Do you know what happens to water vapor when heated by dragon fire? They won't try following me that way again. They tried to teleport to me but I just fly off again. They have set some fun traps but they did not work very well. The cold that one wizard used was bad. It hurt a lot so I ate him quickly. Now I eat the magic users and ignore the fighters.

When they are not chasing me I destroy a building with fire and eat at least one human that runs out. Normally the one that is dressed the fanciest way. Grab, fly away, then eat. I figure that I will have all the humans eaten in about three thousand years. I also visit their main hives each day and set them on fire. Their hives are not looking very good anymore. Sometimes I see humans on little floating hives out in the water. They call them ships. I sink each one I find. I haven't seen any for a few days now.

I made it to the other mountain and a Wizard was waiting for me. I saw him as I was coming down. I started to fly back up but he motioned that he wanted to talk so I flew down after looking for ambushes and traps. Humans are sneaky so you need to be alert.

I landed and said, "Ah, the King Bug's messenger. What you want little Wizard bug?"

"The King wants to know what it will take to make you leave his lands."

"I'm not going to leave without all my gold and platinum back. Then I'm still not going to leave. This is my home. But, if the King Bug returns my bed and makes all his other bugs leave me alone then I will leave him alone. That is fare."

"I'll let him know. Any chance you will hold off your attacks until I return with his answer?"

"Nope."

"I thought not." He teleported away.

The Wizard teleported to the city and the castle. He quickly walked up to the throne room, entered, walked past all the others waiting for an audience, and bowed before his King.

The King impatiently said. "Well?"

The Wizard stood up, "Majesty, the dragon has agreed to stop his attacks and live in peace here in his lands if you return his gold and platinum bed."

"That is unacceptable, Wizard. I told you to negotiate with the hideous creature to leave this land. I also said that return of his treasure is not part of the negotiations."

"He seems somewhat immature, my King. He has a one-track mind. He knows very little about humans. He sees us as insects, I think. You are the top bug in charge and therefore responsible for the other bugs and steeling his bed."

The King sat in thought, "He is not intimidated by my being a King?"

The Wizard smiled knowing full well that intimidation is a King's best weapon. "No, not in the least. It just gives him someone to focus on, Majesty."

"Is there any chance of any kind of negotiation without giving him back his bed?"

"No, Majesty. I do not believe so."

"He is ruining my kingdom. Shipping has stopped, travel has stopped, crops are being destroyed, people are going to starve, and I spent his gold and platinum on the ships he sank. I don't have his bed to give him."

The Wizard wanted to say, "Whoops," but prudently decided to keep quiet.

"I cannot have this continuing. General!"

An old scared man came up, "Majesty."

"Destroy that beast. I don't care how you do it, just do it and do it quickly."

"As you wish, Majesty."

The General turned and started giving orders as he departed.

I was sitting on another mountain top about two mountains over from the main hive when I saw several humans trying to sneak up on me. I flew off toward the main hive. I did a strafing run down one side and set a large portion on fire. I waited until they were all on that side putting out the fire and did another strafing run down the other side. They were not ready for that but a lot of arrows flew up at me and several stuck. I flew off, pulled out the poisoned arrows, and let myself heal. I'll eat almost anything so I built up an immunity to poison while eating poisonous plants. Still, they may find one I am not immune to. I will have to be more careful.

The next day I saw a caravan leave the city. I attacked it. The little things they make horses pull, called wagons, opened up and there were hundreds of human's shooting sticks at me. I flew away to lick my wounds.

I decided that the main hive was too dangerous at this time so I picked on other humans. I flew over this very big river and into another section of land that has humans. Lots and lots of humans. I attacked that hive and they were not prepared. They did have many little Wizards that came pouring out and they attacked me with cold. I flew away and healed up. Then I attacked them some more. It was fun. They gave chase and I ran. When I saw something worth destroying I did and then continued to fly away. I circled while they followed and I attacked their city again. This time there were very few Wizards with cold to use. They tried acid. I like acid as it tends to clean out old wounds and removes scars. I bath in it when I can find it. I set the hive on fire again and then flew off. The Bad King Bug had not warned these bugs. That was a mistake. There was this very big and tall section of the hive and I concentrated all my fire on it until it fell. Then I ate the most colorful human I have ever seen. Nice shiny coverings with gold and platinum parts. He tasted very bad but he seemed to be important.

As I was flying away a little human Wizard came up to me and said in my language. "Dragon, we know you have been destroying the land to our east. Why are you now attacking us?"

"You know."

"No, I don't. Please, enlighten me."

"Your King Bug human steal my bed and attack me. I want my bed back."

It thought for a second and then said, "You are in the land of another King. He did not steal your bed."

"There is more than one King Bug?"

"There are five King and Queen bugs on the landmass."

"Oh, sorry. What section belongs to Bad King Bug?"

"Pretty much, everything you attacked before you came over here. Everything on that side of the big river belongs to the Bad King Bug. He owns the east coast."

"Your King Bug Good Bug?"

"Yes. He would not harm you but he is very mad now."

"You tell him I sorry. You tell him he can have the east side when I get my bed back. I nearly have half of it back now."

The Wizard looked shocked. "How are you getting back your bed?"

I smiled and said, "I eat the human bugs on that side and they have copper, gold, silver, and platinum on them sometimes. Mostly copper and silver. I dump that away. The gold and platinum I process and remove for my bed. I figure I'll have a full bed when all east cleared of human bugs. Then your King Bug can move in. I no attack him if he no attack me. Fair?"

"That seems fair to me. In truth, our King has been thinking of confiscating the east. Their King Bug is rather bad and tends to cause a lot of trouble."

"It's all yours when I am done making the bed. Good hunting over there, but bad King has been killing for no reason and causing bad hunting. Your King is good and not ruin hunting."

"I'll let him know. In fact, could you spend some time setting the wall on fire."

"Wall?"

"There is a wall on the east side of the river at a bridge where human bugs cross. If the wall was down it would please my King Bug very much."

"I'll set it on fire then. I burn it down. I'm sorry for attacking the wrong King Bug. I hope this makes it all better."

I turned to follow the river to the place the nice Wizard said and there was this little place where human bugs cross. On the east side was a big wall. I set it on fire and then ate several of the people trying to put the fire out. It burned down quickly.

The Wizard returned to his King. "Majesty, the dragon was the same one that was attacking Goldman. He did not understand that there was another 'King Bug' in the land. He thought that King Richard was the only King Bug. He was very apologetic when he found out he attacked another King Bug on mistake and agreed to burn down the tower wall at the Helton Bridge for us."

The King's eyes widened. "Bug! BUG!" Then he calmed down and asked, "When?"

"It's probably on fire as we speak. Please understand that to this dragon we are just bugs. It is the only way he can conceptualize us with his limited intellect."

The King yelled, "General! The tower wall is on fire. Mount the attack!"

The Wizard said, "Wait, my King."

The King asked, "What? That fool King Rickard has been a pain in my side for decades. He is weak, his forces are in ruin, and we have a chance of removing him from the land and to take over the eastern coast. Explain to me why I should wait."

"The Dragon is remaking his bed, Majesty. The gold and platinum bed that King Richard took from the dragon. It seems that when the dragon eats us, humans, he also eats our money pouches. He processes the metals and he is using that to rebuild his bed. He is only halfway to his goal. He dumps the copper and silver."

The King smiled, "I would not want to be the one assigned to dig the copper and silver out of his dumping. Though, I can think of a few that disserve the job." He stopped to think for a few seconds. "Can you deliver a message to this dragon?"

"I believe so. He is very easy going when not being attacked."

"Great, tell him that if he helps us take over King Richard's Bug place then we will let him collect all the Gold and Platinum he needs to build his nest and if he can't find enough to make it like it was then we will supply the rest."

The Wizard said, "I will tell him. There is one more thing he seemed to be concerned about. It seems that King Richard's people were wasters. They kill the food off just for the fun of it. I am betting he is the one that has been poaching from our eastern forest. Notice it stopped when this war began."

The King sat in thought. "It's not the dragon's fault he was poaching. First, he doesn't understand borders. Second, he never takes more than he can eat. Third, he never takes owned animals. Tell him that we do not waste and will allow his hunting grounds to repopulate with good game. We may even import some for him. Remind him that we are a race that is constantly fighting among ourselves. We will treat him well because we may need his help in the future to protect his and our lands."

"I will do as requested, Majesty."

The Wizard departed.

I was up on the top of a tall mountain watching the sea. I had just destroyed eight ships with funny little markings of a human skeleton. They did not fight well and the ships sank easily. One was loaded with Gold and Platinum. I could smell it. I ate that one. The nice Wizard showed up along with the Bad King's Wizard. They looked at each other and started casting spells. I ate the Bad King's Wizard and asked, "What you doing here. I set the wall on fire. It burned down."

"My King wants you to know that he is going to end this battle you have with the Bad King Bug. The Bad Bug King has been bad to us also. He is going to take his humans into the east and stop the Bad King. He says if you help he will ensure you get the gold and platinum to remake your bed exactly the way it was even if he has to give you part of his bed."

I looked skeptical, "That very nice of your King Bug. Why is he being so nice?"

"The Eastern ports will make him able to feed his people and create large armadas to protect his lands and sea lanes." The Wizard noticed that he had lost the dragon and so he restated. "The King needs the land that meets the big waters to make ships. Those ships will be used to move food back and forth to places where it is needed. He is very interested in keeping the food for both you and the humans plentiful."

"If he not waste, food be plentiful."

"True, for you, but we eat other things."

"I know. I have been concentrating on destroying all food supplies for this bad King Bug. His people very hungry."

"Our King so good he will take these humans and make them part of us. We will help feed them. We will make your hunting grounds plentiful. My King Bug will even import some good food you may like."

"Let me see. I help you kill Bad King Bug then I get my bed back, I get plenty of food in my hunting grounds, I will be left alone most the time?"

"Yes."

"I help. What you want me to do?"

The Wizard said, "We will cross the river at the bridge. You make sure they are not on the other side in numbers to stop us. Then we will march up to the Bug Nest and try to get in. If you could open the doors so we could get in quickly we would be very thankful."

"You have deal little Wizard Bug. You go tell good Bug King, I will be waiting at the bridge."

The Wizard departed.

I flew over to the bridge and they had started rebuilding the wall so I set it on fire and then attacked them so they could not put the fire out. Then I flew away enough to watch without being seen. Humans have such short sight. It was only two days before the Good King started to pile up his army on the west side of the bridge. I attacked the east side and they ran toward the western army begging protection. The Good King Bug rode a horse across the bridge leading his army without being attacked. I perched on a piece of the cliff that was still on fire. The flames felt good. I watched the good King Bug ride by. I could feel his fear but he became bold after he saw I was not going to eat him. I took to the air and the force of the wind from my wings knocked several humans from their horses. I flew over the Wizard and said, "Sorry."

He waved saying, "No harm done."

The King Bug rode toward the Big Hive and as he rode his army grew. Humans from the Bad King's army joined him. He looked surprised when another General rode up with his. His General said, "Majesty, the Goldman army is asking to join us. They are half-starved and need food. Their King has departed the land and taken to sea with some pirates. It seems that the dragon sank the pirate ships and the King is dead."

The King said, "We will stop here for the night. Ensure there is plenty of food for all that swear allegiance to our kingdom and her King."

"As you wish, my King."

The next day, to the surprise of everyone, they rode right up to the gates and the gates were open and people were cheering the new King. I flew over their heads and the cheers turned to screams. The King motioned me to talk. I landed on the ground near him. The ground moved with my landing and the shaking put a crack in the city wall. Whoops.

The King said, and the Wizard translated, "Thank you, my friend. I will keep my word. Your hunting lands are yours. I will find you enough Gold and Platinum to remake your bed. And, we will let you rest in peace without worry of anyone attacking. Please, if someone does something wrong you let me know and I will fix the issue."

I smiled and his fear returned for some reason. "Thank you Good King Bug. I will not harm human bugs. We live in peace. I took enough gold and platinum from a ship with skeleton markings to make the bed very good. I go home now."

I took to the air returning home and saying to myself, "Finally, I can stop talking baby talk. Little Bug humans would never understand grownup talk. Their minds are just too tiny."

BETS (MIKE PART 1)

I STOOD BEFORE THE KING, MY UNCLE FIVE TIMES removed, a young warrior of grand ability with wisdom lines around his eyes and a grand sense of humor, waiting expectantly for his pronouncement of punishment. I knew it was coming because I caused it, I needed it, and the punishment was part of the plan. The Royal Wizard Karmic, a tall man in his late years with the longest beard I have ever seen, and the King's Cleric David, a short fat old man with a clean-shaven face and meticulous robes were standing there answering his Majesty's questions and complaining. As a fifth cousin to the crown prince, I was beyond being beheaded. Besides, for minor things like borrowing without permission, beheading was not the normal punishment. Still, I had pestered these two enough that my Uncle would have to do something. I was hoping for ninety days in the dungeon. That's my Uncle's favorite sentence.

Being magical, a very accomplished rogue, a fighter without equal, and having a thirst for knowledge was not my fault. Mother was half fairy and half changeling. Father was half-dragon and half-human. I look like a young, very lovely, and well-muscled human. However, I can change my appearance at will. I never do it where people can see me so few people know. Being magical gives me all kinds of abilities that make it easy to learn and practice the arcane arts. I can't do divine magic but not from a lack of trying. I think the Gods are holding me back. I became a wizard out of fun, but I am a Rogue and fighter from necessity. When our castle was attacked, and Mother and Father killed, I had a choice. Either sneak to friendly lands or die. I became very sneaky and each time I was seen I fought like a demon. You would too if your head was on the line. They looked for me everywhere, and in the hunting nearly stepped on me several times. It took a long time but I made it here and have been here for two years now.

This kingdom is a good place to practice and the castle is a good place to live. Being a relative I get free room and board. I do chores for my sixth Uncle now and then. Normally the King needs rogue work or spying done. I am very good at finding out things and I always warn him about possible dangers. In fact, I have saved his life twice that he knows of. He is happy that I am around but others are not.

The Royal Wizard Karmic is upset that I barrow his things when I need them. I never ask and that upsets him more than the borrowing. I also never use his consumables. Consumables cannot be put back and therefore considered stealing. I don't steal! I just borrow his books and study magic. I tried asking once but he flat out refused to allow me entrance into his library. After that, I practiced sneaking past his protections and reading anything I wanted. David, the King's Cleric, is just as upset. I am always borrowing his books and his Rod of Enlightenment. I find it difficult to read clerical books without the rod to help read past the incorrect opinions of the bigoted writers. Wizards write facts but Clerics write beliefs. Beliefs are at best unbelievable. The Rod of Enlightenment lets me know the truth behind the beliefs. I don't suppose that practicing being a rogue on the two helped. They always check their hands and purse after seeing me even if I don't come anywhere near them. Go figure.

The Princess is another reason I need to be imprisoned. She is a beauty, tall, skinny, long luxurious blond hair, a face so lovely it would be a pleasure to get lost staring at, and lips like the...the... Gods, there are no words in all I have read or studied to describe those lips. Heavenly I would say, but that is playing them down. Not long ago I stole a kiss from her and she became very mad. I still don't understand that. She chased me for months and I paid no attention. When I finally realized that she was chasing me; I caught her and kissed her and she flew into a rage. I became mad and bet her that she would kiss me again willingly and she would insist on kissing me. She laughed and told me she would not kiss me again if I was the last man on earth.

The King was sitting straighter now so it was about to happen.

David was saying, "Furthermore, Majesty. Mike is impossible to be around. He cannot be controlled and he constantly takes our things. Mostly our magic!"

The King's eyebrows rose and that's never a good thing. I said, "You must admit, Father David, that I always return the items and normally before you notice. As I said, I am simply practicing." The King smiled and his eyebrows descended and that's a good thing. I don't want him thinking I'm a thief.

Karmic added, "True, but the boy has been told constantly to stop and has ignored our orders and yours, Majesty."

I said, "I bet you, Karmic and David, that you will willingly give me your precious magic items before the summer solstice."

Karmic and David both said, "Never!"

I smiled, "I am willing to never touch your stuff again if I lose the bet. Are you willing to give me free access to your books and the rod if I win?"

Karmic asked, "Let me get this straight. If within the next three moons, I do not turn over my magic to you willingly you will stay out of our belongings unless given permission?"

"Yes; however, if you give me your belongings willingly within the next three moons you will do so from now on without my having to ask."

David looked at Karmic and then turned to the King. "It is a bet. Majesty, I think ninety days in the dungeon would be sufficient punishment."

The shocked look on my face must have said it all as both had the widest grins.

My Uncle asked, "What makes you think you can keep him in the dungeon? He is the sneakiest rouge I have ever had the pleasure to know."

David said, "The cell, Majesty. The one prepared for just such a person. I don't think he is going to go anywhere."

The King looked at me and smiled at the glaring look I was giving the two. "It does not seem that you were ready for such a possibility. It does seem that they were prepared. I so order it. Ninety days in the dungeon starting right now."

I looked up at him, "Any chance I can take a few minutes and set some things straight in my room, Sire?"

The King laughed, "No. I am not going to allow you to go to your room and prepare."

An eager look crept into my face but I quickly changed it and said almost happily but trying to look sad, "One thing then, Majesty. I set traps in my room. They are deadly. Please tell everyone to stay out of the room. And, for goodness sake, don't try magically entering the room. I do not want to be charged with murder."

"I will have the word spread. Anything else?"

"No, Majesty." I looked nervously toward the opening of the thrown room.

The King looked thoughtful and asked, "You look nervous about something and nearly eager to get put in the dungeon. Why?"

"Oh, nothing important, Sire."

He looked skeptical. "Take him away."

Karmic and David took my arms, and the Sergeant and five guards escorted me to the Dungeon. I was stripped except for my Ring of Essentia. My hair was combed thoroughly looking for lock picks and my body searched including inside my mouth. I was made to throw-up so I couldn't have something hidden inside my stomach. They checked me completely. Then they took me down eight levels to a single room where there was no door or window. It had only one small opening. They put me in shifting proof shackles so I could not magically leave the room and chained me against the wall, tied me tighter with magical chains, set protections from dimensional travel in the room, tied a vial of magical air in my mouth, walked out the only opening, and created a stone wall at least three feet thick. Then they laid down traps of all kinds, both to keep me in and to keep others from helping me. Some were very deadly.

The Sergeant asked, "Is this really necessary? The boy is goodly of nature and hasn't done anything wrong. I saw you ensure he has air, but what about food, water, and waste disposal?"

Karmic answered, "The magical bottle we tied in his mouth supplies him with fresh air. His ring takes care of food and water. Without eating or drinking he is not going to have waste problems and with the water we shoved inside him to clean out his backside, where I may add we found two lock picks, there is nothing left from anything he has had in the past. He is clean and now cannot leave that chamber. I cannot reach him without a lot of trouble and neither can anyone else. In ninety days we will come down here and release him."

While they were putting me away for ninety days the King was upon his thrown laughing. The Princess, Prince, Queen, and the entire royal family were having a great time at my expense.

The Prince said, "Did you see his face? I cannot believe he was actually eager to go to the cells. He was learning some new information before his next adventure when he got caught. Does he think he can escape so easily?"

The King stopped laughing for a moment to think. "He did seem eager about leaving. I am told he had packed some things for travel and seemed to be in a hurry. Goodness, he just returned from somewhere. He may have looked eager but he also looked nervous. What was he nervous about? That's what worries me." The King looked around in the hope that someone had answers. A young lady walked in and that caught the King's eye. Not because she walked in, but because she was wearing a diadem and because she seemed to be looking for someone and had a hand on her sword. She was about the size of Mike and had his long hair but hers was red and she was a beauty. Long and skinny. Looks that most women would die for and many men would kill for. She was wearing male clothing and a look that screamed someone was in trouble and she was the trouble. He asked, "Who's the redhead?"

Everyone turned that direction. The Captain of the Guard said, "That is Princess Amanda. She comes from an island so far away I had to look it up on the maps and still could not find it. I asked the Admiral and he had heard of it but never visited that distant of port."

"What is she doing here?"

The Captain said, "She came with a written message, Sire." He pointed to the messages on the desk of his Clerk.

The Clerk came over with the message. The Queen asked, "How long has she been here?"

"Two days my Queen. I am very surprised you did not know."

The Queen frowned, "I will have words with the castle staff about this."

The King grinned, "She was sent here for a class in royal etiquette. However, there is an underlying tone to this message that speaks of Mike." He handed it to the Queen and she read it out loud.

"Dear King George,

It is with great pleasure I present my daughter Princess Amanda. The Hero Mike was visiting our Island and mentioned that Amanda should obtain training from the ladies of your court. He proudly mentioned that your wife would be an excellent person to teach my little girl proper etiquette. I believe that is a wonderful idea and have sent her there for the same. It is apparent to me that she cannot obtain her heart's desire without this training. Please forgive my daughter's lack of ladylike behavior as she was raised with five brothers and bred for combat. Her mother died at an early age and here in Pontara, the women fight alongside the men.

Best regards,
King Steadfast the first."

The Queen said, "Bring her before the crown."

The Captain went to her and led her back. Everyone noticed that she was looking for someone. As she approached the King she asked in a tone of impatience. "Where is Mike?!"

The Queen stood up and looked down on the child. "What horrible manors! Is that how dignitaries approach your father?"

Amanda glared at the Queen for only a second and then bowed of all things. When she straightened without permission she asked politely, "Oh great and wonderful King, where is the Hero Mike?" Her hand was on the hilt of her sword and turning white with suppressed anger.

The King drew his sword and set it across his lap as twenty archers came and pointed over the balconies. Guards drew their swords and the Captain of the guard drew his very slowly but with a purpose that made Amanda think twice. The King said, "I can see why your father believes that you need to be taught some manners. If your hand does not come off that sword I will put you over my lap and teach you several right now!"

She looked down at her hand and blushed. She unbuckled her weapon belt and tossed it to the Captain. "My apologies, good King. I am so used to wearing a sword I sometimes forget that in other kingdoms it is not necessary."

The Queen said, "Here, it is death to draw a sword in hostility in the King's presence. You have much to learn."

She looked at the Queen thoughtfully. "I will learn anything needed to catch Mike. Where is he?"

The Prince asked, "What do you want with my beloved cousin? A Prince of this kingdom."

"A Prince is he. He did not tell us that. I am hunting him to bring him back to our Island so that my Father can marry us." The shock reverberated throughout the room as the word passed around to those that could not hear.

The Royal Princess and Queen were smiling. The Queen said, "So, you are why he was eager to leave."

Amanda said, "Interesting that a man can fight great battles, save many lives, challenge evil and win against unbelievable odds just to have access to some silly books. Yet, runs away at the mere mention of marriage."

The King's interest was perked, "That sounds like our Mike. Please explain what Mike was doing in your lands and I will tell you where he is."

She looked longingly at her weapon belt but the Captain was not going to give it back. She turned to the King and said, "Mike came to our island two moons ago. He was sitting in the Wizard's library when he was first noticed by a servant. They were giving him food and drink and he was sleeping in the room near the library. It was five days before the Wizard noticed him. He kept a watch on Mike and took great interest in the 'boy that loves to learn.' He waited another three days before saying anything to the boy. He found out that Mike was from your country and that he was looking for information about an ancient family that has not been on this Plane of existents for thousands of years. The Wizard and Mike took a liking to each other and he helped Mike with his studies."

"I first saw Mike down in the courtyard. The Master Swordsman was teaching his two favorite pupils and Mike was watching. I was watching because one was my brother and I am very proud of him. He was about to receive Master himself. They saw Mike and my brother said, 'Learning anything good, little boy?' in a somewhat snide tone. I think Mike took exception and instantly in his hand was a quarterstaff. He said to my brother, 'Not really. The two of you are beginners and I could take you both with a simple staff.' That upset my brother and the fight was on. Mike trashed them both and Clerics had to be called for. Two days later, during training, Mike showed up in the courtyard again. This time he went over to the practice swords and started going through them. He finally found two he liked and turned to the Master and bowed. He said, 'The two I fought before have been saying things about me that are not true. I have come to teach them another lesson.' My brother and his friend stood up and came forward while others stood back. Mike trashed them again and this time with their preferred weapon! THEIR PREFERRED WEAPON! Clerics were called in and Mike left. I started watching him a lot closer. At one point he caught me sneaking up on him and he turned just in time to steal a kiss. I – was – so - mad."

"One day, about a moon ago, we were attacked by the King of the Island of the Dead. Mike was a lethal ally. He fought like a demon destroying many undead and not the little ones either.

Mike went after the leaders. At one point my youngest brother was about to be killed by their champion. Mike ran in and fought the undead beast. The battle raged around them and gave us enough time to pull my brother to safety and get him to a Cleric. Mike and the undead beast fought for hours and when the fight ended the undead beast was dead and Mike was still standing. Cut up and bleeding from a hundred wounds he still fought on. Spells shot from his hands, his blades were a blur, and when he stopped it was because he had killed the King of the Island of the Dead. Clerics healed him, Father made him a hero of the land, my brothers call him brother, and I fell in love. Father is raising a statue to Mike in memory of his brave deed killing their champion and saving my brother. He proclaimed that we were to be wed and instantly Mike's eyes became as big as horseshoes and he disappeared. We looked all over for him. The Wizard scryed on him and he is here. Father sent me here for two reasons. To find him and to learn what it will take to make him mine. Tell me, Great King. How is it that a man can be so brave and still be afraid of marriage?"

The King's smile brightened, "Mike has saved my life twice."

The Captain of the Guard loudly cleared his throat. "Pardon Sire, remember the war issues with Harcome? The issue is passed but Mike has saved your life four times, the Prince twice, the Princess twice, and the Queen once. That I know of."

The King blushed and so did the Queen. The Princess was looking thoughtful. Karmic and David were just coming back up with the Sergeant so the King said, "Well Princess Amanda, our 'Hero Prince' got himself sent to the dungeon for the next ninety days. He is not allowed visitors."

Amanda looked about to blow her top. "He did that on purpose!"

The Queen stepped down from the thrown and took Amanda's shoulder saying. "He probably did, but it gives us enough time to teach you how to win him over."

Amanda looked up hopeful. "Really?"

The Queen and Princess Jennifer left with Princess Amanda. The King heard the Queen say, "You just leave it to us. We'll get you ready for Mike. He won't know what hit him." His daughter, Princess Jennifer, took the weapon belt with her but there was a strange, far away, look in her eye. One the King recognized and hoped fervently that this Amanda did not find out.

It was fifty-three days later when the Queen and both Princesses were sitting alone in her sitting room. The Queen said, "You are learning very quickly, Amanda. The new dresses fit you wonderfully and show off your figure to great advantage. You take to dancing delightfully but you still need to stop trying to lead. Now we are going onto another type of training."

Amanda asked, "What type of training is that, Majesty?"

Princess Jennifer said, "How to properly kiss a man." Princess Amanda's eyes widened and her hand started for a weapon belt that was not there. Princess Jennifer quickly added, "You don't want Mike stealing a kiss and feeling like it came from a little brother do you? That is no way to win a man. He needs to continue to look at you as an object of great need. You need to learn to kiss him in such a way as to cause him to need."

"How do I do that?"

Princess Jennifer said, "Relax and I will show you."

"You're going to kiss me?"

The Queen said, "This is preferable but we can call in a servant if you wish."

Amanda said, "No. I can do it. It may be difficult but I can do it." That night Amanda learned to take and receive with kisses from Princess Jennifer.

When they were alone Jennifer said to her mother, "I don't think we should do that again. She was getting too good and I was starting to like it too much. She kisses like a man, though she reverts to kissing like a woman when I remind her. Still, I was finding myself reminding her less and less."

The Queen said, "Then the lessons continue until she kisses like a woman all the time." The lessons continued for weeks.

One day, in the throne room, the Princesses were practicing thrown room etiquette when several adventurers returned from a mission the King had sent them on. They stopped in front of the King and bowed appropriately.

The Leader said, "We have returned, my King." He sounded sad.

The King asked, "Where is the Rogue?"

"We cannot find him, Majesty."

"Did he run away? I would find that difficult to believe. He was the second greatest Rogue in the country."

"We believe him dead, Majesty."

The King was a little upset. "That is the third Rogue I have sent with you. What happened this time? How far did you get?"

"I am sorry, my King, but we did not make it to the front door. There is a trap in the only opening we can find and every time a rogue goes into the cave they die quickly and quietly. We are not close enough to see what is happening. The one time we sent someone in with the Rogue they too died and disappeared. The opening is impassible."

The King called his Wizard and Cleric over with the Captain of the Guard. "I need this group in that mountain. They need to find out what our enemy is up to if we stand any chance of stopping it before things get out of hand. You know the reports, if what I am led to believe is true, this could devastate our kingdom."

The Fighter of the adventurers said, "There is no way passed the opening and nothing comes out. We waited and watched."

The Captain said, "There is one person that can get into that mountain."

The King and Wizard said at the same time, "Mike." A murmur traveled throughout the room.

The Fighter asked, "Who is this, 'Mike?'"

The King said, "Prince Mike is probably the greatest rogue in the known lands. The little sneak is down in my dungeon as we speak. To keep him there we had to undertake extreme measures. Until now no place could hold him and no lock that could keep him in or out. He walks right through some of the best-laid traps as if they were not there. He is that good."

The Fighter asked, "Then how did he get caught?"

The King glanced over at Amanda and said, "He wanted to be caught to escape marriage."

The Barbarian said, "Understandable." Everyone glared at the barbarian.

The King said, "The crown and this country come before marriage and punishment. Wizard, Cleric, go bring him out."

The two started toward the dungeons but Princess Amanda stepped in front of them. Wide-eyed she exclaimed, "My friends, are you truly going to go down to the dungeons loaded with magic items like that? Are you going to release Mike while holding the items he may want to pay you back with?"

They looked at each other and said, "No way." They started removing their magic. The Cleric said, "Hold out your hands, Child." Amanda held out her hands and received all their magic before they headed down to the Dungeons.

Princess Amanda returned to the thrown and laid the magic before the King. "Did you note, Majesty, they gave me their magic items freely and willingly?"

"Yes. Why?"

In front of them all, I changed back into Mike. Princess Amanda was gone and I was standing there in a dress. I turned bright red and disappeared. In my room, I quickly changed into my royal robes and returned. The thrown room was in turmoil but when I walked back in it quickly became very quiet. I walked up to the thrown and started a curtsy but remembered at the last minute and made it a clumsy bow.

The King, my Uncle, said with an enormous smile. "I cannot believe this. You were trapped in that room. I was assured that no one could escape. I hired experts to design that room. And, you spent the last eighty or so days as a girl!"

"About the room, Majesty. You should ask for your gold back."

"How!"

I smiled saying, "I was never really in that room in the beginning. I was never really in the dungeon prepare room being searched. I was controlling an illusion. It was a good one. You could touch it, smell it, everything. That is what I was studying the two days before I was punished. The Wizard and Cleric, fools both, took an illusion down into the dungeon. Still, the room would not have been that difficult to get out of. I went down there and through their traps several times to reset my illusion just in case they scryed on me. It wasn't hard to do. As for being a female for a while – I won another bet, though there was nothing bet."

The King asked, "With whom?"

Princess Jennifer took a step forward and she was not in a good mood. "With me, father. I spent time chasing Mike mostly because he was the only one not paying me any attention. All the other boys were chasing me while he ignored me. It took weeks to get him to realize I was paying him attention and when he finally realized he stole a kiss. I pretended to be upset and tried to slap him but he is fast and ducked away. In a fit of rage, we exchanged words. I said I would never kiss him and he said I would willingly and it would be my suggestion."

The King asked, "How did he win that heated bet?"

Jennifer blushed and said, "I brought up the idea and taught Amanda how to kiss Mike so that she would be ready for him when he was released."

It was about that time the Wizard Karmic and the Cleric David came running out. "Sire, he escaped. He wasn't ther..."

Their voices trailed off as they saw me.

The King said, "The two of you lost your bet."

Karmic asked in shock. "What?"

The King smiled. "You gave Mike, disguised as Princess Amanda, your magic items willingly. You did know that my nephew is part changeling? I remember us talking about just that. I do hope you keep your side of the bet. I would be displeased if you didn't after what he went through to win." He turned to me. "You had this planned out before that bet."

They were speechless. The Queen asked, "Was it so important to you to obtain a willing kiss from my daughter that you found it necessary to disguise yourself as a female? It must have been extremely embarrassing. Especially some of the training I put you through."

Princess Jennifer exclaimed, "You! You lied to me. There is no Princess Amanda and you are no hero." For some reason she was in tears.

I walked to her and placed a hand on her chin and raised it to meet my eyes and said in my most humble voice, "I never lied to you. Everything I said was true, though I did so as if I was Amanda. I did not and would not lie to you. The training was embarrassing but I learned a lot about what a female goes through. I have a much greater appreciation for the gender now. I love you, Jennifer."

It was then that we heard a disturbance in the lobby. Everyone looked up and the crowd parted. Standing in the great arch were several fancy looking fighters escorting the red-haired Princess Amanda. She looked around until she saw me and she exclaimed, "Mike!"

Princess Jennifer was fast. She pulled my sword and took two steps to place herself between us. "You cannot have him! He is mine!"

BETS (MIKE PART 2)

I SAT MY HORSE RIDING DEEP WITHIN THE FOREST OF Hieden thinking that I was glad not to be in the King's shoes. Princess Jennifer and Princess Amanda were both extremely upset when the King told them to both stop their nonsense.

"I am sending Mike with these good adventurers to check out an impossible situation and the chance of him coming back alive is very slim. Therefore, fighting over who is to marry a dead man is foolish."

It took me several days to research the situation and possible solutions and during that time I had issues with both girls until I pointed out something they both understood. "Ladies, Princesses, please. I am trying to study the issue that the King is sending me on. If I miss something due to the distractions you are causing it could mean my life."

They left after that but twenty guards, ten from each land, were constantly ensuring that I was not disturbed. I was even let into the Wizard's University and given free rein to study anything I needed and a Master Wizard was there to ensure I quickly found what I was looking for.

I found out what I needed. The mountain they were going into belonged to the family I have been researching for nearly three years. There is only one way into and out of the mountain unless you know the password for dimensional travel and that did not show up in my research. I know there is a password because I found the password to add for removing protected items. I destroyed that document.

This family was unique. They were a family made up entirely of sorcerers. It is said that they created thousands of spells and their deeds, both good and evil, are renowned. Their magic has been lost to this world for centuries. What I have been interested in is the fact that they kept records, had a grand library, and made many magical devices. The problem here is I was researching this to grab everything for myself. I have a little greedy streak when it comes to books. Now the King was asking me to go do this for him. That always means that anything found belongs to him and we get paid in gold. Normally a small amount compared to what can be found. I went and had words with the King.

"Hi, Majesty."

"Hello, Mike. You look upset. Are you ready to leave yet?"

"I am ready but I am upset. For the last three years, I have been studying and preparing for tackling a specific obstacle."

"Yes. You have kept it quiet as to what that was and we thought it was revenge. However, when all that attacked your family died during the war you continued to study and research something. I have been most curious."

"I am finished studying for that obstacle. It is in that mountain."

The King's eyes widened. "This is supposed to be intelligence work only. I need to know what is going on."

"If I am correct in my thinking then I can tell you what is going on, Uncle. I have been studying this because there are books there that I want. There is an entire library of ancient books. Wizards have found 'MY BOOKS' and are studying spells that can give them an advantage in war."

"That is not good."

"No Uncle, it is not. Those are mine and I intend to go get them."

The King sat and thought for a few minutes. "I cannot let those books reside in the enemy's hands and I am not sure that I can allow them to go to the Wizard's University. They tend to allow both good and evil the right to study there. What are your plans?"

"Put in writing that all written materials found are mine and I will gut the place. Gold, gems, jewels, magic that is not evil, artifacts again not evil, will be brought back and 50% will be placed at your disposal after I pick out anything I may need to help interpret the written materials, and Rogue and Wizard use, plus the cost of consumables."

"That does not answer my question about what you are going to do with the books."

"Study them. Learn from them. Just for fun, at first, I will keep our good Cleric and Wizard out of my library."

"Oh, that is going to chap some hides. It may be worth this just to hear them complain."

"I will not allow anyone into the library without they are of goodly nature and approved by you."

"Where are you going to put this Library?"

"Here in the castle. In the Blue Rooms."

The King stood up quickly. "No one can enter the Blue Rooms. You know that."

"I can."

He sat back down. "The Wizards at the University cannot and believe me they tried. The Clerics cannot and they even asked their God how. What makes you think you can?"

"Because I already have."

He looked at me skeptically. "Do you know what's in that room? What was placed there and imprisoned?"

"Yes, Majesty. It is no longer there. I destroyed it."

He stood back up very quickly, "THAT IS IMPOSSIBLE!"

I touched the King's arm and teleported us into the main Blue Room. "What? Where are we? We're in the Blue Rooms!"

"Yes, Majesty. Note that the dais in the center is empty. I took the evil artifact to a plane with creatures that pay well for artifacts. They eat them. They paid me and part of the cost was to allow me to watch them consume the artifact. I assure you it is destroyed. I will do the same with the evil artifacts I find in the mountain. This room has a password for dimensional travel into and out of this area. I found the clue to the password in my studies and then destroyed the text. Note that I did that teleportation silently."

"Yes."

"I do not wish to take a chance of someone overhearing the password."

"Someone could rip it from your mind."

"They could try. However, they still have to by-pass my traps. Good luck with that." I touched his arm and teleported us both back out. The guard was instantly there. They had seen the two of us through the windows. The Blue Room is constantly watched.

The King said, "Stand down the watch on the Blue Rooms. Mike has taken care of the problem."

"As you wish, Sire."

They left but the normal four guards stayed and one slapped me upside the head with a gauntleted hand saying, "Never take the King without permission." He turned and yelled, "Cleric!"

A young Cleric came in. "Yes, Knight-Captain?"

"Prince Mike hurt his head and is bleeding on the floor. Heal him and then get someone to clean up the mess."

"As you wish." The Cleric came over and healed me saying, "You never learn."

My Uncle was smiling but changed it at the tone of the Cleric. "Mike is a Prince. If your tone forgets that again I will send you to have a talk with Father David about humble piety."

You could see the fear in the boy's face, "Yes Majesty."

We left the next day very early in the morning. A party of grand adventurers. The trip to the mountain was uneventful. The cave opening was easy to see and so were the warnings. The opening was thirty feet up the side of a cliff. My research said that the reason they put it up so high was to keep animals from wandering into the traps inside. That was my first clue. "Traps." Plural, as in more than one. I did a soar spell and went up to the opening and started my searching. If there was a spell or magic device known to man that would help in looking for traps, I was wearing it or had the spell cast on me. Most of those types of spells I knew myself, but several are divine. I ensured the Cleric had the spells charged. I found the first trap. The problem was the hidden lever was on the other side of the trap. Arcane Hand, which gives me a magical hand to do things at a distance, took care of that issue. The next trap was in the ceiling and facing down. It looked like a hole to let in light but the light was diffracted just the tiniest bit, and that is not natural. Staying out of the light I flew up and checked out that trap. I disarmed it and took the Artifact Glass Rod of Obliteration out of the hole. Nice. I put that away in my belt sack. Then I checked for more traps in the hole and attuned to the light. I found six more. Gods! They wanted people to stay out! So how were these others getting in? It wasn't through the front door. All in all, I found twenty-one traps in the front section leading to the front door and another five traps on the door. After disabling the traps and taking any magic, I walked the cave front to back several times. I wanted to ensure I found all of them before letting the rest of the party inside. The door was locked from the inside so I needed the fighters to bash it down.

I walked out and they were surprised. I said, "Let's go." I flew each up to the cave and they entered. I explained everything to them and they set to bashing in the door. It was magically protected from spells. I found that out the hard way. It turned my Annihilate spell on me and disintegrated my cloak. They were thinking about keeping out Magic-Users and forgot about fighters. Our barbarian had a heavy war ax made of adamantine that cut it to shreds fairly quickly. Then the fight was on. All that noise let the ones that made it inside know we were trying to get in. They were waiting.

The moment a hole was available, and they had seeable targets, they cast and we backed off out of the door section of the cave. They were using area effect to try and get any that were hiding in the door chamber section, but we were back far enough to not get hit. The Cleric healed the ones that took damage and we all put protections on each other. When they slowed down I went in and let them see me and they started back up with their area effect spells. I am fast and protected so I took no damage. Eventually, they ran out of convenient spells and I started doing some of my own. I did a spell and then our Wizard did a spell and then I did one and then he did one and then we waited. I looked in after the smoke cleared and five were dead. The fighters started bashing again. We opened the door and I started looking for traps. Sure enough, the reason the others stayed back and cast area effect spells was because going forward would have been deadly. Eight traps were found and disabled.

I looted the bodies and on one Wizard I found the keyword for teleporting into and out of the mountain. All five were wizards. No clerics, no fighters, and no rogues. They were in here trying to take the information out and could not. They had the keyword for getting in and out but not the words or the spell to remove protected items. We slowly gutted that entire place. The treasures found will keep the Kingdom and my Uncle happy for decades. I found enough magically preserved furniture to completely decorate the Blue Rooms and enough shelving to house the entire library and all the books I already had three times over. The magic I found and kept is enough to fill another library. I also found eight items of evil intent. Five were artifacts and three of those were aligned evil. The party of adventurers received ten percent of the treasure. That was enough to start their own kingdoms. I put mine away in the lower blue rooms where it could not be seen. The King knew I had it and knew I was not likely going to spend it. I sold the evil artifacts for more gold than I made on that trip and the King knew I had that also. I took him on a tour.

"This is the den, Majesty. Note the chair, table, and permanent lighting for reading." The den was stuffed with books also. We walked through the door. "This is the library." The library was over thirty feet by thirty feet, twenty feet high, and stuffed top to bottom with books so magical even the King could feel the power in the room. The isles were so close together you had to turn sideways to travel between them. There were thousands of books on spells and magic; far more than the Wizard's University library. The unbreakable glass walls showed the Royal Wizard and Cleric watching us. The Grand Wizard of the University was there also. We could not hear what was being said but it was a heated conversation.

The King said, "Boy, you're getting me in trouble. Half the world is going to want to get in and study. The other half will want to take it from us."

"What do you suggest, Uncle? You know I am not good at politics."

"How long will it take you to build a catalog of these books? Put them in order?"

"If I work hard at it I would say three months."

"Why so long?"

"They are not written in the common tongue. I studied enough to understand the language but the translation is slow at best. To read enough to know what the book is about and then write up a card on each will take time."

"Then get started. I will let the others know what you are doing and that I told you not to read the entire book until the cataloging is complete and you can give us a list. That will have to pacify them. Your biggest problem is female in nature." He looked over at two Princesses with their noses pressed to the windows.

I smiled, "I have a place to hide. This library is the perfect place to not pay attention to them."

"YOU WILL NOT! I want you out eating all three meals with us. And, when the Queen sets up a dance you will attend. If you hide they will be all over me with demands. You're not pushing your problem off on me, and that's an order."

"Oh darn."

"Yes, well. What are you going to do with all that treasure? You have enough to buy this kingdom ten times over."

"True, Sire. However, the gold is not really mine. I am a Prince of this country and therefore the gold belongs to this country."

"True that. Even as King I own nothing but the clothes on my back and not all of them."

I laughed, "And, people think we have it easy. Sire, I figure you are going to spend the treasure I gave you to upgrade roads, bridges, etc.?"

"True. They needed fixing years ago. It's time and we have the funding. I am also shoring up the city walls and castle."

"Good. No one except you and I know of the treasure. They know I am now wealthy, but not how wealthy. Goodness sakes. If the Emperor found out what I have below our feet we would be overly taxed until he has it all."

"I think we need to keep our resources to ourselves. I already had to pay him twenty-five percent of the crown's share. He sent his Wizards to collect and count it."

"Exactly, Sire. When you need funding it will be here. No one needs to know where it came from. You simply have a backer."

He smiled. "That's a good idea and I could get things fixed up all over this country. We could build some new ships and upgrade the others. Our soldiers could get paid better and the posts can be fortified. I could cut the eastern forest down and build more farmlands."

I put a hand on his arm. "Sire, I implore you. Don't cut into the forest any further. Instead, dredge the rivers and ports and mix the suit in with the depleted soil of our current farmlands. You know they need dredging and the river soil will make our depleted soil fresh and new and last for many decades. Two things fixed for the price of one and you won't be starting a war with the Elves."

"That's good advice."

"Another bit of advice, Sire. Plant trees that you can harvest. Ask the Elves to help by telling them you need trees and instead of cutting further into the forests you plan on making forests you can cut on a rotating basis, but you need their help to make it work."

"Oh, that's good and may get them talking to us again. Not to change the subject but what are you going to do with those two?" He motioned to the two girls.

"Just between the two of us?"

"Sure."

"Order me to marry Jennifer."

"WHAT!"

"I cannot marry Amanda and stay here in this kingdom. I would have to move back to her island and take the library and the treasure with me. You want that?"

"No."

"Then as King, you need to ensure I am tied down to this country, this city, and this castle so you can keep an eye on the library and treasure. Don't you?"

"Yes, but why marry Jenifer?"

"I love her and always have. However, if I send Amanda home then Jennifer would have no incentive to chase me anymore."

"I see where you're going. If she's not chasing you anymore she could lose interest. I will have a wonderful time with this. You keep acting upset about getting married."

"Sure. Not hard to do as I am upset." I changed to a discussed look and said, "I'm too young and too inexperienced."

The King frowned and said, "You will do as ordered!"

We pretended to argue for several minutes and then he motioned for me to send him out so I teleported him out but stayed inside where I was safe from the girls.

As soon as he was out he walked over to the two and said. "Amanda, it is with great regret that I have to tell you this. Mike will not be leaving this kingdom. If you get married to him you will have to stay here at this castle for the rest of your life. Mike is not going to give up his books and there is no place protected as well as the Blue Rooms. Top that with the fact that you are not my subject and so I cannot order Mike to marry you. I tried and he told me he wasn't old enough to marry."

Amanda sat down on the bench. She was fuming. She didn't truly love Mike, she was just used to getting her way. "I cannot stay in this country. I am needed back home. I can see that Mike is never going to leave his precious books. It's a shame he lived through that adventure. It would be easier to tell father he is dead than tell him I failed. I will pack and leave on the morrow." She got up and left. Jennifer left also.

Two days later marriage was brought up at breakfast and I pretended panic. I instantly left for my books.

The King went into his private study and told the servants to tell the rest of the family to attend him. When they showed up the servants were told to leave and the doors were shut.

The King said, "We have a problem and the answer eludes me."

The Queen asked, "What is it, my love?"

"Mike! I need him tied down. I just found out that he is looking for someplace else to house his library and that means he'll take his treasure with him. This does not leave this room, but his treasure is ten times what mine is and I need a big portion of that without the Emperor taking it all in taxes. He has it hidden away. Another thing, he is looking at going after another stash of books. If he obtains that and does not bring them back here? The loss for the empire and this country would be indescribable."

Jennifer said, "Order him to marry me."

The King said, "Sweetheart, you do not need to make such a sacrifice for your country. I know you pretended to have a crush on him when Amanda was here, but this is for life."

The Queen said, "Men! Husband dear, your daughter does not have a crush on Mike. She is in love."

"Father, I will not treat Mike like I have treated everything else I have won. You have seen me over and over using an attitude to win it and forget it, or quickly lose interest. That is not going to happen. I am going to marry Mike if I have to kill every female in this kingdom so that I am the only one left. I have plans for being married to Mike that will take the rest of my life to execute."

The Prince said, "Mike is not someone you can make plans around. He is the most elusive man in this kingdom, if not the entire empire."

"I've noticed, brother dear, and I believe he will be just as allusive to keep. When we were teaching Mike to be a woman we spent many hours together. I was falling in love with Amanda and not as a sister. Mike will make me very happy for the rest of my life. We are completely compatible and the Cleric told me that our God has given blessings for the marriage. Order him to marry me. He will not do so on his own. Once married I can assure you he will stay here and be very happy to do so. We are fifth cousins and so easily distant enough to marry."

The King stared at his daughter for a moment. "Do you have any idea what you will be marrying?"

"I believe so, but enlighten me."

"I believe that Mike is becoming the most powerful man on the face of the planet. He is already more wealthy than the Emperor, more deadly than a dragon, and more dangerous than a rabid Jataelcat. The books he has are worth more than this kingdom. He will be studying those books and others he is going after. He will grow in his abilities and surpass the Emperors Royal Magi. The one he marries has a difficult road ahead. She will need to keep him deeply in love and of goodly nature or he could end up evil and destroy us all. This is not just a position as a wife. This is a job to raise and guide the most powerful person on the face of the planet.

Jennifer smiled, "Oh really. How interesting. That means that the woman that tames him and keeps him tamed is going to be the richest most influential woman on the face of the planet."

The King smiled, "You cannot tame him."

Jennifer leaned in. "Are you willing to bet on that?"

THE GARDENER

I ENJOY WALKING. I COULD CONJURE A HORSE OR A dragon mount but walking allows you the time to experience your surroundings; see, touch, taste, and feel the trees, flowers, weeds, and rain. Being a greater Dark Druid Remsant that can change into any animal at will, I don't normally take the road either. Roads are for people that want security and simple lives. I cut through the mountains and valleys, fly over the rivers, and wade in the streams. In doing so I find all kinds of spell and potion components. I found a grand place for Desmire plants and harvested enough to make a hundred potions of soar. I also replanted so that there would be more when I come this way again. Waste not want not. Always replant.

That was the problem now. I was standing out in my garden after returning from a week-long trip and it was destroyed. There was nothing to salvage. All the foliage I so lovingly and painstakingly found and planted, nourished and maintained was pulled up. All the seeds were missing and anything usable for spells or potions gone. Easy to see it was a spell caster as many of the plants are food and the food was still there but the magic components were stolen along with the seeds. Whoever it was, he knew he was stealing from another magic-user. He flew in and flew out leaving no tracks. A good person would have harvested the magic components and left my garden intact and left me the seeds. This was cruel and in my opinion tantamount to murder. War they must have wanted so war was what they would get. Many of those plants are rare and cannot be found on this continent. Anyone using or marketing them, or their byproducts, would be traceable. And, they were my plants and I could find them.

The next day I completed a Find Direction spell. Not the little "Detect the Trail" spell but "Find Direction." I only needed to know which direction they were in and on the map I made a line in that direction. I teleported to another place in the kingdom and completed another direction spell and drew a line. The two lines intersected at the Castle of Darkest Light.

I had to think about that. So, the old vampire Markma was up and about again, or somebody was using his castle. Then it hit me. The seeds taken could destroy him if made into the correct spells. I did a mental sending to the old white-haired human fool and received two words. "I know."

That night Markma showed up in my home. I said, "Hello, old friend."

Markma sat down. I pointed to his chin and he cleaned off the blood. Apparently, he just finished feeding. "Hello, Frank. How's seed hunting doing these days?"

I laughed, "It was doing fine until some fool stole my garden."

Markma said, "I noticed that on the way in. Not like you to mess things up so completely, Frank. People maybe, but not plants. They are at my castle trying to destroy me."

I asked, "You kill the chump that did it yet?"

"He has protections. A Cleric of Solbelli and a Paladin. He has two other Clerics with him and eight fighters, two rogues, and four war wizards. All protected by their God."

He looked ashen. I smiled and said, "Someone must want you completely dead very badly. That sounds like a very high level and high priced group."

Markma frowned, "It is, and that someone is King Smith."

"Rosy?"

"Yes Rosy! I swear that fool never learns. He is still after my amulet."

"You sold that."

"I know it and you know it but Rosy does not believe it. I'd buy it back from you if I had the gold and shove it up his back end. You do still have it don't you?"

I opened my shirt, "It never leaves my body. You need to barrow it? I would lend it to you but not to Rosy."

Markma said, "No. It's better left with you. I cannot be sure when Rosy will pull something again. Like now. His choice of people to hunt me down is deadly."

"Did you bring your coffin or are you going back in the morning?"

"I placed it in your basement. I hope you don't mind."

"Of course not, my friend. You are always welcome at my home. It will be good to have someone intelligent to talk to for a change."

Markma smiled, "You never cease to amaze me, Frank. Here I am a Vampire heading toward Lech status and you willingly invite me into your home."

I laughed. "Because we are good and trusted friends. Still, it doesn't hurt that I am immune to your bite and can easily destroy you."

Markma laughed with me. "And, Rosy thinks I am the dangerous one."

"Tell me Markma. Does this group hunt at night or only during the day?"

"So far only during the day."

I took a few minutes to think. "Where do they go at night?"

"They teleport out."

"Can you not attack during the day when they are below ground?"

"They have spells that cause daylight that sticks to the wall and does not go away. Nearly got me killed. As soon as they saw me they let that spell off and then hit me with a bottle of something. I escaped with my undead life, but just barely. The potion they hit me with made it so I could not turn to vapor for several hours. Little by little my home is being lit up. Soon there will be no place to hide."

I looked at him and said, "The plants they harvested from my garden are for many rare potions; perfect dragon flight, advanced mass healing, stuffed anything, and various other high-level potions. I had enough Volooee to make five potions of minor wish. The problem is they can also be used to make chemicals that will stop any creature from changing form for short periods, like vampires into vapor, and they can be made into permanent sunlight spells that cannot be dispelled."

Markma said, "Not your fault my friend. You did not plant them to use against me. Your reasons were honorable. Theirs are not."

I picked up several magic items and looked at my friend. "Markma. You go after Rosy and don't leave him alive or capable of being resurrected. I will take care of this Cleric." I teleported away before Markma could complain.

At the Castle of Darkest Light, I could not believe my eyes. After seeing all the Greater Sunlight spells emanating from every window I realized that poor Markma will have to find another name for his home. People were taking the place apart. Doors and windows removed so that nothing could block up the light.

Where the light was too little either a new spell was placed or they knocked down a wall. Systematically they were removing all possibility of darkness or shadow. My kind of place. Maybe I could exchange homes with Markma. He always liked my tiny place.

I walked up to a worker that was all by himself and quickly killed him. I did this several times before someone noticed that his friends were missing. He ran back inside and told the Clerics. They all came out and started casting about. I teleported inside and waited.

It was about an hour before they came across a casket. They placed a "Greater Daylight Spell" directly above the casket and then drew weapons. One Cleric drew out a potion. A Rogue checked for traps and found the two I placed there. He easily disabled them. A fighter opened the casket and as they stabbed in and tossed in the potion, I attacked from the back killing two before disappearing. The poisonous snakes I put in the casket took out another.

They were now very upset and teleported out to make plans. The rest of the day and that night I spent placing traps on places they have already been. I also put back many of the doors and windows and trapped them. Then I did the spell "Stone Barrier" behind the front double doors.

The next morning they showed up on top of my first trap. I could easily see where they had been teleporting too. It was a spot where people walked away from but no one walked into. I had some friends rip a hole in the ground and fill the bottom with spikes. Just as I thought. They were not using the ground for their memorization of the place. They used trees and castle placement. They ported in and fell thirty feet onto sharp spikes. Two of the rogues evaded the trap until they looked over the edge at their fellow party members and I walked up, invisible and silent, and pushed them over. I magically shifted to the castle.

Three died in that fall. Not the high ranking party members of course. That would be asking too much. It was the grunt workers, the window and door removers, that died. If this keeps up they were going to have a difficult time finding help.

They stood around healing each other and fixing in their mind a new place for teleporting. I watched. They came to the castle and tried the door and my fireball went off. Three took damage. Again they used wands of healing. This was going to be expensive for them. After the rogues said all was clear, two fighters tried to open the doors but they wouldn't open. A big one went into a rage and ran at the door putting his shoulder into breaking it down. Broke his shoulder and the healing wands came out. One of the Wizards used an "Open" spell. Of course, that didn't work as the doors were not locked. They were barricaded. Finally, another Wizard used an "Annihilate" spell and blasted a hole through the door and stone barrier.

They walked in at the ready and it was dark. I had used a "Stone Configure" spell to make a cover from the rocks outside to fit over the "Greater Sunlight" Spells and then used "Stone Configure" again to attach the wall and stone cover trapping the Daylight inside. Then I used some "Brass Barrier" spells to block out the windows.

They lit an Illumination Stick and tossed it into the room. A fighter walked over and pulled an ax out of his magical backpack. He used it to destroy the stone cover and then put it away. That was disappointing. Tomorrow when he pulls that out I am going to have a "Teleport Item" spell ready. I waited for hours for them to reach me. They took their time as I placed a lot of traps. Most were simple easily seeable traps. Some were not. I was in a hurry to set as many as possible so that the good ones, I actually took time to make, would be a surprise.

They came to the door I was behind and as the Rogue touched the door I set off the trap. Three lightning strikes shot down the fifteen foot wide hall catching every one of them except the two rogues. The healing wands came out.

When they were ready, and hiding behind the wall leading into the last hall adjacent to this one, the Rogue touched the door and I let off the second trap. A Stuffed Fire Ball in the cross-section of the two halls. Caught everyone except the rogue by my door. The wands came out and this time two were discarded after being used up.

One Cleric said, "This is becoming costly."

A Paladin retorted, "So!"

They went further away and the rogue touched the door again. Nothing happened so they returned and I set off the third and last trap. An acid cloud filled the hall making it impossible to see. I walked into the floor and up to the other side of the fog and tossed in a coin with a "Soundless" spell on it. Then I placed a stone barrier to keep the fog in with the people. The yelling and screams were wonderful until I tossed in the coin. They broke down the only door and ran straight into another trap. There was no floor. I placed a portal on this side of the door that opened up into walking off the castle tower. Three made it to flying, one teleported out, one magically shifted to the ground and four died. It was a long fall and with the acid damage on top of it, there wasn't much left to kill. They gathered together and teleported out.

I set up new traps including their new spot for porting in. The next day they fell into a new spiked pit, I placed in their new spot, killing four workers. The others came out alive. They teleported away. The next day they came back riding horses. Great! I love the taste of horseflesh. I let them go in and waited for their screams from my traps to diminish before attacking the horses. Two got away and I had to chase them down but I'm faster and it was a lot of fun.

They made it to their last spot before I showed up looking for them. They were easy to follow. Just listen for the cussing from the dwarf. Each trap that caught him he yelled and cussed. Most were little traps designed to use up resources. At one point I heard a Cleric ask, "Anyone have any more wands or potions of cure wounds? I'm out." They all confirmed that they were out. That was what I was waiting for.

I did a Travel Lock spell into their area and attacked with invisible claw and teeth. I killed the wizards first and then I left them alone so I could lick my wounds back to normal. Nice having instant healing in my licking. I did not need to worry about them getting help because, without their wizards, they had no way to teleport.

Next, I sat in wait for the rogues and after killing one I ran and healed up. Then I repeated the process until all the rogues were dead. At one point they gave chase but the traps nearly killed them all and they had to stop. Spells were thrown my way each time I attacked, but being able to go invisible I was difficult to target. As soon as someone used a "See Unseen" spell I went away until it was off. "They tossed "Twinkle Flakes" on me and I ran until it dissipated. At one point I reached up from the floor and pulled a Cleric down into the floor with me. Only to his knees but he could not go ethereal and get out. The wizards were dead so they could not magically shift him out. He was stuck. That gave me an Idea. I started pulling the others into the walls. Soon I had them all stuck including the dead and all in the same hall. Twelve high-level adventurers. I came out and became visible. As I pulled other parts into the wall to make a nice mural for my good friend I also stone shaped hands going over their mouths so they could not get away so easily. Then just before I turned them all to stone, I asked, "Which one of you tore up my garden?"

A Cleric mumbled, "I did. Let the others go and I will take your punishment."

I walked over to him and said, "You die first, slowly, and very painfully. But know this as you are dying. The others are next and they die because of you."

Six days later I returned to my home and Markma was waiting for me. "How did it go? Is my castle safe to return to?"

"You can return any time you want, my friend. I have removed the light by replacing the sections of wall they were attached too. I'm keeping the lit sections for myself. I destroyed your enemies and made them into a nice ornament for your main hall. The doors and windows are back in place and everything is ready for your return. Oh, I forgot the snakes I left in one of the caskets. But they should be no problem for you. How did it go with you?"

"Rosy is dead and so is all his kin except his youngest daughter. I'm keeping her as a plaything. I found the place where they were making the potions." He held out his hand and several bags of seed gently ported to my table. "There's not much left but I saved what I could." He saw that I could not speak through the tears. He stood up and patted my spiked shoulder and then ported to his home.

SHOP KEEPER

IF THERE IS ANYTHING I CANNOT STAND IT IS HUMANS. They are interfering, fast breading, stingy, overly possessive, thieving, mongrel pests. Yet they do have some redeeming qualities. I enjoy their food and wine and that's about it. They can keep that rabbit piss they call beer, and grog is for the poor and the poor can have it. Still, here I am, a Tree Elf, in the center of their city making a living off the humans. Can't beat them as there are far too many. So, I decided to join them. Works for me.

I own a store on the edge of the better end of the market district directly across from the Wizard's University, and the Fighter's Guild is on the left. I cater to the guilds and universities. My wears include most things magical. I create potions, wands, scrolls, magical arrows and bolts, staves, and my specialty is deep pocket haversacks and quivers though my love is the bow. The great Goddess Natura created the first magical haversack and quiver and you cannot change perfection.

Natura made all her haversacks the same. Great quality but purposefully looking used and almost warn out using leather with old copper hardware. The haversack is the same size as any normal haversack. Hers has four small side bags of magical holding that look about the size of a small hand but can hold 10 lbs or one cubic foot each. The central bag of holding takes up to 100 lbs or 10 cubic feet. The central section and four pockets are enchanted so that the item you want is always the first to hand. No fumbling around. Just reach back and grab what's on top and continue with what you were doing. It's quick and handy during combat, climbing a cliff, or finding yourself suddenly underwater. You can fill the haversack with one hundred and forty pounds and it will only weight three pounds. It weighs one pound empty and three pounds full. Limitations are no sharp objects and no extra-dimensional spaces. Punch a hole in a Natura's Deep Pocket Haversack and possibly lose everything into a rift in the dimensions. Bags of holding are non-dimensional spaces so you dare not open one while in a non-dimensional or extra-dimensional space and you dare not put one non-dimensional space inside another. That could cause a rift that would destroy you and everything around you. You can only place a maximum of 140 pounds or 12 cubic feet in the haversack. Still, few people are ever in an extra-dimensional space, sharp objects can be sheaved, and 140 pounds for the cost of three pounds is very handy when traveling.

I took it a few steps further. In addition to the traditional haversack, I make smaller and larger models. I have a Wizard friend that cannot carry an additional three pounds so I made a one-pound version for him. He took it back to the Wizard's University and what do you know. I now sale more of the small version than any other. I sale the small version to the wizards and sorcerers, merchants and money changers, several to the guard, and many to the Halflings. It cost half what the original haversack cost because it is half the size but surprisingly people love it. I'm told the Princess has one.

I also make a larger version. It is still the same and magically changes size as does the original but the center section can carry 20 cubic feet (200 pounds). All four side sections can carry 2 cubic feet (20 pounds) each, exactly twice the carrying capacity of a normal haversack. I charge just a little less than twice the price of a normal haversack for this. The Fighter's Guild and the army snatch them up as quickly as I make them. Having a soldier that can carry 280 pounds on his back for a weight cost of only six pounds can be very handy. There is one other thing I add to my haversacks and this requires a special order. I can add one or more magical sections for sheathing weapons. No chance of cutting the haversack. I reinforce all around that area. The interior of the sheath is made of the same material as a Natura's Deep Pocket Quiver and that cannot be cut or punctured. I sale very few of those additions as that ups the cost by a multiple of five and Gauntlets of Holding are cheaper. I make those also.

I am most proud of my quivers. The normal Natura's Deep Pocket Quiver is a wondrous thing with four sections. The first two sections hold up to 60 objects the general size and shape of an arrow. The third section holds five objects the general size and shape of a staff. The fourth section can hold up to two items the same general size and shape like a bow. This is great for a bow and staff using fighter. However, most bow users do not use the staff. You can put five quarterstaffs in but the rest of the area is wasted unless you are a bowman also. The Great Goddess Natura, I would guess, uses a bow and staff. Advantages: weights only four pounds even if full, items come quickly to hand, not instantaneous but close, and only cost 2000 GP (Gold Pieces). Limitations: wasted space if you don't use staff or a bow. If upside-down or hung horizontally across the spine an arrow may fall out before you can grab it so only good for over the shoulder which makes it not very flexible for use.

I changed my quivers so that you have a choice of non-dimensional spaces. Also, I fixed the problem with arrows and weapons dropping. You can wear my quiver any way you want. I still call it the Natura's Deep Pocket Quiver. I wouldn't want to upset the original designer.

You can purchase a standard quiver (weapon slot for bows, two arrows areas, two small pockets for only 1900 GP, or you can get a very special, top of the line, custom made quiver for 52,150 GP and anything in-between. I sold one of those to a very rich Barron. Most people turn away from buying the instantaneous option as it is rather pricy. Still, some adventurers need that potions section to be an instant draw and don't want to pay the 15,000 GP for a bandolier of instant potion use. I make those also. Wizard and Cleric adventurers are the same way only they always include wands.

I am very good at making magical bows and magical arrows. That is a passion of mine as I am a very good shot and enjoy hunting. At first, I wasn't selling much magical equipment due to the pricing but then an idea hit me. I started running credit to the guilds. I don't give credit to individuals but I extend credit to the guilds. Why? Because, even if the Guild Master dies, the guild is obligated to pay or the magistrate will shut them down and pay me with their landholdings. There is only one guild I do not extend credit to and that is the churches. First, they're not a guild. Second, they stiffed me calling it donations twice in the past. The Magistrate was upset but the Church has strings and pulled them. Fine! Now I don't do business with the churches, clerics, or cleric want-a-bees. I don't even let them in my store.

That's the rub right now. The King's Royal Cleric, Monsignor Kalnee, just came in.

I came around my register bar and quickly placed myself in front of him and his four brothers, fathers, whatever. "Monsignor Kalnee you and yours are not welcome in my store. Please leave."

"I am here on the King's business, Hardom. Now get out of my way."

I pushed forward and backed him up and just out the door and then grabbed the one brother that came in passed the Monsignor and tossed him out and onto his backside. I'm not very big, but I am strong. "Monsignor Kalnee, please tell my beloved King that he should reconsider his choice of messenger and send his Wizard, or the Captain of the Guard, or the lowliest ash-maid, someone that is trustworthy. I do not allow thieves in my shop."

The Monsignor was highly upset. "I am a High Cleric of Solbelli! I am not a thief! How dare you! I will have the Captain of the Guard down here instantly!"

I knew he was threatening me with arrest but to upset him more I said, "Please do! I can trust him. And, you are a thief. Donations are given, not taken!" I shut the door, turned the sign to "Closed", and shut the curtain. He banged on it several times and then I heard him say. "Father Gormaly. Go get the guard. We are confiscating all this store's goods in the name of the King."

"As you wish, Monsignor."

I knew what he was up to. I had heard the stories and helped one of the merchants before. They confiscate everything and when it is all sorted out and you are proven innocent then they return your belongings minus the items they wanted. I opened the back door and gave an orphan a silver to quickly let the Captain of the Guard know that Monsignor was about to steal all my merchandise. He took off nearly flying through the crowd of people. I quickly opened a portal and removed all my items including my shelves, build equipment, potion-making equipment, office area, and display areas. Everything was gone except for one small item. I was prepared for this and as soon as I opened the portal the items started moving on their own.

I sent them to a secret place in the mountains I owned thanks to the King needing an item and having just taken that land from bandits. We made a trade. My land now and it's free and clear, and with hunting rights for the entire northern forest. The Prince and I have been out in the forest hunting several times but he and the King don't know about this place.

There was a knock on my front door. I walked over and peeked out the curtain. Sure enough, there was the guard.

The Guard said, "In the name of the King, open this door."

I opened the curtain and said, "We're closed."

The Guard who is a minor officer and a member of the Church said, "Open now or I break it in."

I unlocked the door and as I opened it I said, "My-oh-my, you must have just happened to be close, officer. I seem to recall the same thing happening to several other store owners."

He walked in and I shut the door after three more guards entered. They pushed me out of the way and reopened the door. As the Monsignor entered he said, "Confiscate all this." His voice trailed off. "Where are your commodities?"

I pretended shock, "Commodities? I am in the process of changing out my merchandise for more advanced items. I have been thinking about changing this store into a pet shop. What do you think? Cages over there and food supplies in that corner?"

The officer grabbed my tonic and jerked me toward him. "Where are all your magic items?"

I looked him right in the eye and said, "I seem to have missed one broken arrow in that old broken barrel. You can have it for free."

He tossed me to the side. "You two. Take him outside and beat the information out of him. The rest of you are to tear this place down looking for that magical equipment.

They beat me continuously until the Captain of the Guard came by with twenty men. I was badly hurt and could not talk as most of my ribs were broken. I could have easily destroyed them all but then I would be up for murder. Right now they had nothing to charge me with. When I could I finally looked up, my place was on fire and torn to shreds. The Clerics were standing there with the guards.

Monsignor Kalnee said, "Captain, we caught this fool burning down his store. I had the guards teach him a lesson. Meanwhile, I and my friends ensured that the fire did not spread to the other stores."

The Captain looked around, "Monsignor Kalnee, you're a lying fool. I will get to the bottom of this and if I find out that you are guilty of what I believe to be the truth then I will come find you myself. Now, get out of my sight!"

The Monsignor said, "And, what will you do, Captain? You have no authority over me."

Monsignor Kalnee and the guard started off, but the Captain said, "Not you Sergeant! I want these six guards under arrest for questioning. I do have authority over them. Orders from now on are that no guard is to help a Cleric of Solbelli." The Captain leaned down to pick me up. "I am surprised, my little friend. Why did you not kill that fool?"

I painfully choked out, "Because, Captain, he is the King's friend. You cannot touch him and nether can I without losing our heads. He will continue his greed and there is nothing you can do. He will have the order renounced and the guards will continue to help him. Most of the guard belongs to his God."

The Captain asked, "How much did he take?"

I frowned. "Nothing. I moved it before he could get the guard. They were beating me to get information on where I moved it to. They took everything I was carrying. You wouldn't happen to have a healing potion on you? My ribs are broken badly and it's becoming difficult to breathe. Besides, my hands are shattered so I cannot do the spell myself."

He pulled out a potion and started to hand it to me but I was in so much pain that my hands were shaking and most my fingers were broken. He poured it down my throat. It helped a little. I said, "Thanks. I own you one."

The Captain said, "I'd call a Cleric but I don't think you're on their good side right now."

I looked concern, "Yes. I will be hounded until they find my products. This isn't the last I will see of them. They will simply wait to take me when you are not looking, thinking to beat the information from me. That will force me to fight back." I looked up into the Captain's eyes and sincerely said, "And, next time, I will fight back."

The Captain said, "That's a problem. You harm the Monsignor and the entire church will be after you. So will the King."

I started to cry, "I hate doing this. I love this city but I cannot stay here. Tell the Prince that I said Monsignor Kalnee has chased me out and why. I have no store anymore and my wears cannot be brought back to this city. I am leaving. I give you my city land, Captain, for a city guardhouse. We need one in this section of town. Staff it with people not belonging to Solbelli. Goodbye."

He started to say something but I had already magically disappeared. I went to my hideout as it was protected from magical scrying. I used a Wand of Major Healing to fix the rest of my body. Even so, I was going to have a massive headache from the stress of what happened. Healing is wonderful but it takes a complete heal to relieve stress and fatigue.

I waited three months while scrying on the Monsignor. The day after he attacked another merchant, one I did not like, I teleported in and killed him in his bed. Then I killed the four he was always with. I used a knife and made it look like an assassination. No possible way to blame it on me. No magic used and no arrow.

There was great sadness in the city at first but it turned into a grand calibration when the populace found out that it was Monsignor Kalnee that was dead. The Church tried to resurrect him but their God Solbelli refused. He let the Cleric attempting the resurrection know that Monsignor Kalnee and his four friends were evil and not truly his disciples.

The King was upset at first and ordered a complete investigation but the investigation started providing the truth. People came forth once they understood that Monsignor Kalnee wasn't there to 'destroy their soles.'

The Prince sent a message for me to return but I was very comfortable doing what I was doing now. I was hunting and selling magic and pelts to Duke Edward and his people and generally having a grand time making bows and arrows for the fun of it. Though my stockpiles were getting high I was finally enjoying life.

FINE WITH ME

THERE IS A NEW ZEALOT, SELF-PROCLAIMED PROFIT, bigot in the world and he has a lot of mob followers. They run around in bands on horseback proclaiming that all should worship this profit. Those that do not are killed, everything they had taken, and their homes burned down. It's fine with me. Normally I would not care what happens to others as long as it is not affecting me.

I'm a big man and strong as an ox. People normally don't mess with me. However, I was sitting on my porch when they showed up. I started to yell out a warning to my family. "Militia!" But something hit me in the head and I collapsed. When I came too my home was burned to the ground along with my barn. All the livestock were missing and everything in my home taken. I was left for dead so close to the fire half my body was burnt. My fingers, on one hand, were missing but that's OK because the hand was so burnt it couldn't hold the fingers anyway. I was in pain. Not so much from the burning but from the loss of my family. They were tied upside down in the big Kelor shade tree and then the tree was set on fire. They died slowly. Probably very slowly.

It took a good long time before I stopped crying. I lay there praying to my God and received no answer as to why. Slowly and very carefully I healed myself. Slowly and carefully because my mouth was burnt off and I had to cast the spells non-somatic and non-verbal. I thought back on my life and why I was here while I healed myself, grew back the parts that were missing, cleansed the scars, and generally made myself the way I was before.

I took up farming and ranching because I was becoming something I did not like. I was becoming extremely evil. I met this very nice woman with two lovely children and I fell in love. I changed my ways for both her and myself. I put away my spellbooks, wands, rods, and staffs for a plow and hammer. For the first time in my life, I was happy. Oh, I kept up on spells but mostly the ones that help in farming and ranching. I did so many spells for my ranch and the ranches nearest me that I grew in ability but I did not turn evil. I became good which is a big change and in that change came a change of Gods. This one never listens. I receive nothing from him. So I prayed to my old God, the Laughing God, a God that delights in chaos. "Oprepo! I call on you. I have been forsaken by the God of my wife. I have lost all that I loved and I am in the mood to create some CHAOS! If you don't mind some slaughter mixed in with the chaos then I require a God to put this Profit in his place."

Instantly I felt refreshed, powerful, my old knowledge poured into me and I knew what I knew before I put it all away for farming and I knew more. Spells I would have known if I continued on my old path. In an angry voice, and condescending tone, I heard in every fiber of my soul. "It's fine with me." Then the tone turned angry. "However, leave my stable again and I will be the cause of your pain. Take your revenge and should you live I need you for some other issues."

I looked up and yelled, "And, you shall have me!" Anger like fire erupted from my spirit and when I was done the only way you could tell there used to be a barn, tree, and home was because of the shape of the deep holes.

When I calmed down enough to think straight I headed toward my old underground hideout. It was six hundred miles from my home and so well hidden and so magically protected none had ever found it. I teleported to the opening and walked in passed the deadly traps. I stopped and petted my pet Chaos Monster. The guardian, a rather large Dire Rippemnor said, "Hello boss, long time no see." Then backed off when he saw the look on my face. The Killer Creeper touched me in a familiar sign of welcoming and then coiled back up.

I went straight to my library and chose some highly magical clothing. The burnt rags I was wearing were about to fall off. I started donning magic; Circlet of Telepathy and Greater Intelligence, Choker of Storm Thought and Insight, Amulet of Greater Custodia with Shielding and Greater Dodge, Vestments of Terror with Greater Dexterity, Robe of Blending with Luck that adds to dodge, Bracelets of Maximize Force Armor and Skin Armor, Robe of Chaos and Calamity, Belt of Greater Dragon Strength and Breathing, Cloak of Improved Greater Invisibility with Greater Charisma, Gauntlets of Deaths Touch and Holding, and Boots of Advanced Shifting, Exceptional Fly, and Etherealness. I picked up my staff of Advanced Horror, loaded some wands, a couple of rods, a Ring of Minor Miracles on one hand and a Ring of Elemental Control on the other. Then I sat down on the Stone Thrown of Frenzied Thought and planned.

As with all big businesses this Profit had a large following. Even Kings were afraid to do anything against him. Mobs can be dangerous and he had a few thousand that would die for him on his whim. I teleported into the Profit's rooms and killed the guard and took the Profit down to the underworld to a friend of mine.

About three weeks later I was sitting by the side of the road waiting. I could hear them coming and I had already prepared. They came riding around the corner and saw me but thought nothing of the vagabond sitting on the side of the road. I put out a hand for alms and received spit instead. I yelled as they passed, "Worship the Profit!"

It was about that time they hit my trap. A fireball went off in front of them and then one to the side and one to the other side and again in the front. That drove what was left of them straight back to me. I killed them all except one that was the correct size and shape I needed. Him I took to the underground lair of the Drow and to that Brain-Eating friend of mine who was keeping the Profit for me. I changed the way he looked so that he matched the Profit and the Brain Eater changed his mind so that he had the life and history of the profit and thought himself the same. I took him back up top and dropped him off in an area where his men would find him. I did the same thing twenty-nine more times. They now had thirty false profits. I then took the real Profit and released him in the same place. A week later I added another. They had thirty-two Profits and only one was correct.

If he had been a true profit I am sure some Cleric could get a calling from his God. No God was going to help this group. Thirty-two Profits and everyone was giving different orders. Some were good-natured, some evil, and some did not care one way or the other. I had my Brain-Eating friend ensure they were a mixed lot. I sat back and watched as groups were splintered and fought over which one was the correct Profit. Some Profits tried killing the others and so they had to be kept separate.

Meantime, I attacked small groups of his followers in different places. Whenever I found some of his mob burning and sacking they died from my spells. This was cutting into his most ardent followers deeply and they had to do something.

It was about six months into the campaign when all but one of the Profits died. They killed the first Profit and kept the one that matched what they wanted doing and was the most manageable. I saw through a viewing pool who "they" were. That was what I was waiting for. No Profit could grab the followers he had without backing. Someone of intelligence was behind the systematic attacks. It was an old friend of mine. Simon the Scandalous was behind it all. Funny, Simon is a follower of my God. I went home and prayed.

"My God, is not Simon one of your Champions? I need to know as I am about to destroy the fool."

"I have watched you and enjoyed your antics. You know the meaning of Chaos. You are one of the few that does. Simon started on this task to create Chaos but he has become mean and greedy. He has allowed his people to kill for no reason and has angered many Gods who are now angry with me. He is trying to instill some law into this group so that he can control them. I am greatly disappointed in him. I have told the Gods that you will remove him and the false Profit. Do it chaotically. Others are watching and I do not want them to think we are simple-minded."

I sat down on the thrown and thought hard on the matter. For weeks I made and changed plans and then something crossed my mind. I teleported to where I knew Simon was staying and I placed a curse of insanity on his Ring of Essentia. He never takes that ring off. He went insane and started killing. I allowed the Profit's Clerics to cure him but the curse was repeating. Weekly he went insane and weekly the Profit's Clerics cured him. One day he was talking quietly at a meeting and the next instant killed the Profit in front of the others and they mobbed him. The ring passed to a fighter and he killed many of his friends. I took the ring back after that as the word was spread that the Profit was dead and the mob dispersed saying, "He died. He was no profit."

I then turned to the King and Queen and ensured they knew the leaders were dead including the Profit and his backers. They ordered the deaths of all his believers. The mob ran after that. Many died and many hid or blended back in. But I was not done. I then had them set up courts to place on trial the accused and made this person turn in that person just to see what would happen. Talk about Chaos; everyone accused everyone else and the courts were deadlocked so that no one was executed because to do so would be to kill everyone. I reminded the King that you cannot collect tax form zero subjects. He pardoned everyone which was a big surprise.

Many of the mob became bandits. Oh, did I have fun with them. They would find themselves in all kinds of predicaments. Chasing a group of wealthy merchants one moment to be facing a few hundred of the Kings Guard the next. I personally liked teleporting them onto pirate ships. Pirates don't like it when twenty bandits with horses show up on their decks at sea. Insect swarms that constantly followed them around were fun and a wagon full of girls being exchanged for an upset dragon was hilarious. One of my favorites was to magically put them to sleep, remove all their belongings, and teleport them into the hills. It was great fun watching them wake up buck naked and surrounded by little Kobolds. I'd teleport a leader to a Dryad, or the Fairies, or the Pixies, and sometimes to the Drow. One day I found the group that destroyed my prior life. I could feel the Gods watching and waiting for me to destroy them. They were waiting for justice. However, I am Chaotic. I do not care about justice. My vengeance was simple. I changed them all too petit sexy effeminate men, put them in chains, and teleported them all to the demon realm. There I sold them off to Demon Lords.

It's been years since that time and I am told they are all still alive and that's not good for them. However, it's fine with me.

GUARDING

"WHY DO PEOPLE THINK THAT ALL GHOSTS ARE EVIL? Sure, I'm undead and most good-aligned clerics believe that all undead are abominations to their God. Look, my father, his father, and his father back twenty-eight generations protected this treasure. I spent my entire life protecting the items here and when I died I had no son to carry on the tradition so I continued with the tradition even after death. That's not hard to understand is it? Not my fault I had daughters and no sons."

The Cleric said, "It's not your fault. Back when you were alive we could not decide the sex of the child. Things are more balanced now; though, I don't believe in changing what my God determined should be. It is God that picks the sex of a child and Clerics should not interfere. They have overstepped their charter."

The Cleric continued to back away from me and I allowed it for now. "Why Cleric? Why did you come into my home?"

"We were told that there is great treasure here. We are adventurers looking for treasure."

I bent down and touched him again and drained his constitution a little more. He screamed in pain. "Were you not warned about the protections upon this place?"

"Yes! Yes, we were told but we foolishly thought we were capable of defeating you."

"Well, it is plain to see that you were not. Your God protects you from becoming one of my little helpers but as you die be aware of two things. Your friends were not so protected and now they are wraiths and they protect an object that if fallen into the wrong hands could bring the planes of the Many Hidden Hells directly in alignment with this world and therefore this plane of existence. The treasure you so desire would be the cause of death for the entire human race." I reached down and touched him again and sent him back to his God.

It was not long before another group of adventurers graced my doorstep. This group was different. They set up camp outside in the forest within sight of my home. There they started building a temple to Solbelli. Within a few years, the temple grew until my home was blanked off by a secret door.

A Priest came to that door and sat in wait. After a few days, I asked, "What is it you are waiting for, Priest of Solbelli?"

He looked around and seeing nothing said, "I wait for the one that protects this world by keeping evil from reaching his treasure."

"Ah, the Cleric told someone about the item I protect."

"Only that in the wrong hands the planes of hell would be connected to this world in some way. Our God is worried and has ordered us to help protect your home. He has told us not to try to harm you or your minions. So, undead and Solbelli's clerics have a truce at this time. He told us to create a place for his help in protecting this sight. I need to know if you would mind if we consecrated this area to Solbelli."

"As Solbelli was and is my God, though he does not listen now that I am undead, I have no issue with any blessings from that direction. But be warned, my brother. I have seen pretend brothers of our faith who are evil. They come searching treasure and kill any in their way. That is how I died. I will not promise to withhold my touch from them."

The Cleric smiled, "As it should be; however, they will never find this door."

The Cleric stood, walked out, and the door closed and sealed shut with no seams.

DRAGONS AND THIEVES

WHAT AM I DOING! I SHOULD KNOW BETTER! THE GUILD taught me better than this. I can see no other way to achieve my goal. Revenge is a demanding goal and one of the key things in my plan is to become capable of taking out each of the enemies one at a time. Find them alone, attack without warning, and get back what was mine or payment so I can repurchase what they took. Difficult to get enough to pay me for the loss of my father's gifts; however, their deaths are not enough to pay me for trying to kill me let alone taking my father's sword and armor. Every time I close my eyes I relive that attack.

I was minding my own business. I had stopped off in a nice tavern and had a good night's sleep and a good meal. I left on foot toward the caves in Dagger Edge Mountains. I purchased a mule and lots of equipment to get me up the mountain and into the caves. The treasure map that I memorized and burned showed me where there was supposed to be an old abandoned Dragon horde.

I had just entered the forest road when an arrow hit me in the back. Then a fireball went off around me and a Ray of Harm spell smacked me right in the back. I fell down but as I was getting up a Fighter and Cleric attacked me and cut me up bad. Then a Wizard came out and did a spell that caused me to stiffen up and I could not move. They stripped me and took everything. Before they left their Rogue backstabbed me nearly cutting my spine in half and they picked me up and dumped me over a small cliff and into the forest. The last thing I heard, the thing that stood out the most in my mind, the thing that has bothered me beyond everything else, the thing that I hear every time I close my eyes is their laughter while saying:

"That's another one boys. We have his powerful sword and grand armor. If this keeps up the Golden Talon will be the most powerful group in the country. I told you this was easier than adventuring."

What they apparently did not know is I have a little gift from a God I did some work for. It's called regeneration. It's a supernatural minor regeneration. Though I was near death, and the fall should have killed me completely, I held on to the tiny little spark of life that was left in me and waited – waited with a burning need to find them and kill each and every one of them. Slowly, very slowly I regenerated. It took two days before I could sit up and another day before I could painfully stand. There was a stream at the bottom and food and water were in abundance. Raw fish – yum. After five days I could climb back up to the road.

Now, here I am doing the adventuring. I need the tools to fight them because I can't go up against then in my birthday suit. I am going for that dragon horde in my bare hands and feet and everything else. The problem now was no one told me that the dragon was still sitting on the treasure.

I came out of the side cave and saw the treasure. The problem was it was not an old abandoned treasure. There was a dragon laying on it sleeping. I went back in a little way and yelled, "Pardon me. Do you happen to have some clothes I can borrow?"

The giant red dragon's eyes opened and she growled. She got up and came over to the opening of the side cave. Her eye looked in but I had backed up further and she could not see me. She breathed fire into the cave but I was too far back. "So human, when are you going to come out of that hole? If you would have been so kind as to use the front door I would have eaten you by now. You do understand standard don't you?"

I said, "I have a problem. I will make a deal with you. Bring me some clothes and I will come out when you're back far enough that you can't burn me before I duck back in."

The dragon looked confused before saying, "Clothes? You come to steal from me naked?"

"That was not my original plan. I was told that there was treasure up here buried someplace in this mountain. I packed up my belongings and headed out to find unattended forgotten treasure. I did not know it was still owned."

The dragon asked, "So, you did come to steal. Why are you without clothes?"

"I did not come to steal. I am not a thief. I came treasure hunting. I would not take what is clearly owned by someone living. If I was a thief I would not have yelled to waken you."

"Fair statement. Still, why are you naked?"

I relayed the story of the ambush.

"Not a very nice thing for them to do. Tell me. Do they now have your map?"

I chuckled. "No. I memorized it and burned it."

"Oh, that is too bad. I could use a snack."

I said, "I will ask again. Do you happen to have any clothes I can borrow? I will return them. Right after I kill every last one of those murdering rats."

The great Red said, "Oh how nice. You may or may not be a thief but you are not necessary of goodly nature. Revenge is considered evil in most places."

I said, "That's because normally the goody butt wipe doing the evil deed that causes others to need to take revenge is the one that makes the laws."

She sat down and placed her hands under her chin. "You seem to be evil of nature. I agree with your opinion of Good."

I retorted, "I have been accused of many things and most of them I would refute, but when accused of being evil I proudly answer, 'I am not but I would not be upset if I was. Besides, you are just as evil as I may be.' They argue that they are not and I put them through several situations and they always end up doing evil. Most people have an evil streak when they think they can get away with it. Most claim to be good. Hypocrites! I am neither good nor evil, I do what I think is right for me at the time of doing. And I am proud of what I do. But there is nothing wrong with being evil when needed."

She stood up and backed away until she was a good hundred feet from me. "Come out, come out, little human. I would see you in the flesh. You have my word that I will not eat you, yet."

I walked out and stood at the front of the small side cave entrance.

She laughed, "You are naked. What is your plan for revenge?"

I told her that I was going to become strong enough to hunt every one of them down and kill then, one at a time.

She smiled, "I can help with that."

I looked skeptical. "How?"

"I can deck you out in some very nice equipment and then let you borrow a minor artifact of mine. With it, you can touch the person that attacked you and teleport him directly to this cave. I will eat him for you. I am near starving and need food."

I thought about that for a minute and said, "For your help, I will ensure you never go hungry again as long as you never attack me. Anyway, you can change my appearance? They know my face."

She said, "Let me think. Um, yes – I know a way. You may not like the outcome."

"I was almost dead because of them. I don't care about the outcome as long as it does not impede me from completing my revenge."

"Oh, I do like you. This will be so much fun. Wait there." She did a few spells and a Demigod showed up.

The Devil Demigod looked around at his surroundings. "What do you want Lorasisteraus? We completed our deal a long time ago."

The Dragon said, "Oh, I thought you may be interested in helping with a little revenge considering you claim to be the Demigod of Retribution."

His face brightened up. "What did you have in mind?"

She told him my plan and he said, "A disguise. Easily done."

He started to cast so I yelled, "Wait! Wait please."

He looked irritated. "What?"

I said, "I do not care what you change me to look like as long as I am still recognizable as human and I can still take my revenge."

He smiled, "Is that the only parameters. You do not care how ugly I make you?"

I smiled back, "I don't care if I am so ugly children run from me screaming. If you want you can make me so ugly full-grown men run from me screaming. But I want my revenge."

He said, "Good attitude – done. He raised his hand and I changed. Then he departed."

I felt the change. A devil did it so do you think he was nice about it? When I stopped screaming from the pain I stood back up and wiped my eyes. My hand was different. It was smaller, delicate, tiny. I turned to the Dragon and she was rolling on the floor laughing so hard she was in tears. I asked, "What did he do?"

She said, "Look down at your chest."

I did and there were two small breasts. I looked at the rest that I could see and I was defiantly a female. My manhood was completely gone.

I asked, "He made me an ugly female?"

She started laughing again. "No fool. He made you the loveliest young female I have ever seen."

"How long will this last?"

"Ah. The price you paid for help in your revenge is you are now female and will always be female." She looked around and found a large mirror. "Here."

She held it up for me to look at myself. I was not only lovely, I was so sexy and beautiful I would have stared at myself for days and had wonderful dreams about me. I looked to be about eighteen and just becoming a woman. I had no hair on my body except a little tuff of blond hair down below and some nicely curved eyebrows and long blond hair, on the top of my head, cascading down to my knees and long thick eyelashes. The color was a naturally light golden with slightly darker roots just like a natural blond. I stood about five foot six or seven and could not have weighed more than a hundred and five or ten pounds. Skinny wasted and slight of build in the other two areas giving me a natural curve that any man's eyes would be drawn too. My eyes were another story. Green. Only royalty has green eyes and mine are bright green stating that I have to be from royal stock and not mixed. I said, "I can disguise the hair and eyes."

She laughed and said, "All of the ones that attacked you were male. You should have no problem enticing them to come with you alone."

"I could entice the King away from the Queen. Shoot, I could entice the Queen away from the King. You're right and that may work for one or maybe two. The rest will become quickly suspicious when their fellow thieves start disappearing. Besides, I don't know how to entice a man."

Again she laughed, "Enticing a man is easy. Show up and smile at him. That's all you need to do. Your body will do the rest. Walk a little toward the opening and away."

I did and I must say walking was different.

She said, "It is said that Royalty cannot be faked. Yet you have a natural royal walk. Your stance is perfect with no slouch. Sit here."

I sat down on the chair that magically appeared.

"No slouch at all. Perfect sitting; straight-backed, neck held straight, and chin up. That devil made you completely royal. You scream royalty in every move. That is impossible. Royalty is protected by the Gods."

I said, "I wonder what he saw that made this necessary?"

"Hard to say but I am sure it will come in handy somehow."

"Why do I feel more naked now than I did before?"

She said, "You're a female. Females are more aware of their body." Then she smiled, "Stay right there." She started digging into her treasure and putting things aside. She asked questions while she rummaged. "You were a fighter before?"

"Fighter with a little training in Sorcery."

Her head came up, "Sorcery! What circle?"

"Third."

"How good are you at fighting and what is your preferred weapon?"

"I am very good. Good enough to adventure by myself fighting many creatures and undead. I have spent many years perfecting my techniques. I prefer the long sword and composite longbow. I am very good with both."

"Tell me about your strongest most fearsome opponent."

I said, "My most fearsome opponent was not that strong. It was a Lech that lived in a tower they call Grayrock Lean."

"You killed that Lech?" She stood up and she looked worried.

"Yes, and I have killed Dragons that are more powerful than you. If not for being taken completely by surprise I could have taken on that entire group with the weapons I had at the time."

She said with concern, "You could kill me if given the weapons to do so."

I said back, "I don't kill for fun or profit. I killed that Lech because it was attacking a village. I went to talk to it and he attacked me. I killed the three dragons of Dorfair because they attacked me for walking on a public road. I killed the horned black slad lord because he burned down my favorite Inn, and I destroyed the King of Kellor because he overtaxed me thinking I could do nothing about it. I don't like thieves and I am not a thief. I would never attack you unless you attacked me. Still, I would try to find out why you attacked me first. As you seem to be my current and only friend I would never even think of doing something to displease you."

She smiled, "I will not attack you because you are going to bring me food. I am getting very old and flying is difficult at best. There is a gargantuan black dragon only ten leagues from here. He'll kill me if he catches me out of my cave. I need that food to survive."

"You shall have it and much more."

She stopped what she was doing and looked at me long and hard. Then she waved a hand and a very large tub was in front of me. "Stand in that tub please."

I climbed into the tub and stood up. "Do I need a bath already?"

She smiled lovingly, "We need to ensure that all things, including dirt, are off your body." She picked up a picture and started pouring water. It was cold but I started scrubbing myself.

"Do you know what happens to a human when it is covered in blood from a dragon given willingly and with the correct spells?"

"No. But I don't want you to harm yourself."

She did a spell that removed the water and dirt from the tub and me. "Lay down, child."

I laid down.

"I am going to cover you with my blood. You must ensure that the blood gets into every crack and crevice while I am chanting the spell. This will protect you."

I started to get out. "I don't want you harmed."

She pushed me back in. "Losing enough blood to fill this tub is nothing. Now lay down child, and thank you for the concern."

She cut her arm and held it over the tub. It filled quickly, and then she said a spell and she was healed. "Start now." She started chanting.

I emerged myself into the blood and turned over while opening every place on my body. Lifting my breasts, opening my legs and such, opening my eyes, lifting my hair and ensuring my hair was completely submerged, tilting my head so it got deep into my ears, breathing it in through my nose and mouth, and swallowing it.

I continued this for some time before she stopped chanting and said, "Let's get you washed up. Stand."

I stood up and she did that cleaning spell again. Then it was back to the magical picture of water with which I made sure I rinsed my mouth and nose out. Soon I was completely clean.

She asked, "How do you feel?"

"Cold, wet, other than that I don't feel any different."

She blew hot air on me and I quickly warmed up and dried. I started to climb out of the tub but she said, "Don't move. No sense getting your feet dirty." I stopped and sat on the side of the tub with my feet pointed in. I started using my hands to smooth out my hair and remove any tangles. Then I mentally pictured something I saw a girl do with her hair and did a spell called 'Décor.' Instantly all tangles were out, my hair was brushed one thousand times, and pulled back and braided in a fancy weave. The problem was I had no ribbon to tie on the end so it started to come unraveled. Oh well.

She saw the predicament as I held the end and she handed me a white ribbon. I said, "Thanks." and used it to tie off the braid.

She smiled, "You did that just like a little girl would who has been doing it all her life. He gave you natural femininity. I wonder what you lost to gain it."

I said, "That's a good question." I started going through my recollection. "I remember training with the sword, staff, and bow. I remember all my fights. I remember my travels and how to track and survive. We spent a lot of time hunting and moving. Ah, what I don't remember are any women I may have been with. I seem to recall fighting off several men. I don't remember my family. Only that my father was very kind and when I was leaving said, 'Sweetheart, Jennifer, I am loath to tell you this but you must know before you leave. I am not your father and Susan is not your mother. Your father was pure blood and your mother was also. Their union and the resultant child at that time would have plunged their countries into war. I was tasked to raise you the best I could.' I remember hugging him and thanking him for being the best father possible. I also remember hiding my lineage. I remember doing a spell that changes my hair and eye color for about a moon."

She said, "Hold on." She did a spell above my head that created a view of a woman giving birth."

I said, "On the side, that's my father and mother at a very young age. Who's the one giving birth?"

She said, "That is your mother and your father is standing in the corner nearly in tears."

I watched as I was born and then given away. The man said to the man who raised me. "Take him. Leave while I can stand to do this to my son. I will be heartbroken forever as will my love.

Go. Go far away and never speak of this to anyone. You know the spell for his disguise. Teach him. Teach him well to hide."

The spell dissipated. The Dragon said, "You were of Royal birth before. The Demon did not change that. He could not. You were in disguise."

I said sadly, "I did not know. I have hidden my hair and eyes for so long I sometimes forget. I wake up one morning and see I have changed to blond with green eyes and do the spell instantly always saying that's better."

She said, "Oh, little human child. You are the firstborn son of the King and Queen of Kayland. You were born out of wedlock. Your father has been looking for you for nearly your entire life. You see, they married. It was arranged and they were so happy. However, they had only one child beside you. Another boy and they are worried about you showing up."

"No worry. I'm not going to show up. I have some revenge to accomplish."

She added, "Yes, but that Devil just fixed their problem. Why would he do that?"

I laughed, "Because he knows that my being changed into a girl is going to mess with the King in some fashion. I am not some good-aligned bigot and I would not get along with my Father. If we met and he found out there would be all kinds of problems. So, I think I will just stay away. The spell lasts for about a moon." I did the spell and instantly changed. Now I looked about the same except my hair was a natural fire red and my eyes bright blue.

"Oh, that's nice. But the spell 'Correct Vision' can get right past that."

I said, "I found that out the hard way. I was entering this town about two years back and the local Wizard was checking people with a Correct Vision spell. He went to his knees before he thought to check without the spell. I turned around and left. Some stupid Baron has been after me for two years now. Something about a major bounty."

She said, "Just a moment." She closed her eyes and said to no one, "Hello Royal Master Wizard......... I know I never contact you anymore.......... No, what I want to tell you is not important to me.......... Yes, it is important to you......... You know that Prince you were looking for?.......... I found him........... Yes, he is alive but he is not what you would expect......... What I mean is the Demigod of Retribution turned him into a her. You now have a Princess...... I don't need to prove anything...... Just getting you up to date...... Bye now.......... No. I really must go.......... Nope, can't say anymore........ Bye."

She fell down laughing so hard her sides hurt before she got back up.

I asked, "What did you just do? I hope we are not going to have company any time soon. It's getting cold again."

She stood back up saying, "He does not know where I now live and he cannot scry on me. I have protections. Still, he is going to try and I am expecting him to open a conversation soon. As he may try to open a portal. I think you need to get dressed." She went back to rummaging through her treasures until she found a tiny, highly decorated, upright clothing cabinet carved out of ivory. "Touch this and say 'Enlarge'. Then open it and try on some of the items inside. Let's see if you know what goes on first."

I touched it and said "Enlarge" and the cabinet became six feet high and four feet wide. I opened the closet and there was one outfit hanging up in the center. The outfit included all the matching undergarments and shoes. I said, "I was hoping for something a little more for traveling. I can't climb down off the mountain wearing that." Instantly clothing started moving to the left and another dress came from the right. Things sped up until it was just a flash of clothes going by. This continued for thousands of dresses until it slowed down and settled on one dress. This one was perfect for traveling. Long, but flowing enough to allow for movement and hiking the dress up for climbing or descending. Good strong material with little to no frills. I pulled out the bloomers to put them on first. As soon as I touched them the entire outfit magically transferred to my body. The mirror on the inside of the door showed a gorgeous redhead wearing working clothing fit for a Princess.

The Dragon said, "That will work." She touched the closet and said, "Reduce." Then she picked it up and placed it inside a Natura's Deep Pocket Haversack. "You say you're good with a bow? Try this one." She handed me a Natura's Deep Pocket Quiver saying, "The keyword is 'Swish'.

I took the quiver and said swish as I looked through it; two bows, sixty arrows, three staves, and five spare bowstrings. One bow was on fire and one was cold. I pulled out the fire bow and held it close. I said, "Warm. I like."

She placed a hand on her mouth saying, "Oh my. You did not swallow any of my blood, did you?"

I said, "Of course. You said all crevices."

She looked concern saying. "Hold still." She breathed fire on me. It felt good. It did not harm me or the dress. Then she did a cold spell and that hurt far more than it should have. I screamed in pain. She did a healing spell and said, "I am so sorry. I should have warned you. You swallowed my blood freely given while I was chanting a greater natural armor spell. In doing so you took on some of my characteristics. Fire is wonderful and can heal a bit, acid is not bad at all and can clear scars, but cold is deadly."

I smiled up at her concern saying, "That's wonderful. I never liked the cold anyway. Now you say I am immune to fire and acid? That is grand."

She smiled back, "You child," She touched a claw to my nose. "are immune to fire, acid, slashing, bludgeoning, poison, disease, fear, and piercing. However, you are highly vulnerable to cold and smell based attacks. Do you smell anything strange?"

I raised my head and smelled the air. "There is a rabbit outside trying to sneak by and it is afraid. I smell fear. I will be right back." I ran outside and shot the rabbit. I ran back in and asked, "Snack?"

She smiled and nodded. I took the rabbit off the arrow and tossed it up. She swallowed it whole – fur and all. I asked, "Doesn't that fur tickle going down?"

She said most seriously. "On a bear it does. I normally skin them and eat the fur separately."

I laughed, "What you can eat and what I can eat are two different things."

"When you're starving, as I am, you will eat anything."

I looked sad, "If I had a way to get the food back to you I would go get you a few deer and a bear or two."

She reached into the tiny pile she was making for me and said, "Attach this to your belt. Kill the bear or dear and then touch it while saying 'Transport' and thinking of this place. You and the food will return here."

I said, "I will be back soon." As I left she started looking through her treasures again. I headed outside and it wasn't long before I found that bear that chased me into the caves. Two shots with the fire bow and it was dead and half cooked. I touched it and thought of the dragon's cave and said 'Transport'. Instantly the bear and I were in the cave. I said, "Cut a small piece off the cooked section for me and the rest is yours."

She hungrily ate the entire thing. She said, "I am so sorry. I know you are hungry also but I have not eaten for three years."

"Three Years! That is horrible. Did that fill you up?"

"Not even close."

I said as I left again, "Leave room for adventuring thieves."

She said, "There is always room for thieves."

I left and returned six times before she stopped me. She ate three bears, one minotaur, and three big mule deer. I got two of the dear in one trip.

"I am full now. I do not know how to repay you. You are very good with that bow. I counted that you used only eleven arrows and everyone hit. Is this correct?"

I smiled, "Yes. It seems my agility has increased greatly."

She said, "Becoming a female caused you to lose some strength; however, you do make up for it in dexterity." She handed me a long sword.

I buckled the belt around my torso so that the hilt was over my left shoulder. Then I reached back and pulled the sword so quick the Dragon blinked. I practiced for years to be able to draw a long sword quickly and I am very fast. To say the sword is magical would be an understatement. It did not glow or speak but I could feel the effects as I held it. The blade was a little long and thin for a long sword but it could fall into no other category I know of. It had a beveled belly with an edge on both sides that was sharp and seemed to vibrate. The back was straight and thin and the tang full and shaped like a Dragon. I asked, "What are the properties of this grand weapon?"

She looked a little frightened while saying, "That is a Dragon Blade. It is made of adamantine folded a hundred times. How they folded adamantine is beyond me. The darn blade bends. It is not stiff like normal adamantine and cannot be sundered. I know. I tried over and over. It has a razor vibrating edge. Do you know what that means?"

"I have trained to have the ability to do extra damage when I hit well and trained to hit well more often. Razor edge enhances that ability making it easier to hit harder, and does a lot more damage."

She frowned, "Vibrating Razor Edge doubles that ability and triples the damage. The sword also has something called Sprit Energy which bypasses all armor both natural and artificial. What is worse is it has a thing called Dragon Smite. One hit and a Dragon could die instantly. It is blessed by a God that did not like Good or Evil so only Natural can wield it without nearly dying. It is not aligned but it has Holy Smite and Unholy Smite both. How he did that is far beyond me."

I sheaved the sword saying, "A dragon killing blade. I am surprised you would allow anyone to have it."

She said, "I am old and cannot leave this cave anymore because I have a black dragon problem that the sword may be needed for, and I need someone to feed me. I am not loaning you any of these items. They are gifts to the person that stated that for my help she would ensure I never go hungry again. I am decking out my champion."

I smiled, "I will keep that promise and you will never regret our friendship."

She said, "Good, then let's continue." She picked up a knife and handed it to me. "This is a simple knife. Always sharp, never rusts, a good utility blade until you say the activation word and then it becomes 'The Dagger of Danger.' By touching the hilt and saying 'Watch' it will warn if danger is within thirty feet by vibrating. If you are holding it while pointing it away from you and you say 'Watch' it will glow brighter when you point it toward the danger."

I said, "Nice." I added it to my belt and touched the hilt saying "Watch." It did not vibrate which is good."

She said, "Checking to see if I am going to eat you anyway?"

"I was thinking you were decking me out with nice tasty magical spices."

She laughed and the laugh sounded stronger than before. Not louder, just more healthy.

I said, "You're sounding better."

She said, "Eating will do that you know." She picked up a headband and placed it on my head. It snapped into perfect placement. "Oh darn. I forgot, that one is cursed when it comes to royalty."

My hands moved to it instantly trying to pull it off. "Cursed?!"

She said, "Don't worry. It is picky about who uses it. You must be female and have an outstanding charisma for it to animate at all. I was thinking that you are so beautiful and so easy to get along with that you may have a high enough charisma for it to work. I was right. It was made specifically for blonds. Being that you are female, royalty, and blond, the item loves you. The curse is it will not come off. Like I said, it is picky and when it finds female royalty that is captivating enough to activate it, you cannot remove it until death."

I said, "Before I cut my head off what does it do?"

"It holds your hair back out of your face."

"And?"

"It is called 'The Intellectual Circlet' which is to say it grants the wearer great intelligence and wisdom. For some stupid reason, the creator of the Headband thought that his daughter, which was blond, female, and royal, was lacking in intelligence and wisdom. She killed her father for putting that on her and she was beheaded for doing so. The headband has made its rounds over the years. I have a little royal blood and am considered very lovely for a red dragon. That darn thing keeps trying to attach itself to me. It's now your problem. Besides, you got surprised and accosted, walked into a dragon's cave, and then asked for clothes, and then made a deal with a devil. You haven't shown much intelligence or wisdom that I can see."

I was just about to yell at her but then it hit me. She's right. In her eyes, I have been a silly little fool. A very lucky fool, but still a fool just the same. "Very well. I concede the fact that I have been rather silly in my actions but what choice did I have? No more cursed items without my approval please."

"Um, it does one more thing. You're going to like this."

"Really, what?"

"The King wanted his daughter to be able to be an ambassador to several nations. The Headband grants you perfect knowledge of all languages. I am told that even ancient and rare languages are included."

"That will come in handy."

She smiled, "We were just talking draconic."

I looked confused and then said, "We were. I understood everything just like it was my natural language. I did not even realize I was speaking another language."

She smiled, "Good. The standard language is difficult for me." She picked up the haversack. "This has some necessities and a few other things. It is all yours."

"I saw you put the clothes closet in there and a brush and comb. Thank you."

"I also added a bedroll, tent, ground cloth, flint and steel, water bag, some sacks, rope, and a magical carved horse."

"Magical carved horse?"

She smiled, "Yes. You pull it out, place it on the ground, and say 'Enlarge' and it comes to life as a light warhorse with all the needed tack and saddle. This one was a gift to the Queen of Horbor a few thousand years ago. It is decked out nicely and has a side-saddle. It's a long way to the nearest town. I thought you would need a ride."

I walked over to her and hugged her neck. "Thank you so very much."

"You're very welcome. There are a few other items in the haversack including some gems and gold for traveling. Now go find those fools that tried to kill you. When you return I want the full story. This will be fun."

I hugged her again and said, "I am off then. I will be back." She settled down for a long sleep as I left the cave. I climbed down the mountain and three weeks later rode that horse near the closest town. I reduced it and placed it in my haversack, cleaned up, and changed clothes before walking into town. I must have made a sight as everyone was watching me. What they saw was an extremely beautiful redhead, wearing a lovely dress that had to be made for high rank and fit like it was cut exactly for my body, a sword and quiver over my shoulders, a haversack on my back, a knife at my side, and a staff that glowed being used as a walking stick. I was stopped at the gate and almost everyone stopped to stare. I had thought long and hard on what I was going to say and do. Especially since some gates have spells on them that let the questioner know if you are lying.

The guard standing duty bowed low and asked, "My lady, are you alone? You should not be out alone. There are bandits, dragons, and bear eager to find a young lady out by herself."

I smiled and my smile lit up the hearts of everyone there. "Thank you so very much for your concern. I am looking for a nice place to stay for a few nights. An adventuring Inn would be welcome. Do you have one?" I knew they did. It is where that group hung out looking for prey.

"Yes, we have an adventuring Inn, my Lady. Pardon, but I must ask you some questions."

"Please go ahead. I know you have to do your job. I will not take offense, kind Sir."

He loosened up at the 'kind Sir' remark. "My Lady, what is your business?"

I answered, "Adventuring and catching thieves."

He nearly choked. "That is dangerous work, my Lady."

I said, "After my Step-Father trained me in weaponry and survival he kicked me out on my own. He was a Ranger in the Black-eyed Forest. It is difficult, but I've gotten along so far. I was not trained in sewing or cleaning. I am a fairly good camp cook. Least I think so."

"Your Step-Father was a Ranger? That makes more sense. Who was your Father?"

I frowned, "That is not up for discussion. He gave me away at birth and that was the end of that relationship. Next question."

The Guard asked, "Reason for coming here?"

"Passing through, rest, dinner, a good bed, shopping, and possibly killing thieves if any try. I looked over at someone that looked like a thief to me."

The Guard smiled, "That is our rogue. He is not a thief. Last question. Are you wanted for anything?"

I said, "Not for something I did and not for anything illegal."

The Guard had to think on that answer and asked, "What are you wanted for?"

"Being me."

He looked me up and down and said, "I can understand that also. Very well. You may pass. The Inn is down the main road and on your left. The sign will read 'Bull Tail Inn'."

I said, "Thank you." and headed that direction. At the Inn, I entered and stood in the door until my eyes adjusted to the darkness. They use few candles, as candles cost. It also helps you not see how dirty the dishes and glasses are or if the meat is green. My staff glowed enough to light most of the place fairly well. I tapped it twice on the floor and the room lit up as if noonday. Nice staff. The other two are equally as nice. I did some experimenting with them on the way here. This one does several little things that cost a charge, but light, greater light, and daylight are free. Now that I had everyone's attention I walked over to a corner and sat down with my back to the wall. They were all right in the center staring at me. This was going to be easy. If I took out the Wizard first and then the Cleric I could probably take them all right now but the deal is food and I will stick to the plan.

I glanced at the room and when my eyes touched the Wizard I increased my smile just a little. The barmaid came over.

"Is there anything I can get you, my Lady?"

"I smell some food in the back. Is dinner ready, and is it fresh?"

"Father killed the dear only two days ago. It was hanging until this morning. It was freshly butchered today. The bread was baked this morning also. You are lucky, my Lady. Everything is fresh."

The wench was lying badly. I said, "Wonderful. I, of course, will check when I receive my plate. If it is not fresh I will kill everyone in this Inn. Well, except that Wizard and Cleric. I may want to romp with them later."

The Fighter and Rogue were slapping the Wizard and Cleric on the back. The Fighter said, "It seems like your female luck just changed and to the very good side. When the two of you are done with her let us know. I'd like a bite of that."

The Rogue said, "You hold her and I'll tie her up. We can have her for weeks."

The Wizard said, "Not until I'm done placing spells on her. She will beg to make love to the two of us."

The bragging continued for some time. If they only knew I could hear them. The bar wench had run back to the bar and told the Bartender what I said. He came around the corner carrying his club.

He walked up and I pulled a small stick from my belt. He said while looking apprehensively at the stick, "You planning to start trouble in my Inn, Wizard. If you are then you can leave."

I said, "No trouble, good Sir, unless you cheat me. I don't like waking up in the middle of the night with stomach issues because the dishes are greasy and the food rancid. I can taste stale or non-fresh food instantly and will react very violently. So bring me the dinner as promised. Freshly butchered this morning, fresh bread, fresh food. I will have a glass of good wine with that. You do have fresh food? I was not lied too, was I?" I placed my hand over the stick and looked upset.

He backed off just a little saying as he bowed. "The food will be fresh though one day old and the bread hot from the oven."

He nearly tripped back to his bar. He whispered to the Wench. Go tell your mother I need her finding us dinner. Fresh meat, hot fresh bread, and everything else fresh or we will lose the Inn. I think she intends to burn it down with us in it if we lied. And, warn the Sheriff."

She ran to the back room and out the back door. It wasn't long before a fat man came in with a badge of office hanging from his neck. He went up to the bartender. "What's the problem, Mac?"

"Two issues. That rowdy group of trouble makers in the center still hasn't paid for anything. Their tab is getting big. It looks from their clothes that they can afford the bill but I am starting to wonder. Second, the female Wizard in the corner by the fire. She has threatened to kill everyone in this Inn and the town and burn the place to the ground if her dinner is not just perfect."

The Sheriff laughed, "You lying fool. First, I'm betting you're going to try to bilk those men for the room and board. Don't! That rogue will slit your throat. Second, I cannot believe any Wizard would say something like that. I will check her out but I am very skeptical."

He strode over to my table while passing the center table. "I hope you boys intend to pay for all this."

The Fighter said, "Don't worry Sheriff. We may need to come back this way so we will pay."

The Sheriff reached my table. "Young Lady."

"Yes."

"Mac seems to think you are planning to burn down the town and kill all the people if your dinner is not perfect."

I raised my left eyebrow and asked, "And you believed him?"

"Not really. What was actually said?"

I answered, "I only said I would kill everyone in the Inn if the food is not as promised. The guard at the Gate was a nice man. I would not kill everyone in the town for what the owner of this Inn did."

His expression turned to concern and a little fear. I could smell it. He was not expecting me to admit I would kill anyone. "My Lady. If you harm anyone I will have to step in."

"Then ensure they bring me what they promised or let me know how you would like to be buried, or at least what is left of you," I said that exactly how I practiced it and the effect was perfect. He immediately backed off and went to the bar.

"Mac, you had better meet your words or kiss you backend goodbye. I'm out of here."

As he was leaving two large but short women came in. They went right to Mac and they were carrying baskets and the food smelled wonderful. "You want to point out who we are giving our dinner too?"

He looked chastened and pointed me out. One said, "Your lying is going to get us all killed someday." They came over to me and started setting up the table. They even brought dishes. They were mumbling so I acted very pleased and said as planned, "This is almost as good as the Castle's food. Thank you."

Their eyes went very wide and they looked closer and noticed the stiff posture, the look and the style, and it hit them. One whispered in awe, "Royalty."

The seed was planted. Now it was "If there is anything else we can do for you, my Lady? Please don't hesitate to ask." And, "Are you staying long, Mistress?" We talk for only a few moments and they left for the bar. They hugged and kissed Mac for bringing then in and then left. He was so confused until one whispered to the other. "Royalty. no wonder her stomach is so sensitive. The poor dear." Then his eyes nearly popped out. The wine he brought me was his best. When the thieves heard their leers increased.

After dinner, I smiled at the Wizard and stood up. "Are you and your friend busy?"

He smiled back, "No, my Lady. This way."

The two of them took my arms and led me up to their room. As soon as the door closed I placed a hand on each and teleported to the Dragon Cave. Their turn to be surprised. She picked them up and swallowed them whole. I smiled and teleported back to the room. I went through all their stuff and found nearly everything they took from me. Problem is, none of it fits anymore. The armor was far too heavy, even if it did magically change the size, and the sword was difficult to pick up. Still, they had acquired a lot of items. I gathered them all up and teleported them back to a small place I found on the way here.

I teleported back to their room, waited about two hours, and then messed myself up some and walked downstairs. "Guys?" The Fighter and Rogue looked my direction. "The Cleric asked me to fetch you. He said to bring rope. Do you know why?"

They quickly got up and headed my way. The Rogue stopped off in their room and grabbed some rope. I asked, "You guys have horses?"

The Fighter said, "Not at this time but we have our eyes on some in the stable out back."

As they opened the door I touched both and teleported to the cave. They fought but I killed one and she killed the other. I teleported back and waited. Later that night I climbed down a rope and went into the stable. I teleported out four of the best horses with tack and saddles and enough supplies to feed the horses for a few days stuffed into saddlebags. The dragon was very pleased. Then I teleported back into their room. I took everything and showed back up at my hidden place and then teleported to the cave.

She said, "Looks like your revenge is over."

"Yes, it is."

She tried to grab me but I was ready. I knew she was pretending to be weak. I also knew she was going to eat me the moment my retribution was over. She had to wait until that Devil was satisfied before she could finish her plan. However, she made a mistake and made me very fast. I teleported out.

Back at the Inn I set the rope out a window, stripped, spread some blood in proper places, and used a spell to put me to sleep.

"Hay! Wake up!" It was the Sheriff and he was shaking me.

An old Wizard pulled the covers over my body and then did a spell. He said, "That will wake her up. Give it a moment. She was magically put to sleep. Sheriff, they used her as a diversion to steal the horses and leave without paying the bill. This is not her fault and she probably knows nothing. Although, she is going to be upset when she becomes aware. That was a nasty spell. You may ask her to help you find them. If you do you may need to protect them from her wrath." He looked over at my gear. "They did not take her equipment. The blood on the floor was evident. She set protections their Wizard could not get through. Smart girl. Be careful Sheriff that headband is cursed."

He quickly pulled his hand away. I fluttered my eyes a little and fought my own spell and his. The Wizard said, "She is fighting our spells. They probably knocked her out and then did the spell. She is a fighter. See that blood. She cut one and probably two before they had her."

I opened my eyes and instantly started to cast. The Wizard was ready and dispelled the fireball. "CHILD! Stop this instant! Your attackers are gone."

I looked around and saw my equipment and smiled. I stood up on wobbly legs and started for my stuff. I put my clothes back on and inventoried my possessions. I looked at the blood on the floor and smiled bigger. "That one will be looking for some healing. So will the one that poured the knock out drug down my throat." I turned to the Sheriff. "Where are they?"

He said, "Now look. This is a matter for the authorities and not some vengeful royal outcast."

My surprise told him he was correct. The Wizard asked, "What land and why outcast? And, don't think of telling me it is none of my business. I am a Master Sage from the local Baron and I will find out in ways you don't want."

I looked at him long and hard as I completed putting my equipment on. "I will tell you for the price of one fourth circle spell of your choice."

He smiled, "Only know third circle, Child?"

"Correct."

"Done."

I smiled and sat down on the bed. I dismissed the disguise spell and said, "I am the son of a certain King and Queen. They had me at a time when they were not supposed to be together.

They gave me away at birth. A Demigod turned me female for reasons of vengeance. Do I need to tell you any more? I hear there is a price on my head."

The Wizard said, "You are Prince Robert. Or should I call you Princess Robert?"

"I am called Jennifer."

The Sheriff said, "This does not make sense. Why poison you when they could have simply knocked you out?"

I pulled my knife and put my hand on the table. Then I slammed the knife point into my hand. It should have pinned my hand to the table with lots of blood. It did not even scratch me. I said, "After the first two had their way with me they had me call up the other two. The fighter hit me hard and was surprised when I not only did not fall but I pulled his knife and tried to cut him. I got him and the rogue. I was taken from the back and pinned. The rogue poured a potion down my throat. I immediately started blacking out. I fought it and heard then say something about, "Time for hunting adventurers in another area." And, I think one screamed and cussed at my equipment. Then the Wizard saw me fighting it and did a spell. It took him three tries."

The Wizard looked shocked and then angry. He sent a message to someone. "We figured out who has been killing off adventures. I will be at the Baron's place shortly." Then he turned to the Sheriff saying, "You will keep this child in this town for three weeks. I will not have her messing up our hunt for those men."

I smiled, "I will not need to hunt them. I know where they went."

They both looked at me.

"You think I give away my body to just anyone. I was soliciting their help with an old feeble red dragon that can't even fly anymore."

The Wizard chocked out, "You were planning to try to take out Lorasisteraus?"

"Is that its name?"

The Wizard shook his head. "They may have done you a favor by trying to take the dragon on without you. That dragon is not old or feeble. It cannot fly very well due to a run-in with a black dragon it killed over our main city. But it is not feeble. Hundreds have gone up against her and died. She gets most of her food by eating adventures or tricking them into getting her food and then eating them."

I opened my eyes real wide as if in shock, "Really?"

He shook his head and pulled out a scroll from thin air. He handed it to me saying, "Your fourth level spell, Child." He turned to leave and just before disappearing said, "Fool child, stay away from that dragon."

I put the scroll away and looked at the Sheriff. "Where is a good place for breakfast?"

He smiled, "My house. The wife would skin me alive if I didn't invite you."

We started walking out and I said, "I am glad they stopped me. I can't fight a full-grown dragon in its prime."

The Sheriff held the door open for me and said, "I'm glad that Wizard didn't ask me to come along. We both have something to celebrate."

I smiled and left it at that.

FOOL KING

THERE'S THE OLD TALE OF VILLAINS THAT HAD THEIR heart removed so you can't kill them without finding the heart and destroying that first. Tried it, does not work. You can still bleed to death as your heart is still magically pumping blood through your veins and if the veins are opened you die.

I tried becoming a vampire so I could not be killed and found several ways to kill myself. Oh well. I have tried everything and have found nothing that can make me incapable of dying. Even Gods can die. Oh, they are very long-lived but several gods can gang up on one and destroy it. They don't do this often because it can quickly happen to them. It's kind of a taboo. Ancients and OverGods can die, they went to war and proved that. The True Gods can die or what will happen during the big war? I think they can die. It is said that certain artifacts can make you immune to death. If that were true then where are the last owners? Dead, that's where. I gave up and fix myself back to being simply human.

I have slowed down aging, reversed aging, stopped aging, sped up aging on enemies, but even if you are immortal, you can be killed. That's the rub, someone wants me dead. Why? I have no idea. For over a hundred years I have been doing nothing but studying here in my tower. Most people I had ever known would be dead.

I guess I had better go down and ask the goon squad banging on my door what they want.

I walked down the stairs and up to the front door. As I unlocked it I heard swords leave scabbards. I did a check and a quick spell of protection. As I opened the door a man was standing there.

The man said, rather nervously, "Are you the Wizard Oron?"

"I am Oron."

He held out a parchment unrolled it and started reading in formal tones, "Let it be known to the Wizard Oron that he needs to remove his tower from the place it is sitting. A road will be coming through this area and his tower is in the way. In addition, he needs to pay 50 % moving tax on his tower before moving. Also, he needs to pay the 50 % relocation tax before placing his tower in a new location. As the taxes amount to 100 % of the total worth of the tower and everything within the tower, if the taxes are not paid and the tower not moved within thirty minutes of hearing this message, the tower will be forcibly confiscated. Pined this day, Third Day of the Dire Moon in the year of the Snow Wolf. Signed, Magistrate Pooleicthy, head of the legal staff of Castle Goron." He looked at me and asked, "Do you understand?"

"Yes."

He smiled, "Are you ready to pay the taxes?"

I smiled, "I have a parchment from the King granting me this land and tax-free for life. As I am still alive that tax does not apply to me and the land is mine so it cannot be used as a road without my permission, then I would have to say no."

The man boldly said, "The King said you would say that, but read that parchment again. This is a new King and he is not beholding to that paper."

I smiled and raised a hand. The parchment was instantly in it. I opened it up and moved where he could read it. "To all that read this document. Be it known, for services to the crown, and for paying six million three hundred and ninety-five thousand in gold, I declare the Wizard Oron free and clear of all taxes for life, knowing full well that Oron is long-lived and will be around long past my time I make this land his and him tax-free through all future Kings."

I rolled it up and magically put it away. "The King has a copy and knows this. Please go back to your King and this Magistrate Pooleicthy and tell them that I am not moving, no road is going through my land, and I am paying no taxes."

The man looked a little nervous now. "I am ordered to let you know that if you do not pay and leave, the King will have your head."

Now I became a little upset. "Tell the King I said please try! I haven't had a good war in a century and need to test out some new spells."

That did not go over so well. A Paladin clamored up in his shimmy plate armor. "You are breaking the law by staying here."

I said, "You are breaking your covenant with you God Solbelli. I know and have met Solbelli and he is a God of great good and would be upset at any Paladin that went against the law to force a man from his home and confiscate it just because of the wishes of some greedy new King. You saw my proclamation from the old King. It is a legal document and by all good laws must be kept. To charge me 100% tax, exempt or not, is robbery and you know it. Rethink your position because I can assure you Solbelli will not protect someone breaking the law to steal."

"I will think on what you have said."

"Good. Commune with you God. I am not afraid of what he says. He is a good God. However, if you continue to work for a thief, Solbelli is going to become angry. I would leave the services of such a King if I were in your position. What is more important to you? Your God, or your King?"

"My God. I will commune. If you are correct, I will leave the services of the King. If you are wrong, I will return and ask you to leave or I will kill you."

He turned and started to leave, but several attacked him and he died, but not before killing eight of the thieves. That gave me a chance to see who the real power was. A rogue in the back of the crowd was the top issue. I dominated him. Simple spell. Then I sent him a mental message, "Take your time and let no one know what you are doing. But, kill the current King and Magistrate. He did not move but his thought turned to plans on doing my bidding. I resurrected the Paladin.

I said to the others, "This is foolishness. Tell your King that I will give it one week in contemplation. At the end of that time, I will either move without paying taxes, or I will remove him from power. He has that long to prepare." I shut the door and instantly there was a loud knock.

I opened the door and the man with the proclamation said, "Your time is up. We are going to tear this tower down and take everything."

I raised a hand and made every one of them incontinent and unable to become aroused. "Let me know when you change your mind." I shut the door and locked in my protections. They attacked with magical pickaxes and massive weapons and did nothing. After all the time I've lived, you would think I placed some very powerful protections on my tower and you would be correct. Now that I knew it was not a grand wizard I had no worries. Only a God or DemiGod would make it passed my spells. However, just in case I summoned a gargantuan silver dragon to chase them away. They left and quickly.

I thought about leaving. I don't like it when I am constantly bothered by the peasants. The King was sending little nothing people to work at digging one side out from under my tower to topple it. Fool! They could dig the entire bottom completely out and this tower would stay in place floating in the air. However, they ruined my rose garden. I am normally goodly of nature so the King figures that I won't attack them. He's correct. However, I will attack others in his name. An Eye Sundry is an evil little creature with many eyes on long stocks and each eye can shoot out a ray of light or magic arrow. I sent an Eye Sundry into his bedchamber late at night and it killed him and the man he was with. Then I sent the Eye Sundry into the Queen's chamber and then his children's rooms.

They all died and a new King was placed on the thrown. Guess who? You're right, it was the Paladin. He came to my tower one day alone but wearing the crown. I answered the door. I released the rogue from domination. No need now.

"Good day Paladin of Solbelli and now King. How is the kingdom this morning?"

"Better, now that evil has been removed from the seat of power. We will do well. However, after looking into his records I have concluded that the road is very much needed. Is it possible for you to move the tower over just a little and grant us the rite of passage through this spot? We will not without your permission."

"I can easily move it over and help with the road while I am at it. It is nice to work with someone that asks."

"You would have done this for the old King?"

"If he had asked."

The Paladin turned around while saying, "Fool King!"

FOREST DRUID

I WAS FLYING THROUGH THE FOREST LOOKING FOR NUTS and barriers, just doing my own thing when a stupid Dallit Frog struck me with its extremely long tongue. I pulled my silver sword and cut the end of the sticky tongue cleaving it in two. The tip was still attached and pumping poison into me, the rest returned to the frog to be regenerated. In a few short hours the darn frog would be as good as new. And, during that time he would find me and eat my paralyzed body. I could feel the numbness already spreading. Time was short so I flew down and attacked the frog. The only way to keep from being the frog's dinner is to kill the frog. It wasn't hard to hit or stab, but the thing jumped around so much it was difficult to catch. I killed the frog and sheaved my sword just as my arms went limp. I flew up into the trees and landed on the smallest branch I could. I wrapped my wings around it and changed color to match the branch just before going completely limp. It's not good to be helpless in the forest. Almost everything is deadly and hungry, but that's a chance I have to take every day as I get hungry and need to find food.

While I am stuck up here I may as well introduce myself. I am Clear-flame. I am a miniature fairy. Some fairies call me a freak, or puny, or a thousand other names. Fairies have grand imaginations and can think up some interesting things to upset humans and others. In this case, it is one of their kind.

Fairies don't get named until they metamorphous into their wings. My mother named me Clear-flame as my wings are clear with translucent rainbow colors so bright they look like flame. My wings glow at night. I am one of the few. I have learned to control that as it tends to attract predators.

Because of my size, I got beat up several times. Mother didn't care and neither did the rest of my family. My sisters would have nothing to do with me as I "crimped their style." Even the old wizard would have nothing to do with me. I asked him if he knew a way to make me grow. He laughed and told me to leave his home. I left that tree and finally ended up at the tree of the Queen.

Our Queen is known for her wisdom and kindness. I got in line and listened to all the foolish talk. The line moved slowly and I was the last to see her that day. I think being the last was helpful as she granted my wish instantly, but not as I was thinking. I asked, "Dear Queen Bright-Light, I am small and get beat up a lot. I seem to have no ability to stop this as hiding does not help. Can you make people leave me alone?" For some reason she looked tired and not in a very good mood.

She said, "Of course I can. I grant you the silver sword of returning for your protection and I exile you from our kingdom. You are never allowed to come here again. There, now no one can beat you up because after receiving your sword you will be escorted away from our lands."

The Queens Clerk said, "Majesty, the sword is our most prized possession."

"I know this, but when he dies the sword will instantly return to our pedestal. How long do you think he will last in the great forest? A week? A day? I would bet an hour at most. We will know the time of his death when the sword returns."

They handed me the sword and scabbard and escorted me to the limit of our lands. I tried to explain that this is not what I meant, but the ones escorting me said, "Never be the last to see the Queen. She takes it as laziness not getting up early enough to get a better spot in line."

On the way out one guard told me many things about the forest. I listened intently as my life was on the line.

"First, don't ever let your wings glow. There are a thousand monsters that will be attracted to the glowing. Second, stay up high but not too high. On the ground are far more creatures that can catch you and in the air are the dreaded birds. Try staying in the trees, but not close to any branches. Third, keep your eyes open and listen. Make no noise. Monsters are attracted to sounds. Forth, don't let yourself smell. Monsters are attracted to smells. Fifth, don't let yourself be seen. Monsters have keen eyesight. Sixth, when you land, instantly hug close to the branch or leaf and change into its color. Seven, NEVER TRUST A HUMAN! Eight, some monsters are friendly and will let you land on them. Be careful, other monsters will fly down and pick you off."

We came to the end of our lands two days later. We had traveled up over the mountains and into the neighboring valley where they knew no Fairy lived. The Deep Forest. At the edge, they said goodbye and left. I flew in the opposite direction.

I have lived on the edges of the deep forest for over a year now. I know the creatures. Every one of their types has attacked me at one point or another. Many have died before they decided that I don't make an easy dinner. Even the local birds leave me alone. One attacked me once and I killed it and was working on killing the others. I destroyed two snakes and a hawk when I was messing with the colorful birds. They decided to talk with me and found out I am a vegetarian and I am no threat to their eggs or young. However, I can protect them from others and they allow me to stay in a small hole in the tree. I've dug out that hole and made a home.

I constantly find dead creatures, mostly after the carrion have finished stripping the flesh. Every once and awhile I find dead humans. Adventurers, the birds call them. I search these as they carry things I like. The tree I stay in is very big and sits back into the forest about seven trees in. I dug out a large room, without harming the core. We fairies know how to take care of the trees. I have filled up that room with brass, copper, silver, gold, and platinum; built two bigger rooms and filled them also. In addition, I took bits of this and that; cloth for clothes, a bunch of silver needles for traps, all kinds of things that I can use. I had to leave much behind as some medals sting when I touch them. I think they call it iron or steel. Whatever, it has iron in it and we fairies are allergic to iron. Still, some rings are magical and changed size and shape to fit my fingers, a necklace, some silver armor, a knife and sword, a bow and arrows, a backpack, and shoes that all changed to fit. I now looked like one of our guards, all decked out in armor and full of weapons. The items were heavy at first, but I kept them on and now they are not heavy at all. Also, I grew. I had to make the hole into my home bigger because I was getting bigger. Not taller, just muscular.

That frog's poison was wearing off. If it would have hit the armor it would have done nothing, but it hit my elbow joint where I am less protected. I could feel my arms again. I waited a little longer until I could feel everything and move my fingers and toes. I unfurled my wings and used my magical knife to scrape off the end of the frog tongue. I turned my top dark green with bits of dark brown, my bottom, sides, front, and feet green leafy. It took a lot of practice to learn that change, but creatures find it difficult to target me like this. Looking from below or the sides I look like a leaf, and looking from the top I blend into the bottom of the forest. I am working on becoming clear, like water, so I am nearly invisible. I haven't perfected that yet.

I cautiously looked around. I am very good at spotting anything and there were several creatures up here with me. Luckily for me, none were the kind to eat me. Two branches down was a lizard that just ate a large praying mantis. A good thing about that. If either would have found me while paralyzed I would be stomach acid by now. Still, when I took off I stayed away from that lizard. It has a fast and wicked tongue. This tree was not a nut or fruit tree so I moved over three trees to find something ripe. Sparkle! The entire tree was covered with Dewberries. I flew into the tree while looking for monsters. I found several and knocked them out of the tree. Then I settled near some berries and waited while munching on one. Other than chewing I made no movement and no sound. Other things made movement but nothing deadly. There was one very large Jagged Edged Nermal, but they won't harm something that does not attack them. The only real concern was the dire centipede. At least three times longer than I am tall and a wicked mouth. Kicking him out of the tree would not work. Far too many legs holding on. I flew down and whispered to the Jagged Edged Nermal. "See the centipede. He'd make a grand dinner."

In a deep voice he said, "As much as I like the taste of centipede, Fairy, I cannot kill the creature on my own. Too many legs and each has sharp claws. The top armor is hard to penetrate. I need to flip it over or get underneath it. Still, it would feed me for a full moon."

I asked, "What if I attack it and remove some of those legs while you are attacking it also."

"Why would you help me?"

"Your species have never attacked me."

The Jagged Edged Nermal said, "You do not taste very good, and there is little meet."

I laughed, "Centipedes eat my kind and I need to harvest some of these berries. Having that monster gone and you well-fed would be a good thing for me."

"Very well, I will start heading that way. I will not take long."

Jagged Edged Nermals normally move very slowly, but they can move quickly when upset or hungry, and this one was hungry.

I said, "Then I will start the attack and distract it."

I flew up and away from the Jagged Edged Nermal. Then I flew down and did a scraping run across the centipede's right side cutting as many legs as possible. Centipedes are fast and mean but pain takes time to register and I finished my surprise attack and flew out of reach before he realized I was attacking him. He turned and followed me but a good half his legs on one side were cut and useless. He roared in anger. Everything in that section of the forest went quiet. I dived toward him again and he turned to meet me. I changed directions at the last moment and he reached up for me and the Jagged Edged Nermal moved under him and started gutting his belly.

I flew down and said, "Thank you."

"You are welcome little Fairy. In return, I do you a favor. The ants are headed this way."

"How long?"

"Before the next light."

"Then I must hurry."

Being in a hurry in the forest is not wise, but ants will strip the tree clean. I stuffed two berries in my mouth and filled my magic bag. It is the first time I used it and I was astonished at just how many berries went in before it was full. I would not need to hurry after all. I had enough berries to easily feed me for the entire winter. Dewberries last a long time, especially when it's cold. It took most of the day to pick barriers and fly home. When I arrived three birds came near me.

"I smell berries."

"Berries?"

"Berries?"

I said, "That way three hours by my speed. Four hours at your normal speed. You must be quick as the ants will come before light."

Squawks went up and a flight of birds took off. I took mine inside and then came out to stand watch over the young until they returned. A berry tree this late in the year is a grand boom and no bird could afford to stay behind. One of the fast green tree snakes noticed the grownup's departure and headed up. I waited.

When it reached the branch it wanted it started that direction. I came down and chopped its head off. Two others tried the same. I waited until they were on branches before cutting them in two. They fell into the throng of creatures and were dragged below the leaves.

Something was wrong. Creatures below were running north. I looked south. The forest was smoking. I looked west and the birds were returning. They came in squeaking and squawking about Humans. One came to me and said, "Pack up and leave. Humans are coming."

I headed toward the Humans.

When I reach the spot where the smoke was coming from I saw five humans sitting around a fire. One was talking.

"We need to find a good path we can cut through the forest for the road. It needs to be above the water level and as few hills and mountains as possible."

"Why don't we just widen the road that goes around the forest. You know the Druid is going to be mad when they start cutting."

"Mad? He'll be killing off-road crews right and left, but the King will hunt him down. Us, we map the path and leave. We'll be long gone before the Druid has a clue."

I turned as invisible as possible, flew down, and shoved my long sword through the ear and into the brain of the one in charge. I flew out, back up in a tree, and hid.

Pandemonium broke out when the fighter fell over dead. One man looked closely at the fighter and said, "Something entered his ear. Some bug or something. It's in his brain. I can see the cut mark where it entered."

That gave me an idea. I traveled back under my tree and grabbed up two bugs that I know love to attach themselves under the skin of animals. I carried them toward the Humans saying. "I have some animals I want you to have. They licked their lips. When they saw the humans they complained, "Too tough and they dig us out."

I said, "Not if you enter their ears and go into their brain."

"They smiled and I told them exactly what to do. Then we waited. When the humans went to sleep I placed the bugs into one ear of each. I waited until they were deep inside before I stabbed another in the ear and he woke up and yelled as I flew off. He did not see me as I was invisible. Three more died that night and the one that was left ran from the woods leaving everything behind. The soldier covered his ears with a cloth before running for safety. I watched him leave and when he was a good minute flying distance he was stopped by another man.

"What are you doing out here soldier? You're supposed to be mapping!"

The soldier cried out, "The others are dead. There is a bug inside the forest that is drawn to our fire and it enters the ear and eats the brain. We did not see them, but four are dead due to bleeding in the ear. The cleric said it was some new kind of bug."

The other calmed down, "Very well. I will report to the King that this part of the forest has killer bugs." It was then that I saw one of the bugs fly into the ear of the new Human. He screamed, swatted at his ear, and dug a finger into his ear, but it was too late. The soldier saw and ran until he was out of sight.

I headed back into the forest and there was an Elf waiting at the edge. I started moving away to enter from another direction, but he disappeared to instantly reappear at the point I was now heading for. I flew up within several feet of him and looked him over closely. He was covered in bark. Bugs and small animals were crawling on him and he did not care. A small wolf cub was in his right hand and he was petting it with his left. I started flying sideways to go around him, but he simply took a step my way.

He said in Fairy, my own language, I was most pleased. "Now, what is an Eastern Fairy doing in the Deep Forest?"

"I live here."

"How did you come to live here, little one."

"My name is Clear-fire. I was exiled from my lands because I was too small and was picked on a lot. The Queen was in a bad mood when I asked for her help so she sent me away saying, now they cannot pick on me because I'm not there."

"I see you have the Grand Fairy Sword."

"She gave it to me expecting it would return to her within an hour."

He smiled, "Surprise to her; you lived. And, now you have stopped the human King from trying to put a road through this part of the forest. That soldier will run to his King and tell about the bugs. They will send others, but now I have a weapon I did not know I had. They are afraid of bugs. I am amazed."

I said, while keeping my distance, "Bugs are probably the single most dangerous creatures in the forest. You should have more respect."

He looked astonished and surprised and then he chuckled, "You are correct Fairy. In my old age, I have lost the respect I should have. The forest is a wondrous thing."

I smiled, "It is that. It feeds so many and all it asks for in return is our secretions and dead for its food. There is a grand circle of life in the forest. My mother used to tell me, 'Clear, if even one part of the circle is broken, all will fall.' She said, 'It is the job of the Grand Druid to protect the forest, but it is our duty, our life, our home, and our survival. Without the forest, there would be no Fairies. That is why we keep a big army and teach the secrets

JOHN RICKS

of killing Humans.' That is what she told me and I will protect the forest with my life." A tear started, "I miss mom."

The Elf looked happy and then quickly turned puzzled and then sad, "How old are you Clear-fire?"

"I am almost six years old."

He turned angry, "Your Queen turned you out how many years ago?"

I backed up some more. "About one and a half."

"YOU WERE ONLY FOUR!"

I took off as fast as my wings could take me. I recklessly flew passed all kinds of monsters and finally into my tree. I sat at the front with bow in hand, shaking from every bone.

The birds asked, "What is wrong, friend?'

"There is an Elf after me. He is mad."

One bird that normally talks for the others scolded, "Why did you make an Elf mad at you?"

I said, "I didn't try too. I fixed it so the Humans would leave us alone and this Elf showed up. He asked me some questions and at one point he asked me about my age and I told him. He seemed mad that I was only four years old when my Queen tossed me out."

"Yes, we have been puzzled about why your queen kept you so long. We kick our children out on the seventh moon."

The Elf was at the bottom of the tree and said, "Normally Fairies leave the nest at ten or eleven years. Kicking one out at age four would be like kicking your babies out at only one moon."

The bird said, "That's murder." Many of the others echoed the same. Her head turned to the Elf. "Grand Druid, there is a mad Elf somewhere nearby. Be careful."

I looked down, "That is the mad Elf!"

The Elf said, "I am sorry, Clear-fire. I was not mad at you. However, I am a little upset with your Queen. Tossing out a little child to the mercy of the Deep Forest is not a nice thing to do. And, you mentioned that you were exceptionally small and that makes it even worse."

I put the bow away and peeked out. "I have paid her back. I still have the sword."

He smiled, "True, but you should let that sword return to her. You have two better swords. They are hidden in your tree."

I looked surprised, "I do?" I went inside and pulled out the six magical swords and laid them where he could see them. "Which ones?"

He smiled and then frowned. "The golden one is a far better sword and it is human bane. It does not like humans and will help you fight them. It suppresses fire three times a day. It can put out a large forest fire. It is very magical and turns bugs and forest monsters that attack you into ice giving you time to escape."

My eyes went wide and I hugged the sword. It was cold but hummed at my touch.

The Druid said, "Oh, she likes you. That is good. However, she is jealous over the silver sword."

I unbuckled the sliver sword and sat it down. I went inside and came out with a piece of parchment. I used green mushroom sprig to write: "Thanks, don't need it anymore." I placed the parchment around the pommel and tied it with string. Then I said, "Go home." It disappeared.

The druid said, "The Black sword is even more powerful."

I said, "I don't care about that. This sword likes me. I will love it always."

With a smile the Elf said, "That is good as it is the Sword of the Forest. It used to belong to me until a Human absconded with it. I made another. The black sword is evil and will help you kill Humans also. It is extremely powerful and will give you the ability to destroy everything; however, every time you use it the sword will turn you a little evil until you need to kill every living thing and everyone you know, even your bird friends. It will make you destroy a part of the forest circle."

I backed up and my hand went toward my golden sword. Anger entered my face. "How do I destroy it?" It actually tried to leave. It trembled.

The Elf said, "You cannot so do not try." Then he called out. "Malificus, trade this little Fairy for the sword. I think the Staff of the Woods would be fare."

Instantly the sword was gone and an old walking staff was in its place. I picked it up as I heard. "He was going to try to destroy my old sword. I was waiting to see what would happen when he hits it with the Sword of the Forest Natura helped you make. It would have been interesting."

The Elf said, "It would have destroyed this section of the forest."

Malificus said, "Probably. Teach this fool some manors. He is very magical. That old Fairy Wizard would have realized if he wasn't drunk on Hilybar sap at the time. I laughed and laughed when my spy told me he was kicked out of their kingdom. The most magical creature to bless this world in a century and he is exiled. Natura is most upset. Did she not send you to find him?"

The Elf said, "She did and the Black Sword blocked my efforts. I wonder how it arrived here in the forest and how he just happens to be the one to find it."

Malificus laughed, "Well, got to go. Bye."

The Elf said, "Figures." He turned to me. "Come here Clearfire. I need to test you for something. I will not harm you."

I came down to his hand. "You are small for your age." He did a spell and I glowed so I depressed it.

The Elf's eyebrows went close together and he asked, "What did you just do?"

I said, "I started to glow and that attracts predators. So, I stopped it."

He said, "That was my spell. I am going to make you glow again. I will protect you from the predators so don't worry." The sword started to hum so I drew it and knew she would protect me also.

He did his spell again and I glowed like sunlight for hours. He did another spell and I glowed another color for hours also. He told me to get some sleep, "I need time to think and pray."

I gladly went back over to my swords and gathered then up and put them away. I pulled out five of my Dewberries and flew them down to him.

He smiled and said, "Thanks."

I went back up and went to sleep deep down in the tree.

Nemar went to his knees after eating the berries and started praying. "Natura, Great Goddess of the forest. I have found the Fairy you sent me for. Malificus's Black Sword was blocking my view. This Fairy, Clear-Fire is his name, has the Sword of the Forest and she loves him. She senses his power. He picked up the Staff of the Woods and carried it like a walking staff and it did not kill him. He is very powerful. He glows in both disciplines for hours."

"He should, Nemar. I touched him at conception. His faithless father abandoned his wife and children when he found out she gave him a 'puny son'. I struck him down in front of the Queen. I am most disturbed that the Queen kicked the child out and most pleased that he lived through it. I created him for your replacement. Train him well."

"Your wish is my joy to obey. And, thank you. I am getting old and tired."

"Rest will come soon my champion. Then you will live with my faithful in my temple."

I was flying through the forest looking for nuts and barriers, just doing my own thing. I did not have to worry about the creatures in the forest. No creature would ever attack me. I am the Forest Druid and it is my job to protect the forest.

LUCK? OR DID A GOD STEP IN

AS I RAN THROUGH THE BACK ALLEYWAYS AND HID IN A trash heap I thought to myself, "Big cities are too small." No matter where I go I end up running into Master Graywall or one of his goons. This time they almost caught me. They were still looking and I lay as quiet as possible. Still, they had their swords out ramming them into everything in the alley. Three times they shoved them into this heap and twice they missed. Luckily the trash cleaned the blade as it left my leg or my hiding place would have been found. I was bleeding badly though, and that blade shoved moldy who knows what into the wound. If I don't stop the bleeding soon I may be hiding here for the rest of my life. I may still die from the infection. Not like I can afford the services of a good Cleric. I waited and waited until they were out of sight for the count of one hundred. Not everyone can count, but I got my education from being the fanning boy for a girl that was receiving lessons. I can read and write and do figures better than she can. She treated me like trash and that is what she saw when she looked my direction. At least I received a bath, clean clothes, and food. She didn't like the smell, look, or the grumble of my stomach. Said it distracted her from learning. That was alright with me. Once a day for two years I fanned her and listened to the lessons. I lost that position when her father arranged a marriage with the Merchant's son next door. Darn, I'm already drifting off. Too much loss of blood. I took a dirty rag and stuffed it into the wound, and then I took another and stuffed it into the other side of the wound and used my last rag to tie the two in place. I limped out and looked around. A man was standing over me. I tried to run, but there was no strength left in me and I passed out.

I awoke to light coming through the window. A lady was running around getting things and a Cleric looking at my leg. I recognized nothing as my eyes did not clear. I must have stirred as a hand pushed my head back onto the pillow and a commanding voice said, "Hold still, boy."

I lie quietly trying to regain my full sight. It took a few minutes but eventually, my sight cleared. I was in the military compound. Darn, I tried my best to stay away from this place. I remember the stories about "boys go in but only men come out." I did not panic. I looked around hunting for an escape route. The man standing over the bed smiled and showed me the shackle attached around my left wrist.

He said, "You're not going anyplace, boy. Not until you're fully healed and I have every bit of information I can get from you."

I whispered, "Dorm."

His look turned cold and bitter and he leaned in. I whispered, "Dorm will kill me."

He asked, "Why?"

"He is Master Graywall's spy in this camp. Master Graywall cannot afford for me to be alive."

The Cleric looked up at the Man and said, "That makes sense. We never even thought of interrogating Dorm as he takes all the notes on the other interrogations. And, as he is always present, he may be why the prisoners are impossible to get information out of.

The man left my side and walked over to another. "Find Dorm, put him in irons, and place him in the room. Don't let that assassin escape. And, don't leak a word about the boy. Not to anyone, not your best friend, not your wife, and not your God, understand."

The man saluted and said, "As you wish, Captain."

Another man dressed in finery sat on a chair in the corner. He said, "If Dorm is the leak I want his head, Captain."

The Captain said, "As you wish, Highness."

My eyes almost popped out of my head and despite yelling and grabbing at me I managed to get off the bed and onto my knees with my head low to the ground.

The Prince said, "Rise, boy. Get back on that bed, and don't you move again until the good Cleric says you can."

As I stood up I said, "Yes Majesty, Sire, Highness, sir." I wasn't sure which one I was supposed to say so I said them all.

The Captain chuckled and so did the Cleric. The Prince said, "Highness is the proper title, Boy. Now lay back and be quiet."

I laid back and did not move an inch. Not even when the Cleric took the rags out and started digging through my leg for other items of trash. He found some too. It was painful and they all could clearly see it was nearly killing me, but I did not move. You follow a direct order from a Prince. That was born and bred into me by a father and family who were highly loyal to the crown.

The Cleric did a couple of spells and my leg was all better. I was still weak from loss of blood, but my leg was healed.

The Cleric said, "That should do the trick. He is healed and I removed all poison and disease."

The Captain pulled up a chair and sat down looking at me. "He needs a wash and clean linen."

The Cleric added, "Food and water also. The boy is near starved."

The Captain turned to me as others got busy. "You the one that sent a message to the crown about an assignation plan?"

I whispered, "Yes Sir, Captain Sir. That is why they were after me. Someone found out and told Master Higel. He is one of the Castle spies. I instructed the guard not to tell anyone except the King. What happened?"

The Captain said, "Guards do not break protocol because of a Rag-a-Muffin. Who are the other spies?"

"Giggles, oh sorry, I mean the Lady Penelope is spying for the King of Landor, Sir Hillman is spying for Lord Walters, Squire Samuel is spying for the King of Diaken, and Garywall has four spies, all servants; Martin the wood bringer, Carroll the scullery maid, Mistress Jayfive the person in charge of cleaning bedrooms, and Master Higel the Day Captain."

The Captain said, "You know this for a fact?"

I said, "I found his list, Captain Sir."

The Captain asked, "How did you find his list?"

"After I lost my last job, because the Lady got married, I went looking for another position. I can read and write and do figures, so I tried to raise myself to something that pays enough to actually allow me to eat. I get hungry you know. Well, one night I was woken in my sleep and dragged by the tail out of my place under the docks. To my surprise, I was taken before the Night Watch of the Thieves Guild. Some big wig Assassin was there. I pretended to still be knocked out so they did not care about talking in front of me. I found out all about their plans and when they went into another room to 'Seal the Deal' with some women I kicked my guard in the privets, grabbed the papers they were writing on, and ran the other way."

The Captain smiled, "What did you do with the papers?"

I smiled back, "I have holes in my shoes and have been using them to plug the holes."

Instantly the Cleric was removing my shoes. I said, "Hay! How am I supposed to escape without shoes?"

The Captain picked up my hand again to remind me I can't escape, but the shackle was not on it. "HOW IN THE!? Sergeant! Don't take your eyes off this boy."

The Sergeant looked at me disapprovingly. "As you wish, Captain."

The Cleric said, "It's all here. The Thieves' Guild and Assassins' Guild agreeing to assassinate the King. In their own handwriting too."

The Prince said, "This will get Father to take action against them. This is proof that the truce is off."

The Captain said, "Protect this boy!" and then he and the others left.

I was instantly attacked by two girls that stripped me down to my birthday suit and started scrubbing me.

I said as I squirmed, "Hay, brushes are not necessary. I am not the floor you know."

One girl said, "No, the floor is far cleaner!"

They cut off all my hair so I would not have lice eggs. They even cut my eyebrow hair off. I was scrubbed from top to bottom. When they found out my feet are ticklish they spent extra time complaining about getting in between my toes. Then I was covered up with a blanket and told not to move. Food was brought in. It was the best food I had ever tasted. I told them so.

The Lady asked, "If it was so good, why aren't you finishing it?"

"I'm stuffed. I'm not used to getting a complete meal. Someone's trash here and some there. I found a dead fish once. I stretched that out for an entire week." I was looking around again and the Sergeant said, "Don't even think of leaving, Boy. The Captain would have my hide."

I frowned, "They took my clothes so I don't have pockets to hide this wonderful food in."

He smiled, "Don't you worry about the food. Stick around and I will ensure you're fed well."

I turned to him and I could not hold back the tears. "I won't go anywhere, Sir. You'll have to throw me out."

He said as he took my hand, "That bad out there, Boy?"

"If you refuse to steal, or work for one of the less reputable guilds, then yes."

He asked, "So you're saying you never took anything that wasn't yours?"

"Except for those documents. No sir. I have never taken anything that does not belong to me. Ask my last employer. I am honest."

The Lady asked, "Who was your last employer?"

"Master Locksmith Jeff Nader, my Lady."

The Sergeant looked surprised and asked, "You were Master Nader's apprentice?"

"No, sir. I was the fanboy for his daughter. It was a great job. She always needed a fan during her lesions and I learned everything she did. That's how I know how to read and write and do figures. I always received a bath, clean clothes, and a meal. It was a sweet deal."

The Lady asked, "Didn't he pay you?"

I said, "Clean clothes and a meal was my pay and I was in heaven."

She was so mad at Nader for taking advantage of me the Lady burnt herself at the fireplace. She was blistered badly and it was getting worse. The Sergeant got up and went over so I did also. I reached out and touched her hand and while saying the same thing the Cleric did while fixing my leg. I made the same hand signal also. Instantly the hand was fixed. They both stared. The Sergeant exclaimed, "How did you do that?"

I said as I climbed back into bed. "I did what the Cleric did to my leg. It seemed like the right thing to do." I grimaced.

The Lady came to me quickly, "Something wrong, child?"

"Now I have a headache something bad. I feel sorry for that Cleric if he gets a headache every time he heals someone. No wonder they charge so much."

She smiled, "He does not get a headache. You did because you overextended yourself." She turned to one of the girls, "Get the Royal Cleric and Wizard. They need to know we found a potential. And, contact Master Nader and find out about this boy."

The Girl curtsied and left. Soon the Cleric came in with an old man following him.

"Brother Lorn, do slow down. I am not the young fool I use to be."

The Cleric said, "I am thinking you need an apprentice far more than I, Master Longstick."

The Wizard barked, "Don't jump to conclusions. We know nothing about this boy or if he can do magic."

They entered just as the maid came back with Master Nader in tow.

Master Nader passed them both up. "Ah, Boy. I am glad I found you."

I smiled and said, "Master Nader, sir. It is nice to see you again. How is your lovely daughter doing?"

The Captain came in and shut the door. His voice was quiet, but you could have heard him over an angry crowd. "I thought I made it very clear that no one is to know about this boy. VERY CLEAR!"

Everyone was intimidated except the Wizard. He turned to the Lady and asked, "Is that true?"

She blushed and said, "Yes, my Lord."

The Captain asked, "Who sent for these people?"

The Lady said, "I did, Captain."

In total anger, he walked over to her and slapped her hard enough to knock her down and then said, "If you weren't my sister I would have you flogged! If this boy dies because of you, I will have you flogged anyway."

The Wizard asked, "Why is the boy important, Captain?"

"He was the one that warned our King of the assassination attempt. He is a hero and the entire Thieves' Guild and Assassins' Guild is after him. Now, all of your lives are in danger also."

Master Nater said, "I just wanted to ask the boy to come work for me; to be my apprentice. My last apprentice left to join some adventurers as their rogue. I need someone I can trust and the boy is completely trustworthy. I was worried when I first hired him and so I set him up. I placed a small bag of gems on a table he would be near and ensured everyone left. He never even touched it. The bag was open and the gems sparkling in the light. He looked at it but never touched it. When I came out he got my attention and said, 'Master Nader Sir, should you be leaving a bag of gems like this just lying around open, Sir?' I was so flabbergasted by his complete honesty that I kept him on longer than I normally would have."

I smiled, "A job?"

The Wizard said, "Wait. Before you sign up for anything I need to check something." He walked over to me and did a spell. It was a simple spell and now I knew it. I glowed for about an hour before the glow started to fade. The Wizard was keeping track of how long I glowed, and the Cleric was keeping everyone quiet. When he was finished the Cleric did the same thing to me but there was a slight difference in the spell. I glowed for about twenty minutes and then it faded.

The Wizard said, "Master Nader. The boy, how long did he work for you and do you know his name?"

Master Nader said sadly, "Two years and a month, and no; I do not know his name."

The Lady said, "He worked for you for two years for only a meal and a bath and you did not even know his name!"

Master Nader looked at me, "What's your name boy?"

"Mark, Sir. Mark Longfellow Jr."

The Captain's eyes nearly popped out of his head. "Sir Mark Longfellow, Night Captain of the Kings Army, Hero of the Great War, a man who saved the King's life six times by count. His son?!"

I smiled, "You knew my father?"

The Captain said, "Send for a litter. I want this boy transferred to my rooms in the Castle."

The Wizard said, "He will be transferred to my tower in the Castle. He will be safe there."

The Captain was about to refuse the Wizard but the Cleric said, "Captain. Did you see how long the boy glowed with arcane magic?"

"Over an hour. So?"

The Wizard said, "The longer the glow the more the potential and the more harmful to himself and others if not trained properly."

The Captain said, "Your point."

The Wizard said, "The Grand Master of the University glowed for forty-seven minutes. He was the longest ever recorded, short of a Godling."

The Cleric said, "The Pope glowed for fourteen minutes."

Everyone was shocked and looking at me. If I had a mirror I would have been shocked and looking at me also. I said, "I'm not magical."

The Cleric said, "Mark, we have looked long and hard for someone like you. Your new Master is getting very old. You are needed as his apprentice."

"Do I get food?"

He smiled, "Yes. You will never go hungry again."

I said, "I'll work very hard for you, Master Wizard Sir."

He said as he tossed my hair, "You'd work hard for any honest man that feeds you."

I was covered completely in linen and taken into a carriage. When we entered the castle I was carried up into the Wizard's tower and set down. Clothes were sent in and I was dressed in better clothes than I have ever worn. Food was brought in and I ate some and hid some. I was given a room about fifteen by fifteen with no view. The candles never burned down. I tried to blow them out to save them when not needed and the Wizard laughed. "Those are spelled to burn continuously without burning. Touch the tip."

I did, and there was no heat. I smiled and asked, "How?"

He said, "I will teach you, but it takes time. It seems you already know one spell. Got it from the Cleric fixing your leg I hear."

I must have blushed.

"What's wrong, Mark?"

Humbly I said, "I know five spells now. Three from the healing and the two used to check my arcane and divine abilities, Sir."

He sat down in a chair and said, "Do the arcane ability spell on me."

I walked over and repeated exactly what he had done, and he glowed. Then I grabbed my head and went to my knees.

He did a quick spell and my headache went away. He said, "You know the spell, but you are not ready to use the spell. It is beyond you and can burn you out. The first thing I wish to teach you are the Articles of Magic. You must learn them and understand them before I can teach you anything else." He handed me a parchment with fancy writing in a strange picture type of language.

I said, "This is not in the standard language, Master."

He said, "You need to use the research library and find out how to decipher it first." He stood up and walked out. I nearly ran to catch up. He opened the door next to mine and inside were thousands of books in stacks and piles.

I asked, "How am I going to find anything in this mess?"

He smiled, "I have the same problem. Good luck and take your time. I am not in a hurry." He turned and left.

I sat down and thought about the situation. I would bet that this will not be the only time I am going to need to find a book in this room. Just to find the book I need I will need to read some of every book this time, the next time, the next time, and so on the entire time I am here if I don't do something. I looked around and there were plenty of bookcases so why didn't he put them up when he was done with them? It looks like he pulls it out, tosses it off to the side and pulls another one until he finds the one he wants. That tells me that he cannot remember what he has. I said to myself, "Old Wizard losing memory." I went back to my room. There was parchment, pen, and ink there. I took it back to the book room. I cleared off a table and sat the writing stuff down. Then I cleared out an area by piling up all the books into one spot. That took most of the day. The lady that cooked for him called me down for dinner. Of course, I came down as quickly as I could. The food was wonderful. I asked the lady if she had something that could cut parchment nice and evenly. She asked what size I wanted. I told her about hand size. She went away and came back with a stack of parchment in exactly that size and said, "If there is a good reason for the needed item, then you can ask and we will provide. Parchment is always an item a young Wizard needs."

I thanked her and after dinner, I went back up and started my plan. I picked up a book and started reading it. Once I knew about what it was, which was difficult as it was the first book I had ever read, I made a card for it and put the title on the top and a short statement of what was inside. As the title started with a 'D' I put it on the fourth shelf. Then I picked up another book and did the same. I was woken up by the lady saying, "Master Mark, you missed breakfast and lunch, are you going to attend dinner?"

She saw the twenty cards and the twenty books on the shelves and smiled, "Did you sleep last night, dear?"

I said, "I did not know it was another day, Mistress."

She said, "Come down for dinner and then go to bed. I will figure out something to help you keep the time."

I smiled, "Thank you."

Dinner, again, was most excellent and I had run out of hiding places to store food so I only took a couple of apples. They said I could have all I wanted, but I figure that once I have the books figured out and placed where they should be I would not be needed anymore, so I had food hidden all over.

The next day I was woken up by the Lady, I seldom see the Wizard. At breakfast she said, "You know, you don't have to store food away. I promise you that you will always receive a good meal at this place."

She said that so kindly that I actually stopped. It was difficult, but I forced myself. It is hard going without and thinking it will happen again. I kept myself busy by reading and filing. I did not know it was called filing until one book I picked up talked.

"It's about time you picked me up. I have been waiting, you know."

I put it back down and left it alone for three days. It was all by itself on the floor when I finished that pile. I picked it back up and it said, "I am sorry, Master Mark. I did not know I would upset you."

I said in near petrified fright, "You won't eat my soul will you?"

"No. I don't do bad things. I am a book of Good. What I would do if you were not good-aligned is to change you to my alignment. But, I am happy to say, you already are very good. Therefore, I will not harm you. You may even find me helpful."

I was writing its name on a card which means I am going to file it away, so it started talking faster in a panic. "If you leave me out and open, I can help you understand what each book is about."

I said, "Many of the books are not in my language."

It said, "I have noticed. You are creating a shelf of unknowns. Pick one up and open it."

I set the talking book down and picked up a book of all drawings that looked a lot like the drawings on the parchment the Wizard gave me.

It said, "That is a book on cantrips. It is written in the language of Magic, the Dragon speech, also known as Draconic."

I asked, "Can you please help me learn each language?"

It said, "That could take years."

I smiled, "The Wizard told me that he was not in a hurry."

It said, "In that case, go over to the third pile on the right. No, one more back. That's the one. Eight books down. Yes, that one. Pull it out and bring it here."

I did as told and took the book over to the other book. I opened the indicated book and it talked. They started chatting back and forth and the new book asked, "Master Mark. I am told you wish to learn the language of magic. Why?"

I said as I pulled out the scroll. "The Wizard gave me this parchment and told me it was the Articles of Magic. He said I need to memorize them and understand them before he would teach me anything more. However, I don't want to just learn the minimum to do the least I can. I would like to go that extra step and learn everything I can while the offer still stands. I don't want you to translate this scroll. I want to know the language well enough to read, write, and speak it. Then I will translate the scroll myself."

The book accused, "You have a hidden motive. I can smell it."

I blushed and whispered, "The Wizard said he was not in a hurry for me to learn, so I plan on learning everything I can. I am going to stuff my head with every bit of knowledge. This is a grand opportunity and I am not going to squander it." I leaned in conspiratorially, "Besides, the longer I take, the longer they feed me."

The Book exclaimed, "Boys and their food!"

The other book said, "Look Melina. The boy is good to the core, I did not have to change him. He has no prejudices because he has no experience. You always said that Humans are wrong-headed and only need the correct bringing up. Here is your chance to train one up correctly."

She thought on that for a moment, "Hum, you do have a point, Hal, but I am not sure he can take my kind of training. I am a stickler and very strict."

I said, "Please. I would love to learn from you. I do not mind if you are strict. I will do what I need to do to learn, as long as I do not have to do anything wrong."

She questioned, "WRONG?!"

I said, "Yes Mistress Melina. I would never do something to harm anyone, especially those that have put their trust in me. I would give my life for the Crown and the Wizard. I will not steal or shirk my chores to do something else. I consider those things to be something wrong."

She calmed down. "Those are the wrong things to do."

I added, "I don't always know what is right or wrong. It would be very helpful to have mentors like yourselves to let me know before I get into trouble."

She said, "Will you listen to our advice?"

"Of course, Mistress."

She chuckled, "He is polite. I like that."

Hal said, "He knows nothing about magic. Oh, he can do a few spells, but was frightened and left me alone for three days when I startled him."

She said, "Yes, I watched that. But, he did come back to you. He finished the rest of the pile, but he got up the nerve to pick you back up. Very well, I will take you on as a pupil, until I think you are ready, or I think you have strayed."

"Thank you, Mistress."

She said, "Prop Hal and I up so that we may watch your progression."

There were several wooden items used for propping up books and I used the best two I could find.

She said, "Now, pen in hand and write this down."

She started teaching me Draconic.

The Wizard smiled before closing his scrying pool.

The Prince said, "I like his attitude toward the Crown."

The Wizard said, "I expected nothing less, being who he is the son of. Still, he includes me in with that giving his life thing. What I like about this, even more, is that he is Very Good as verified by a powerful artifact. Also, he befriended the two books and she agreed to train him. That is extraordinary. My last apprentice, she turned down flat and slammed his finger in her pages when she shut and refused to open for him. She was right, that boy was a fool. Tossed her in the fireplace to burn, and after that, no book would open for him. I sent him off to the Wizard's University and those books would not open for him either. Somehow, they communicate with one another. I haven't figured that one out yet."

The Prince said, "That's very interesting but remember this, Wizard, loyalty only goes so far. If you decide to test him, don't do it by taking away his food."

The Wizard's eyes opened fully in shock, "Of course not. The boy is like a dog in that matter. He is the most loyal to the one that feeds him. On that matter, I am thinking of getting him a Ring of Essentia. With that, he will never be hungry again."

"Good idea. Maybe he'll stop with the storing food. Your Sister is being very kind, but she is getting frustrated."

The Wizard said, "He stopped doing it consciously. But without thinking he still takes food and places it in little kooks. It keeps my Sister on her toes. She likes the boy."

The Prince smiled, "I have feedback from the house Mistress on that. Your sister has been heard saying, "My son is still storing food."

The Wizard looked shocked. "That was not foreseen. She has never had children and has wanted them very badly. She had an egg once, but it was stolen. That is what caused her to destroy that city. I brought her here to help her with this problem. I cannot and the Cleric cannot. She can never have another egg."

The Prince said, "Well, she has solved the issue herself."

The Wizard wasn't so sure, "My sister is delicate. It would not take much to push her into taking her life. A simple rejection on his part and she would be devastated." They walked off talking about the issue and the extreme ramifications.

One night about two moons into my being in the tower the Lady came in saying, "Come on sweetheart. Time for a bath and then bed. You look so tired." I went with her while listening to the discussion between Hal and Melina.

Hal said, "He is tired. We have worked with him three days straight."

Melina said, "She seems more motherly toward him each day. The Wizard's talk has affected her though. She seems worried."

After that, I was too far away. I thought to myself, "More motherly, more motherly, hum. Is there an issue I am not aware of?" I started watching a little closer.

She said, "After your bath it's bedtime. I have already turned down the covers. It is going to be cold tonight sweetheart, keep covered up. I don't want you catching cold."

She kept up the conversation nervously for some reason. It was like she was afraid of something, possibly my harming her, or rejection. I can understand that. I have been rejected lots of times and each one hurt in its own way. When I was in bed and tucked in and just before she covered the light I asked, "Can I have a few words with you please?" I patted the bed.

She came over and sat down and took my hand.

I said, "You seem nervous around me for some reason. I love you so very much. I have not had anyone that returned that love in such a long time. I look at you as my new Mother. I don't want you to be afraid of what I learn. I would never harm you."

She started tearing up and hugged me very close and hard. "And, I see you as my new son. I love you too dear. Now, go to sleep. You need your rest."

I thought to myself, "It worked. She's not afraid of me anymore." Happily, I turned over to go to sleep. I had no idea what I just accomplished, or that the fabric of time just changed its pattern.

However, the Wizard knew. He joyfully flew down the stairs to his sister but quietly walked in when he reached the door to the kitchen. "Well, sis. How are you feeling?"

She smiled, "I am doing exceptional. You were wrong you know."

"I was?"

"Mark accepts me as his new Mother. He told me so. He brought it up. I did not have to say a thing." She came over to her brother and hugged him. "And, I owe it all to you."

"How so?"

"Your talk made me decide to talk to him. I was so nervous he saw and started the conversation. He thought I was afraid of him and what he is learning." She smiled. "Imagine that. He assured me that he sees me as his new Mother and that he would never harm me. My son is so sweet."

"What are you going to do now?"

"Keep things just like they are."

The Wizard looked worried, "He is quick. He will find out."

She said, "Not for many years. Meantime, I have a son. Gods help the fool that tries to take him away from me."

He left the kitchen saying to himself, "God help us all if she loses him. I will have a talk with Melina. She needs to slow down his progression. The longer it takes for him to find out, the better."

The next day at practice I placed the last book on the shelf. I sat down in the chair and let out a breath. Done with my first goal. Hundreds to go. Hal, may I obtain your opinion on something please?"

"Glad to help, Mark."

"My new Mother is different. There is something about her that I don't seem to understand. Not the way she walks, or talks, or anything mentally. It's the way she feels when I hug her. She has a different temperature than most. Her body temperature is closer to mine."

Hal said, "Oh, that's because she is half green dragon. She is cold-blooded like you. The Wizard is the same, but he received the human side. His twin received the Dragon side. She actually has to actively spell up her shape each morning to look human."

Melina was furious at Hal. "You fool! How could you?!"

Hal realized what he said, "Oh my, I forgot. Mark, you did not hear what I just said. You are not supposed to know."

Melina yelled, "As if he is going to forget now. WIZARD! WIZARD!"

I said, "Stop, please. You're hurting my ears."

I stood up and walked down to the Kitchen. Mother was there making dinner. "It's not ready yet son."

I smiled, "I have a question."

She smiled back, "Go ahead."

"When am I going to get to see my Mother in her true form?"

She stopped dead in her tracks and turned to me looking very worried, "What are you saying?"

I walked over and gave her a hug saying, "I would think that my mother, being half Green Dragon, would be more interested in my education about dragons."

Tears started floating down her cheeks. She sat down. "How did you find out, Sweetheart?"

"You and I are a different temperature than others. Therefore, I asked and Hal has a big mouth. In addition, I have been speaking Draconic since I came down and you did not even notice. You speak draconic as if you were born to it."

She looked near in a panic so I added, "I don't see why you kept such a wonderful thing from me. I guess you had your reasons. I will not meddle, but I hope you trust me enough to show me someday." I gave her another hug and left saying, "I love you, Mommy."

The Wizard had finally answered the book's call. He immediately came down to the kitchen. I passed him on the way. I gave him a hug saying, "You and my Mommy are both half Green Dragons. That's wonderful." Then I let go and went back to my books. The Wizard entered the kitchen.

He asked, "You alright?"

She smiled, "I could not be better. I have nothing to hide from my son as you and I both feared. He is truly open-minded and innocent about the different dragons."

The old Wizard said, "Yes. He is a remarkable and loving child."

She said, "Yes, and for that matter, please explain to me how the son of the Greatest Hero this nation has ever known could become a vagabond."

The Wizard said, "I have no idea, but I can check." He left to talk with the Captain of the Guard.

He found him just sitting down for dinner. "Hello, Captain. How is the war with the Thieves' Guild going?"

"Hello, Master Wizard. The war is nearly over. The King has hired a hundred mercenaries and they have scoured the city. Using Clerics and Zones of Truth we have uncovered several rats' nests. They have asked for a truce but the King is not of a mind for any kind of truce. Not when their last target was him. The Assassins' Guild has moved away. Their losses were far too great. Now, what brings you down to the barracks? I know you get daily reports on the war and know probably know more than I."

"I am confused. How did Mark become a vagabond? He was the son of a Knight Captain, a hero. What happened?"

The Captain said, "His father was killed in the big war. We did not know about Mark as the man kept his son hidden. No one had a clue. We took a hair before you took him off. His lineage has been checked and he is the legal son of Knight-Captain Mark Longfellow. However, we could not determine who the mother was. Strong magic hides that from us."

The Wizard asked, "Strong Magic?"

"Yes. But, you'll have to ask Mark that. He would be the only one to know."

"Thank you, Captain."

"No Problem. I hear your sister has adopted him."

The Wizard smiled. "The boy needs a mother."

The Captain said, "I am glad to hear that confirmed. We worry each day having a Green Dragon living in the castle."

The Wizard stood straight, "My sister is no threat and neither am I, and she even less so now that she has a son. The Book of Goodly Alignment changed her a long time ago. But do us both a favor, don't upset her."

The Captain said, "I that." and the men at the table echoed the statement. Many of them had seen what she could do during the big war. They were very glad she was on their side.

The Wizard returned to his tower and went to the Library. Mark was there talking to the two books.

Mark said, "I have translated the Articles of Magic. They go as follows:

D-o not mess with the Fabric of Time!

O-h, and do not mess with the Weave of Life, (watch it if you must, but do not change it)!

N-ever mess with the Weather! Ever!

O- ther than wishing upon, do not mess with the stars!

T-he planet rotations are off-limits, including the moons, leave them alone!

E-verything has a cost, find out what it is and if it is worth it!

V-ice adding to or removing from, don't mess with space!

E-ach time you create something the material comes from somewhere. Know where first!

R-esearch, research, research, research! Know what you are doing!

M-ess around with magic and it will mess back. Be very careful.

E-verything you do affects everything else and everyone else. Be careful.

S-tay away from using magic for longevity, you won't like the outcome.

S-tudy until you know what you are doing and then study some more.

Hal asked, "And, what did you learn?"

Mark said, "Many things, Hal. First, do not make a mess. Second, be very careful. In our studies of different books, there have been many examples of Wizards, or other magic users, that have messed with time, life, or the weather. In all but one case it came out disastrous. In that one situation, it came out well only because the person was intelligent enough to get buy-in from the Gods and was God backed. Still, the plan was not his original plan because he simply did not know what he was doing at first. The Gods showed him the correct way as it was something they all wanted. Third, everyone has agendas including the Gods. If we do something that harms their agenda they tend to take retribution. Or, if we are lucky and listen, they stop us. I would have thought that being a Wizard I would not need a God to guide me. I was wrong. Guidance from a God can and will keep me from doing something that unwittingly makes a mess. Forth, it seems to me that the more powerful the magic-user the more chance of making a mess that he cannot clean up. Therefore, as you gain in power you need to be even more careful. Not to say at the start you do not need to be careful; quite the opposite, being careful, taking that extra step to ensure you're not making a mess, knowing the consequences beforehand, is of the highest importance."

Melina asked, "And if you do not know the consequences?"

I said most seriously, "Then you are not ready. Find out the consequences. Ask your mentor, check with a friend that can help, study some more. Do anything except continue. It is like trade. Only a fool trades without knowing the cost of the trade. I have heard that Wizards study constantly. Now I think I know why. A War Wizard needs to sling spells and change spells instantly. They study in advance to know what the consequences will be in any given circumstance. That takes a lot of thought and experience. That's why the Wizards University. It is also why it requires many years as an apprentice. The Wizard in charge must ensure his apprentice understands and has the basic tools needed to not make a mess."

The Wizard walked in. "Very good. You have done well." He bowed to the books, "And, you two have done a grand job so far. I am most pleased."

I said, "Thank you, Master."

Hal said, "Thank you, Master Wizard."

Melina said, "Of course. However, we are not done with his training yet. He has a long way to go."

I smiled and looked hopeful. The Wizard chuckled, "I will leave you to it then after I have asked a few questions."

He turned toward me and asked, "Mark, who was your mother?"

I said, "Your sister."

The Wizard frowned, "That is good and proper as she loves you being her son, but I was asking about your blood mother."

"Sir, I do not know her name."

"What do you know?"

I looked down and said, "I know this. She was a Dragon."

He stiffened, "And, how do you know this?"

I changed into my sleeping form and then back. The shock in his face registered and I started to tear up.

He smiled and poked my nose, "You are the child of a Rainbow Dragon. Extraordinarily rare."

"Rainbow Dragon, Sir?"

He put his arm around me as he led me down to the kitchen. "Rainbow Dragons are created by Reds, Blues, Greens, whites, and sometimes blacks matting. Your mother was truly open-minded and had to be a mix herself. Going by the brilliance of the scales I would say you have no black in you; mostly blue and green with a little red and less white. Normally the children of such mating are one color, but once in a long while they pick up two tones, even less often are three tones, You have five and they are very prominent including a gold streak down the center."

"Will this upset Mother?"

"I do not think so, but we are about to find out."

We walked into the kitchen. I said, "Hi Mommy." But there was no enthusiasm in my voice and she noticed immediately.

She came over to me and picked me up and sat down with me on her lap. "What's wrong sweetheart?"

I threw my arms around her neck and hugged. I could not talk in fear she would reject me.

The Wizard said, "He is worried that when you find out what he is you won't want him."

"I will always want him. He is my son."

The Wizard said, "His mother was a Rainbow Dragon."

"So. I've known that for months."

I pulled my face back long enough to see into her eyes and went back to hugging her.

The Wizard asked, "How did you know that and why did you not tell me?"

She said as if it was only natural, "A Mother checks on her son in the middle of the night to ensure everything is proper. He reverts to his dragon self when sleeping. And, how is it you don't know? For goodness sake, both books know. He has fallen asleep at his desk many times."

She peeled me off her. "I need to get back to baking. You are my son. Did you think I would take a full human as my son?

For goodness sakes no. You, dear, have wonderful colors. Now go along and study. Be good."

"I will Mommy." I left.

She looked over at her brother. "You may not be bigoted, and he may not be bigoted, but I am. If he did not have prominent green in his scales I would not even think of him as a son. However, I have studied his hide, the Green is slightly more prominent than any other color. And, as no Greens are claiming him, he is mine."

"I need to check him for immunities. You know the issues multicolor can have."

"Please do so. But do not harm him."

The Wizard stood up, "Of course not."

The Wizard walked in as Melina was teaching me to speak Elvin. He said, "Well, that is an issue I can remove from my long list of issues." I looked up at him. "Your Mother has a need for a child and you happen to be mostly Green. She claims you as hers because she is the only Green around to raise you."

I said, "Good. I claim her because she is wonderful."

He smiled, "I need to do a few tests on you. Multicolor Dragons sometimes have issues with health."

I asked, "Are they going to hurt?"

"Some are."

"Oh darn."

He smiled, "Come with me."

We got up and went to see the Cleric.

Three days later we returned to the library. I went directly to bed. Some tests can make you sick and no amount of healing is going to help me forget the heaves. Mommy was right there comforting me and chewing out her brother. She eventually calmed down and asked, "Well, what did you find out?"

The Wizard said, "Healthy as a rock. No issues caused by birth or any other issues. He is immune to lightning, fire, and cold. Acid does normal damage and so does sound. For some strange reason, poison does not work on him correctly. Normal poison does not work on him at all, and supernatural poison makes him ill but does not do any harm. We tried a supernatural poison that should have drained his strength and it did nothing. We were shocked. You were correct. He is mostly Green Dragon and is developing the breath weapon to prove it."

She exclaimed, "You did not force him to use his breath weapon at this age, did you?"

"Of course not. We took samples from the liquid sacks. We checked his blood. Please, explain to me how he can be your son."

She smiled, "We have grown to like each other. And...."

He said, "NO! He is your blood son."

She angrily said, "That is not possible. I have never had a son. My egg was stolen from me. I am a purest. I have never mated with another color."

"No, but you have changed shape and mated with a human; haven't you, sister dear?"

She looked long and hard at her brother, "You know that story. He found me beat up and dying after fighting that Black. He nurtured me back to health. He was a good human and I fell in love."

The Wizard said, "About six foot three or four, plate armor, blond, chiseled looks almost exactly like your son. A three-foot scar running down his left side."

Her eyes went wide. "It cannot be. That was my lover. But, where would Mark get the colors?"

The Wizard said, "I wondered the same thing. After doing some magical checking I found out that his father was three-quarters dragon. He hid it well. Mark is more Dragon than Human; that is why he cannot retain his human shape when he falls asleep."

She said, "My baby. My own has come back to me. Does he know?"

The Wizard said, "You talked to your egg a lot. He knew the moment he heard your voice."

"Why didn't he tell us?"

"He did not want to scare you away."

She said in a huff, "As if." She came up to my bedroom and there I was in Dragon form curled up around my pillow.

Her brother followed her. He whispered, "The boy's small for his age."

She whispered back, "He is not a fighter, he is a Sorcerer."

"Wizard."

She looked at her brother and said kindly, "A little of both then."

One of the Gods watching said, "They know."

Another said, "He is needed or they all will die. We must protect him so he can save them."

In another part of the Universe another God, an evil God, was watching and said to no one, "If he lives."

FINDING A HERO

I TELEPORTED TO THE PLATFORM AT THE DECSPILE castle and was greeted by the watch captain, three wizards, and two clerics. There were plenty of guards also. Always, when there is a party, protections are at the highest.

The Captain said, "Hello Princess David. Welcome."

I stepped off the platform and turned to look at the Captain with a frown.

The Captain said, "Don't be upset with me. Your father has not rescinded that order and your running away just reinforced, in his mind, that you are a coward and a sissy."

I looked over at the Wizard. "And you?"

He smiled at me and said, "I must comply with your father's wishes; however, the Captain is incorrect. You are a Queen now."

I asked, "Why did your King invite me to this party?"

The Cleric said, "I believe he said to your Mother, and I quote, 'Invite our youngest child, sweetheart. We can have some fun at her expense if she is fool enough to show up.'"

The Wizard looked at me closer. "You've changed, Queen David. You're still tiny, but there is something about your look that says dangerous. I must ask you, are you a threat to any member of the royal family of Decspile?"

I said, "I am no more a threat than any King, or Queen, that this royal family highly upsets. Besides, your King has something wrong. First, I am not the youngest, just the smallest. And second, I no longer claim them as my relatives. He is not my father and she is not my mother."

I started to walk over and get in line for the announcements, but the Captain said, "You did not answer the Wizard. Are you a threat?"

I said, "Only if threatened. I have a right to protect myself."

The Watch Captain said, "If physically threatened, not for verbal abuse."

I said, "I am not who I use to be, Captain. Pass the word. I verbally abuse back even if it is your foolish King. Or worse, I may just go along with this insane foolishness and embarrass them more than they could possibly harm me."

I stood in line thinking back on the past. All my life I have been treated badly by my family because I am small and easy to pick on. My size has always been an issue with my father and therefore he trained my two older brothers but refused to teach me combat or anything else as I am considered too fragile. I had to hide from both brothers to keep from being beaten, tied up, and left in some dark hole, clubbed until unconscious and then urinated on, again. Some favorite things for them were placing me in a metal box and setting me on the roof where the summer sun could heat the sides and air making it nearly impossible to breathe and constantly burning my body, and using me to slate their lust in every way possible. The last thing they did was get my sisters to dress me like a baby girl and then shattered every bone in my hands and feet so I would have to crawl for help, and then they left me in the tunnels under the castle. I could not climb the ladders to get out and nearly starved to death before a servant found me weak and dying of blood loss from the rat bites.

My sisters were worse. They would find me and sit on my tummy until I pasted out from lack of air. Then they would fully dress me up as a girl doll. Cut my hair so it was in a female fashion, or glue on a wig, tie my hands behind me and parade me around so all the family could have a laugh. They even took me shopping for dresses throughout the city several times, but that was after the Wizard's spell. They had the royal Wizard place a "Control" spell on me and I had to follow his orders. The orders were simple, dress like my sisters want, play as they want, and act happy about it, including telling my father I want to be a little girl.

When they took me before father in his court during full attendance with all the dukes and barons present, Father was discussed and pronounced that I was to be addressed as Princess David from now on and that I was no longer his son.

Many times I tried to tell him what they were doing and he never listened. He would sit on his big throne and always take their side. I would beg him to use the stone of truth. All he had to do to know the truth was place his hand on the stone while I, or the others, were talking. It was right there imbedded into the arm of his thrown. He never did and I came to understand that he knew the truth and did not care. At one point he got mad and sent me to the Cleric and the dungeon. He ordered my privets beaten hard for thirty days straight, three times a day. Then at the end of the thirty days, they were to beat them completely off since I would never need them. The Cleric was to ensure I did not pass out or bleed to death. I was seven. At just over eight years old I got my chance to escape.

There are several protected places in the castle and city where you can hide from magical scrying. Everyone would be searching those places. However, I figured they would not even start looking for a couple of days. I snuck out at night through the city and onto the road. Three days later I was deep into the northern forest where the forest druid protects from everything, and to protect himself he has made it so no one can scry into the deep parts of the forest. No one would believe an eight-year old would hide in the depths of that dark forest. They would not look for me there. And, if I died, it would be better than living at home.

I took nothing with me except clothes the servants tossed out as far too old and warn. I left a note pointing out that I took nothing and was not the thief my brothers continuously claimed I was. While in the forest I made friends with an old druid and told him my story. He gave me a ring for Custodia, Essentia, and it masked my whereabouts from the Wizard magically scrying on me. He taught me spells, a forest Wizard did the same, and a Dragon taught me divine spells. I practiced constantly. Within three years I could do fifth circle spells in three disciplines.

I killed an evil black dragon and won its treasure. Not my fault. I was running away and got cornered. I had to fight and got very, very lucky. Now I am rich, have my own books on spells, and many artifacts.

I knew my father's people ruined the North-Western section of Decspile. They used it all up and made it worthless. Few things grow in that depleted land. Father, and Queen Linda of Harden, who owned a small portion of the surrounding mountains, put it all up for sale. At the auction, my representative ensured the land would no longer belong to Decspile or Harden and the owner was not subject to my father (the King) or Queen Linda. Father, King Latale, told everyone that the owner would be his own King and that land would no longer be part of Decspile or Harden. We bought it for only 10 gold a square league. I was now legally a King of over 10,000 square leagues of completely worthless land. They saw my name go down on the documents and laughed.

King Latale asked, "So, he is still alive. I am most displeased. You know where he is hiding?"

My representative said, "No, he came to me and disappeared. I am sure he will be by sometime to pick up the papers."

Of course, I picked up the papers, at night, hidden, invisible, and soundless. I left a message for him to contract with Decspile for someone to dredge their two rivers and the three lakes to make them usable for ships. They paid me two million in gold for the project, which is way underpaid. However, I was not interested in gold. I needed the topsoil off the river bottoms to change my land into a grand garden. In the next three years, I worked on just that and now have the best soil and land on the continent. Last year I planted and everything is growing wonderfully thanks to a God that wanted something from me.

I was now at the front of the line. The announcer normally comes back to us and asks how we want to be announced. Then he goes forward and bangs his staff on the box to get attention. One bang for most, two for important people, and three for royalty. With me, he just looked and then walked up front laughing. No bang just a "May I have your attention. The next person does not rate a bang of my staff. Announcing Queen David the Sissy."

Everyone laughed. I must have been red-faced as I walked out in front of everyone. The laughter continued until I reached the throne. It became very quiet waiting to see what the King would do. Rudely he ignored me for a few minutes and when he finally turned to me he said, "Sweetheart, what are you doing pretending to be a Queen and dressed as a boy? Shame on you."

I said, "Funny, I did not take you for that sort, King Latale. Calling another man sweetheart. Apparently, you still like your young playthings dressed like girls. How many did you kidnap to replace me as your pillow?"

He stood up in a rage, "How dare you!"

I said, "I dare because I can. If you want to play this game, fine with me. I'll play too."

He sat down and said, "Then dress appropriately, Princess."

I looked at him long and hard and then I raised a hand. I was now completely dressed as a Princess. The dress is special and grants a major plus to my looks, but not my charisma. That is already high enough. I was now the most beautiful creature in the kingdom. However, I was still small and people were looking at me as if I were a little female child."

King Latale said, "Much better. After all, with your parts missing we would not want to cheat some lady into thinking you're a man."

I asked, "What parts?"

King Latale smiled, "Your privets that I had beaten completely off."

I said as if it were nothing. "Oh, those. I grew them back."

The Cleric said, "I doubt that. I did a full heal on you and they did not grow back, Princess."

I said, "Fool Cleric, of course not. I had to cut off the skin so that it was an open wound, do a complete regeneration, and a full heal after."

The Cleric said, "That would be more painful than having them beaten off."

"It was."

King Latale asked, "Who did you get to do this for you? I thought I made it very clear that no one should help in any way."

"True, King Latale. You are one of the evilest creatures I have ever met. However, it is your party so I will answer, though you deserve it not. I did it myself."

King Latale said, "That is impossible. You would have to be very magically talented to accomplish such a feat."

The Wizard said, "He teleported here without help, changed his clothing magically without help in an area protected from such. He is talented in the arts, Sire."

I said, "Far more than you would think. Enough to have killed a gargantuan Black Dragon by myself. It got in my way." I did not have to tell them I was running away when it got in my way. King Latale's hand was on the stone so he knew I was telling the truth.

He said, "Then you gained in power beyond your siblings. I suppose you came to kill a few."

I said, "I have no intention of harming anyone. I have forgiven you all a long time ago, I have not forgotten, and I do not claim you as relatives, but I have forgiven."

King Latale asked, "Then why are you here?"

I nonchalantly said, "You invited me."

He asked, "Knowing how you will be treated, why are you still here, PRINCESS!?"

"To keep up to date on what is happening with my neighbors. After all, I am a King even if you refuse to say so. A King needs to stay informed."

King Latale said as he waved a hand in dismissal, "Well, go over with the rest of the Princesses, Sissy. There are far more important people waiting."

I said while moving over, "Ah, dismissal from your presence is a joy to my ears."

Again he stood up saying, "How dare you!"

I said as I took my place, "Oh, sit down fool."

He started to say something else, but the announcer took that time to announce the next person.

Only one of the Princesses said anything to me and she was probably one of the loveliest Princesses in the lands. No brains, but very pretty. She snidely whispered to me, "You have such a tiny waist. How does your corset feel, Princess?" She giggled and so did the rest, except Princess Tabitha.

I answered, "My corset is not tight like yours. I do not have to pull in eight inches of pure fat."

Several girls choked, one fainted, and three laughed.

Her eyes went wide in anger.

King Latale got upset and said, "What is going on?"

I said, "Nothing, King Latale. This idiot asked me how my corset felt and I told her it..." She quickly put a hand over my mouth so I bit her hard. "As I was saying. I told her mine was not tight because I did not have to hold in eight inches of pure fat as she does." I said, "Cleric!" and pointed to her hand.

King Latale said, "Why don't you do it yourself?"

I said, "Fine." I turned to her and pointed at her hand saying, "Want that healed, Fatso?"

She fainted. I healed her and then said, "Corset must be too tight." She got back up and tried to slap me. I am very quick and ducked while pulling her forward. She slapped my oldest sister. That started a fight that I magically shifted away from.

King Latale looked around and saw me. "Still running from a fight I see. You started it, at least you could do is stop it."

I smiled, "I left to keep from killing anyone. However, if you want me to stop it I surely can." I raised my hand and did a mass paralyze. Then I walked back over and picked each off the floor and set them up straight. I released several Queens that then helped. Then I removed the paralyzing after saying. "Continue with this madness and King Latale will be upset. Shame on you making such a fuss over her excess weight."

One of the girls said, "I wish we did not have to wear them, corsets I mean."

I said, "Here, let me help." I raised my hand again and removed every bit of magic made especially for making people look better and every corset in the room (except mine). Dress buttons popped, laces broke, and clothes no longer fit. Women were screaming, fainting, and angry. "Isn't that better? Now you can be yourself without being nearly cut in half. Oh, by the way, I sent the hated garments back to Princess Hellen's room for the Princesses and back to Queen Daphne's room for anyone over eighteen. I have no need for them."

There was a mass exodus. Duke George started toward me and was drawing his sword. His wife and daughters are all a little overweight and this was a disaster for him as he was hoping to marry a few off. I raised a hand and in it was a sword of pure blackness. The evil radiating off it made the air thick and difficult to breathe. "You want to fight me, Duke George? I would be happy to entertain you in this folly." Then I did a couple of fast moves that made the fat man back up. He looked at the King for help as he sheaved his sword.

King Latale yelled, "You dare to draw sword in my throne room!"

He was looking at me and I knew he meant me but I said, "Well, are you not going to answer your King, Duke George? You did draw first and I was only defending myself."

King Latale said, "You egged him on."

I turned to him and said, "King Latale, I am simply treating everyone the same as they are treating me. Everyone laughed at me because of you, so I treated you badly and the rest of them also. As long as I am treated badly, so shall you be treated. Treat me nicely and I will do the same in return. Ignore me completely and I will not do the same because I want to know what is going on with my neighbors. This is my best chance of finding out. I am not leaving. How I act is up to you and the rest of these people. What is interesting is you don't like two minutes of what you put me through for eight years. I expected more from a King."

The Cleric exclaimed, "That blade is Evil!"

I said, "That blade is nothing compared to some of the resources I have at my call. It is only a soul destroyer."

People started to back up and a few started to leave. Princess Tabitha, who was not wearing a corset before, came up to me. To me, she said, "Put that away, please." I did. She turned to the King. "It is true, King Latale, that this young man did not verbally attack anyone unless they verbally attacked him first. It is also true that he did not physically attack anyone unless they attacked him. And then, he was willing to heal that person. Every single man here should be thanking him for letting them see which girls were fooling them. Most are far fatter and far less lovely than their clothes and magic items show. Did you not notice their magic, items that enhance their looks, also became disabled?" She turned to my eldest brother. "How does it feel to know what that woman is going to look like when you get married and you wake up next to her the following morning?" She turned back to the King. "Get him drunk at the wedding, he'll need it that night. He did you all a favor and that is why Duke George is so upset. Tell me, Duke. How much of the King's tax money did you spend on those magical items?"

Princess Tabitha is a naturalist. Always has been. On a scale of one to ten, she is eight or nine. However, the others, with the help of magic, are tens plus and so she is never looked at. She is the most intelligent Princess in all the kingdoms. And, in my opinion, the best looking.

Duke George became angry again and his hand on sword started toward her. My clothing instantly changed to Kingly robes, my weapons were at my side and a staff of great power was in my off-hand. I stepped between then and decked him before that sword could be drawn. He fell back and slid several feet. I said in a near growl, "No one ever touches Tabitha. Do not threaten her again."

The surprise and shock on everyone's face was near comical. Including Princess Tabitha's face. No one had ever stuck up for her in her entire life except direct family. I just did with a possessiveness that rivaled true love.

She placed a hand on my arm and said, "It's alright, King David." I blushed and changed back into a Princess.

King Latale exclaimed, "You have changed." As he looked down at the three hundred pound man I just decked. "Get up George. Twice you drew a sword, or started too. Don't do it again. We will have a little talk about where the gold is going too, as you keep asking for more to help our people." Then he turned to me. "Well, should you not be off with the other Princesses?"

I smiled, "Sure." and then turned and left.

The men in the room started arguing and the few women that were left started heading toward the rooms where their peers would be.

Princess Tabitha followed me to Princess Helen's room. I walked right in. There were instant screams. My sister yelled, "Get out!"

Sorry Princess Helen, but your father told me to come be with you and the rest of the Princesses. Not my preferred choice, but this is his house." The girls were in varied states of undress. However, thanks to my sisters I had seen it hundreds of times before and could care less.

They took turns blocking my view from the ones changing until they realized I was not watching. One girl was upset that I would not look at her. With nothing on, she walked up to me and said, "Note; I am not using anything magical, Princess."

Without looking at her I said, "I could easily put the physical enhancements the Cleric did back in place. Let's see, the nose and your breasts. Must have been painful having those enlarged and firmed."

She backed off saying, "Don't you dare!"

I went back to talking with Tabitha. "So, how have you been?"

"I am doing fine, David. You seem to have had an interesting life lately."

"Yes, well; after running away things instantly became far better."

"Where did you run too?"

"The dark forest."

It immediately became quite.

Tabaita said, "That was very brave of you."

I chuckled, "I was trying to kill myself. I failed."

One of the younger girls decided to have some fun with me and turned to me to get her corset laced. "Well? You removed it. Please lace it back up."

I said, "As you wish. You know, the biggest issue with corsets is that they tend to press in on the ribs. That bruises that area making it painful to wear. However, if the corset did not do this then the pain would be cut considerably." I magically changed her corset and then placed it around her waist. I laced it completely closed and she was still comfortable. "How's that?"

"You need to close it all the way or my dress will not fit."

I smiled, "It is closed all the way. Check the mirror."

She walked over to the mirror and exclaimed, "I don't believe it. How is this possible? This does not hurt."

I said, "Don't tell your mother or she will get a smaller one."

Princess Helen said, "Remember the Corset we made you wear?"

One of the others asked with a giggle, "Was it tight?"

Princess Helen said, "Too small for his little sister. It brought his tiny waste in six inches. At four inches his lips turned purple. We had to wait until he could breathe again before bringing it in another inch. At that point, we had to wait an hour before closing it completely and locking it on."

One of the other girls said, "So he knows first hand what we go through."

Princess Helen said, "Sort of."

Tabitha asked, "Sort of?"

I said sadly, "They had the Wizard place a spell on me making me do whatever they wanted including wearing whatever they wanted and acting happy about it in front of others. They made me beat the inside of the corset with sting weed and nettles until the inside was completely covered and then they made me put it on and hold it up as they laced it. It was a full-body corset that went from neck to nearly my knees. Then they beat me so the nettles would enter into my body deeply. Then they tied me up and gagged me and placed me in a metal box in the sun so I would sweat. That way the sting weed would do its worst. They left me there all day. Then they dressed me up very fancy and made me act happy as they took me in front of everyone. I tried to fight it, but the magical domination was too strong. They had me play dolls with an evil little girl they call my sister. She made me stand up and deeply curtsy while wearing that corset to anyone that passed, while swishing the dress and saying, 'Hi, I'm sissy David.' I had to lick my lips if it was male. I broke four ribs trying to deeply curtsy wearing that corset and nearly bled to death before she had a Cleric heal me. I had to continue this for twelve hours. I broke my ribs twenty-six more times. And, during the entire time, I had to smile and act happy. Many of your parents were there and they think I'm a sissy because of that and other times their royalty forced me to dress up and be happy."

Princess Helen said, "Ah, but that wasn't the best thing we did to you."

Tabitha exclaimed, "BEST!"

"Oh yes, remember the special box, Sissy?"

I looked dejected, "How can I help but remember. I have a perfect memory."

She said, "We made a box that looked like a dog with no tail. We stripped her, placed her in the tight box with one hole on each end so she could eat and go to the restroom like a dog. Then we had the box taken down to the front gates for dog guard duty. They let her go three weeks later."

I saw the way everyone was taking this in and noticed they were appalled, sad, and a bit angry so I added to the fire that was building. "That is not the worst thing you did to me. The guards followed your orders precisely; even your King and Crown Price took advantage of my situation. Nearly every boy and man in this castle took advantage. Still, that was bad, nightmarish in fact, but not your worst. I can take the pain, goodness knows I have had my share. However, you wanted to ensure the entire country knew and thought me a sissy. For two years you dressed me as a baby girl with the fanciest dresses and very short. My diapers were always showing and I begged you not to do this. In privet I could beg and cry, in public, I had to act happy against my will. You took me everywhere in the city, country, visiting other countries, all with the orders that I could only say googoo and baba. I had to smile, giggle, laugh, and act like I loved the teasing and torment. At night when we returned I would cry and beg you not to do it anymore, but you constantly did. Where ever I went I had to crawl and I always had to use my diapers. I could not complain. I hid as much as possible, but being on my hands and knees made me continue to look like a plaything. My brothers were worse and made each encounter extremely painful and or humiliating. They have grand imaginations. After that you let me grow up some. I could walk. Now I had to smile and happily curtsy and say thank you after each torment. I was also made to lick clean the privy seats. I was used in ways you cannot imagine, and I had to act happy about it. Beatings, burnings, smothering, and I had to look happy, curtsy, and thank my tormentors. Did you know I was kidnapped?"

Princess Helen asked, "No, when?"

"The week before my eighth birthday. They demanded a ransom or I would die very painfully. Father sent back a message saying. 'Go ahead and kill the sissy.' They sent back one of my ears. Father laughed at the message and sent back, 'You just made the sissy even more worthless.' They had their Cleric regenerate my ear. I begged then not to send me back, but they sent me back just to upset the King. I hid as best as I could down in the sewers coming up for only scraps of food. But, you found me and turned me over to the King. He ordered my privets destroyed over a thirty day period for trying to fool him. He refused to use the stone to know the truth."

Princess Helen said, "So, you ran away."

"I tried to get someone in the castle to kill me. They would not. I jumped off the tallest tower and the wizard, set by the King to ensure I didn't kill myself to get out of my shame, stopped my fall. I then decided to leave. I did not have to run away. I had to escape. How long before anyone looked for me? Weeks?"

"Going by the date on your note, only eight days."

One of the girls exclaimed, "Your brother was missing for eight days and no one cared to look or ask!?"

She retorted, "If I or anyone of my siblings, except Princess David, were to go missing for more than ten minutes people would be scrambling to find us. For Princess David, not even maids would have anything to do with him or his tiny closet of a room. The only reason we looked at all was to show him what we did with his smashed prick and ball skin." She reached behind her and picked up a mask. "We were going to fix this mask to her face so she could never take it off."

I raised a hand and the mask went up in flames.

She said, "That belonged to me. It was a prize possession."

I asked, "You want me to do the same to your breasts. I will cherish that mask always."

Her eyes went wide, "No!"

"Then don't complain. Consider that I just recovered the only thing I left behind. Thank you for keeping it for me."

A girl on the bed said, "If they did even a small portion of this to me. They would be dead. I would find a way. If I were powerful I would be here for killing."

"I am above them and better than them. I forgave them years ago. I cannot forget, but I can forgive."

"Then why did you remove our corsets and magic. That was pure mean!"

"I plan on treating you the same as you treat me. If you are mean I will be far meaner. For example, if Princess Helen tried to put that mask on my face, she would have found her face completely removed with just a little hole for a mouth and ears. What would be left would give a seasoned fighter nightmares."

"Father would have you killed."

"He could try."

There was a Sorceress in the far corner being invisible. She used a few spells to check me out and I allowed them. I looked directly at her and asked, "Here to watch me?"

Everyone looked in that direction but they saw nothing. She dispelled the invisibility. "I am here to watch over Princess Tabitha and Lady Joann."

"Then watch, but stop with the spells."

"I have found out all I need to know."

Princess Helen ordered, "What did you learn?"

The Sorceress said, "I am not under your father's command so shut up foolish child."

"How dare you." Princess Helen stood up as if to slap the woman.

Power nearly erupted from the woman and my ex-sister was slammed hard and fell to the floor in pain. "Do not ever challenge me, child of evil. I am not someone you or your father can push around." She looked over at me expectantly and smiled when she saw the lack of care in my face. "I see you do not care what happens to this fool either. You are acting much differently than with Princess Tabitha."

I said, "Princess Tabitha did not laugh at me and she stood up for me against King Latale. I would protect her with my life." I turned back to the girls, "As I was saying. Treat me bad and I will treat you much worse. Treat me good and I will treat you very well. I figure that is reasonable."

One girl said, "Please don't take this wrong, you make a very lovely girl. Prettier than most of us, but why are you dressed as a girl if you are so powerful?"

"This is King Latale's house and land. As long as I am here, and until someone can talk him out of this foolishness, I will comply with this stupidity; however, the way I am going to act is still 'treat me bad and I will treat you much worse.' He is treating me bad. I suggest he never show up on my land. He will not like being a Queen in the silliest frilly gowns and tightest corsets that cannot come off."

Many giggled. The sorceress asked, "How do you feel about Queen Linda?"

I said, "I noted that she did not laugh at me. I also noted that she was appalled at the way King Latale was treating me. Did she not whisper to her children, "It is apparent we are in a den of evil, trust no one."

"Yes, she did."

Princess Helen exclaimed, "We are not evil!"

I said, "Really. Sorceress, did you not do a check on alignments when you came in. What did you find out, if you would please?"

She said, "Most here are not evil or good. They tend to conform to whatever they need to survive. Princess Tabitha, Lady Joann, and you are goodly in nature as well as a few others. Three are evil. Princess Helen is one of them."

Princess Helen's mouth tried to say something in her defense.

I added, "I did the same check and heightened to get past any artifacts that may be in play. Princess Helen is borderline, just into being evil. The two she runs around with are fully evil. It's rubbing off on her. King Letale is Evil and getting worse. Queen Linda is not evil yet, but close. The rest of that family is evil. They did not start out that way, but their Father did not put a stop to what they were doing and now they are evil, or becoming evil, by their own deeds." Everyone started talking at once.

It took a moment to quiet them down. I pulled an artifact from my dress pocket. I gently tossed it to Princess Helen saying, "The one with the ball has the floor." The ball in undetectable as being magical.

She held onto it and the magic entered into her. She said, "I am sorry for all I did to you. Thank you for forgiving me." Then she started to cry. She handed the ball to her friend who started to say something but broke down crying also. The evilest one of the three took the ball and said, "I will not..." She broke down crying.

I floated the ball back to me and looked at them and then at the ball and then back at them. I put the ball away. The Sorceress knew what I did and smiled, but she said nothing.

It was time. We headed back out toward the throne room. When we entered the Sorceress went to report to Queen Linda.

Whispering she said, "My Queen, if he plays ball, catch it and toss it to King Latale when the chance comes. Trust me." Then she disappeared.

All of the Princesses returned to the throne room at about the same time the Queens returned. They lined up on one side and we on the other, just down from the Princes' and Kings. King Latale asked, "Well! Is that over with? Are we all back together?"

Queen Linda said while giving me a dirty look, "I believe so."

King Latale said, "Good. Princess David. Are you finished disrupting my party?"

Princess Helen said, "Quote from David, Father. "Treat me bad and I will treat you much worse. Treat me good and I will treat you very well. I figure that is fair.' Unquote."

I smiled up at him on his big thrown. Him being so high and big and my being so small does not intimidate me anymore.

He said, "Very well. Let it be known that the way you treat people is the way you will be treated. Except me." He looked at me very hard and said, "Treat me bad, sissy, and you will pay."

I said, "I have no wish to treat anyone bad. However, your treatment of me is painful so the repercussions will be just as painful. Though they are not physical so I will keep mine to verbal only. It will be interesting to see who is the most intelligent with our banter. This is your house so I will comply with your mandated dress code for me. Don't visit my home or you will find yourself dressed like a Queen."

That received several giggles.

"If that were to happen it would be war, sissy."

"Then it would be war, old Fart."

He sat down smiling. Prince Sal, my ex-brother, made the mistake I needed. He pulled his dagger and chucked it at my head while saying, "You dare threaten the King, you foolish little piss ant!"

The dagger I caught and tossed aside. I snapped my fingers and he disappeared. I yelled, "DON'T MOVE." Everyone stopped. "Piss Ants are difficult to see and you could step on him."

The King said in tones of hate, "Bring him back. NOW!"

I said, "I cannot unless I can see him. You will need to find him first. Besides, he tried to smack me in the head with the butt of his dagger." I pretended to look through my clothes for something and then produced the Ball. I said a few words and the ball glowed. I said, "Find the closest Piss Ant. It turned around until one marked side pointed toward the thrown. I said, "I can't move."

King Latlae said, "What, WHY!"

I said, "Because the spell I did works on me too. If I dispel it everyone's feet can move. All it would take is to lean a little the wrong way. I am pretty sure the coward ran for what appeared to be cover. That could be under your chair or the edge of a shoe."

The King asked, "Will that ball work for me?"

"Yes, now that the spell is on it."

The Wizard said, "Let my feet loose and I can find him."

The King said, "Shut up. I have my hand on the stone. He is telling the truth. Toss me that ball, David."

He called me David, how nice. I tossed him the ball. He caught it. "Find me the nearest Piss Ant." The ball pointed to under his chair. He put his hand down. "Sal, climb up on my hand."

I knew that Sal did as told, though he seldom does. The King watched and when the Prince was completely in his palm he said, "David, release the spell, get over here and fix this, please."

I was shocked. He said please. I dismissed the spell and walked over. I said, "Place your hand on the arm of your chair, that way he is sitting on your hand vice breaking your arm with his weight."

King Latale moved his hand. I did the reverse spell and he instantly appeared.

King Latale said, "Get off my hand, boy! Take this ball back to Princess David and pick up your dagger."

He took the ball and walked it over to me and then he picked up his dagger and returned to the King's side.

The ball had stopped glowing so it did its work. I walked back to my place and faced the King. He was about to chew me out but then it hit him. "Sal, you brought that on yourself. I will have no attempt at retaliation. Do you understand?"

"Yes, Father. I understand." The tone in his voice said it all. He understood and was not going to comply. Hopefully, the ball's magic would kick in quickly.

King Latale said, "I don't know how it happened, but let me put that another way. You are fuming at probably the most powerful wizard ever known. Maybe near demigod level. He just did a spell that trapped everyone in the castle including the Sorceress that Queen Linda brought, our Master Wizard, and the Grand Master from the University. Our esteemed Cleric was stuck and so were people outside in a wide area. I could see them through the window. Even the horses could not move. He did it without word or jesters. Grand Master, how high a level was that spell?"

"Far higher than I can do even without the enhancing additions."

Everyone was looking at me. I said nothing.

Sal said, "He is a coward so I suppose it would be a waste of time to challenge him to a fight hand to hand."

I smiled, "I would be happy to fight you without magic. I'll be wearing a dress. Are you sure you want to be beaten by a Sissy?"

"I'd like to give it a try."

"Very well. Have a Cleric stand by for healing you." I walked over to the center of the room and motioned for the others to give us some space.

King Latale said to Sal, "I have a feeling this is a bad idea."

I said, "Don't worry, King Latale. I told you I would not take life at this time. He will be broken up fairly badly though. I will heal him if your Cleric is not capable."

Princess Tabitha said, "Men! This does not need to happen."

I looked at her. "Do you prefer I do not fight him?"

She said, "Yes."

I still needed to stall to give the ball time. I raised a hand and a tree trunk three feet thick and ten feet long was in the room. I motioned for two big Guards to lift it. They tried and could not. Several others tried and could not. Sal came down and tried and could not budge it. I said, "Wizard. I know you checked. Is there any magic on me besides the clothes?"

"No."

"King Latale please place your hand on the stone." He did. "The spell I put on the ball is over, my clothes do not affect me in any fighting ability. They do not increase my strength or speed."

The King said, "That was true."

I said, "Wizard, please keep checking me."

"I am."

I walked over to the tree, lifted it as if it were nothing, and twirled it over my head so fast the wind blew the hair on most people enough they had to use their hand to control it. Then I stopped it and broke it into six pieces with slams from my hand. I turned to Sal and said, "Tabitha does not want me to near kill you this day so I will beg your forgiveness for turning you into what you called me." My look changed to burning hate and I added, "This once." The Ball had its needed time.

Sal looked on in shock and quickly said, "Apology accepted."

I raised a hand and with a shutter, the six parts turned into firewood and flew across the room to stack near the fireplace. I walked back over to the Princesses and stood waiting.

Tabitha said as she took my arm, "It must have been difficult to beg his forgiveness."

I said back, "You have no idea how hard."

The King said, "I think it's time for dinner."

We were led into the ballroom where dinner was just being served. Everyone looked around for their place-marks. Mine was found at the Princess table. I sat down straightening my dress after one of the servants scooted my chair in. All three of my sisters were on the other side of the table. Tabitha was right next to me. First good luck on my part. Conversation and food started going around after the Cleric said blessings.

Boys were a big topic of discussion, but undermining it all was fear. Decspile is the biggest country and its army is very large. No one has had the guts to upset Decspile for a century. Except me. The conversation changed to me.

Lady Dila asked, "King David, how is it you are not afraid of Decspile? The rest of us are."

My sisters listened intently. I said, "I have the ability to destroy their army if they attack me. I cannot and will not attack them in their country, but I can retaliate if they attack me and completely destroy any army that enters my land without permission."

One asked with scorn, "How is that possible?"

I smiled, "Only a fool gives away his abilities."

My youngest sister said, "It is a worthless land so who would care." Then she went back to talking with the girl next to her. She pointed my direction every now and then and they laughed.

The dinner was very good. I, of course, checked for poisons and other issues several times and ate little. Hard to eat with a corset on anyway.

I noticed that one of the Girls looked dejected and was eating even less than I. Looking around I saw that all the girls from

Harden were eating slowly and seemed sad. Two of my sisters seemed to be rubbing something in, but I did not know what. The now Good Aligned sister was trying to stop them. I asked, "Tabitha, what are the three demons rubbing in. They seem to be rubbing something in and the ladies from Harden seem to be sad."

Tabitha started to say something but Princess Lil (my second sister) butted in. "They are having a difficult time finding food for their people." She pretended a poorly faked sadness, "I am told some are starving. We, of course, have plenty of food. They could buy some, but father is holding back most of it due to the bad weather."

Tabitha said, "The price they are charging for food is too much. We cannot afford to feed our people even without a 200 percent tax increase."

Lady Julie said, "King Latale is trying to force us to give him our southern port. Our only way to the sea."

Tabitha said, "We would not be here at all except King Latale threatened to stop shipment on the little we did buy."

I smiled inside but kept my face looking sad. "Sounds like something King Latale would do. How long do you have to stay?"

Tabitha said, "For the entire three days."

I asked, "What else is going on?"

A Dwarf princess said, "We are in the same boat. Food is very hard to find. Now that they ruined the lands you purchased even Decspile is having problems."

The Elf Princess confirmed with a nod when I looked her direction.

Tabitha said, "Decspile is having problems, but they are using those problems to starve the rest of us. We have kept with the treaty, but they are finding ways around it to threaten us and take our lands. Without food, they will get it too."

Two of my sisters were smiling, one was crying.

I glanced up at the head table and Father did not look so happy. I said to myself, "Perhaps plans will change."

Dancing was after dinner and I had a grand time dancing with all the Princesses, except my sisters, I left them alone. Boys cannot dance with boys, but no one thinks twice about girls dancing with girls. We had a grand time and I used that time to lay a plan. You see, I have lots of food on my lands.

When dancing with the Elvin Princess I whispered, "I have an answer to your food problem. At midnight, have your Mother teleport to the old Elvin Tower on my northern border. I know your Wizard knows the place. Tell no one, not even your Father."

When dancing with the Dwarf I did the same. When dancing with Tabitha I said, "I have an answer to your food problem. Tell the sorceress to bring the Queen to this place at midnight. Warn her to tell no one. Please come with them." I placed the spot in her mind knowing that would be enough for the Sorceress and I said no more.

We had a grand time after that until about midnight when several went to bed early. I said my goodbyes and teleported away. King Latale offered me my old room. He said, "We haven't changed a thing."

I said, "I think I will teleport home for the night. If I remember correctly it is still set up as a lock you in the nursery for a big baby."

He laughed as I left teleporting to the Old Elvin Tower.

Shortly several people teleported in and checked the place for traps. They walked around me saying, "Pardon me, King David, need to check for traps and ambushes."

I smiled, "Check all you want."

They did and then disappeared. The Elvin Queen came first with the Princess.

I welcomed then and let them know Queen Linda was coming and the Dwarven Queen. I had sent a message to the Pixy Queen and the Fairy Queen and they both showed up about that time. Then the Dwarf and her daughter, and finally Tabitha and Queen Linda. I hugged Tabitha and then said. "I'm fairly sure they won't believe me. Please Fairy Queen, tell our friends about my worthless land."

She smiled as she sat down on my right shoulder and the Pixy took up the other side.

The Fairy Queen said, "I moved my entire tribe here to this paradise. The 'Worthless Land' has been revised by King David. Who, for some strange reason is wearing a dress."

I said, "Whoops, sorry" and changed into my hunting clothes.

Tabitha's eyes looked over my body differently than before as my hunting clothes showed off my strengths. The Fairy said, "As you know the land was destroyed by King Latale. However, with a lot of magic and hard work, King David changed it into something wonderful. Rivers and streams, forests and orchards, grand lands full of food and all kinds of creatures." She added proudly, "King David loves us and considers us as equals. He shares."

The Pixy added, "That is a rare thing in a human. To love us and treat us as equals. To not hunt us down for pets. When I first met him he had just killed the man that was capturing us. He let us out of the cages and apologized for the evil man. The man had a sign on his wagon, "Pixy dust, made from fresh ground-up pixies."

I had a tear also and said, "These, my friends, understand pain even worse than mine. Pain caused by humans that don't care."

Queen Elowee asked, "We have many pixies and fairies in our forest that have lost their homes because of humans. This paradise; is there enough for all."

I said, "I could feed all of you ten times over. Move your people into my lands and gather. Replant for next year and leave my forests and the lands the Fairies and Pixies are on alone, but otherwise take what you need. I have plenty."

The Dwarven Queen asked, "Why the secrecy?"

I smiled, "First, I want to mess with King Latale a little. Second, I do not trust the other Kings and Queens. They would attack me and I would have to destroy them. I will not allow anyone into my lands that will harm my friends or kick them out of their homes. I am allowing Queen Linda in because I know her people and I know she can and will control them. Besides," I pulled Tabitha into my arms and added, "How could I ever disappoint Tabitha?"

All the Queens smiled including the Pixy and Fairy.

I added, "Send your wizards in tomorrow to check out the lands and see if I am telling the truth. Have them report directly to you and tell no one else. Then you can secretly start moving in and harvesting."

The next day I changed my pants for a dress and teleported back to the Decspile castle. I arrived at the same group that was on duty the previous day. I said, "Hello Gentlemen."

The Captain said, "Hello Princess David. Did you do something to our King?" His hand was not on his sword and he looked pleased for some reason.

I looked puzzled, "Why? Can I change back into pants?"

"No."

"Captain, if I was going to do anything to change your King it would be for me to wear pants. Did you check with the Royal Wizard and Cleric? Has some spell been placed on your King?"

"We checked and there is no spell other than the protections they placed."

I walked off the platform looking even more puzzled, "Then, what is the issue?"

"The Cleric says the King, Crown Prince, and Princess Helen all changed to goodly alignment. Only a God, or an artifact, can do that. I would like to see that ball you carry."

I pulled out a ball and handed it to him. "This one?"

The Captain looked closely at it. "That's the one."

The Cleric tested it for magic. "It seems to be a ball, Captain."

The Captain took out his knife and quickly cut it in two.

I looked upset, "That, Captain, is the only gift of kindness I have ever been given. It is worth more to me than this entire

Kingdom." I took the two pieces and did a mending spell and they combined back together. I bounced it a couple of times. "Do something like that again and we will cross swords." I turned in a huff and left.

The Captain asked, "What do you think?"

The Wizard said, "That was not an artifact. Cutting it in two would have destroyed it fool, and if it was an artifact you and I would be facing an angry God. Don't do that again! As for Princess David, I think he is being honest. He always has been. I also think that putting pants back on would be a top priority and if he was the cause, we would have received orders for the same."

The Cleric said, "We may still. The King is highly upset over what he allowed to happen to his youngest son. Being goodly of nature has changed his look on life considerably."

The Captain said, "Yes, for the better in my opinion. Still, someone is using magic on the royal family. Let them know what we did to test Princess David. He is not the issue. Start looking other places. Nearly everyone here would love for our King to be Goodly aligned. Find out who and how."

I smiled to myself as I teleported the fake ball back to my castle and brought the Grand Ball of Good Alignment back to my pocket. It was truly the first loving gift given me and I would hate to see it destroyed. The Ball's best ability is it cannot be magically detected. It looks, feels, bounces, and checks out as a small ball made from a targor bush.

I did not need to be announced and no one was announced. Instead, people were pointing out where meetings were going on.

I asked, "Where are the Kings discussing issues?"

The guide said, "The Princesses are meeting in the rooms reserved for the Princesses."

I looked at the guide and asked, "Do you like being human?"

"The Kings are meeting in the war room."

"Thank you."

I went to the War room and quietly sat down where I could hear what was going on, but not where they would be disturbed. They saw me and several laughed. The discussion changed at that point for a second.

One King said, "I don't normally allow sissies the chance to listen to men discuss issues they could not possibly comprehend, but in this case, I think it proper to show you what you could never hope to be."

After that, they and their advisors ignored me completely, which was fine with me as I did not know what to intelligently say as I have no training in politics. Servants brought me food and drink fit for a Princess. No strong drink or anything heavily spiced. That also was fine with me as I've never had strong drink or spiced food.

With all the posturing and political niceness, it took hours to figure out what they were talking about, but I finally figured it was the food issue. I did not say a thing. The Elvin King was sitting back saying nothing. I could tell the Dwarf King was arguing for the fun of it; he winked at me twice. Queen Linda had no representative at this position. She would be with the Queens arguing the same thing, but having to say, tell the King this or that. Queen Daphne would have no authority to grant anything. It was a foolish arrangement in my opinion, but men are fools sometimes, and this argument was proving it.

King Latale said, "King Falor, how much of your forest are you willing to give up for a larger food allotment? Queen Elowee took that time to enter. She smiled at me and then motioned for her husband to talk. She whispered in his ear. I could hear as I was magically enhanced. "Falor, my love, I have secured a food source with plenty. We need to leave this place and talk."

Falor asked, "Elowee, you wonderful old Elf, how long to pack?"

"She kissed his cheek, "We are ready and waiting, the children and luggage have already left. It is you, I, and our Wizard."

"Go to the circle and I will be there shortly."

Elowee added, "Tell no one, my Love."

"Understood."

She departed and he returned to the table, "I am most sorry my friends, but something has come up that takes me away." He turned to King Latale and said, "The answer is none." Then he turned and left. It took a moment before that set in.

Advisors were called in and told, "Have our Wizards watch for Elvin army movement." Everyone was anxious except the Dwarf. His wife must have told him last night. It was only minutes before a Dwarven Wizard came in saying for all to hear. "It is confirmed, my King."

The King stood up and said, "Well, got to go. Bye." He left as quickly as his legs would allow while keeping a look of decorum.

Before they could sit back down a page came in to report, "Majesty, Queen Linda, and all her subjects have just departed as well as the Elves and Dwarves. Our Queen is curious."

King Latale said, "Tell her that I said I have no idea unless it is war. Those three may have decided to join together."

The page left as three other Kings got up and decided they had emergencies they needed to attend.

Soon it was only King Latale and me in the room. All had made an excuse to leave; either for preparation for war or thinking that the others may have found food. Many were heading toward Queen Linda's home.

King Latale stood up and asked me, "You wouldn't happen to know what's going on would you?"

"Yes." Then I teleported to the Prince's group.

Both my Brothers were looking to go see the King. I bounced my middle brother the Ball and he took it and smiled as he tossed it between his hands, "What do you want, baby sister? We are busy with men's work."

I pleadingly said, "You never take the time to play ball with me."

He tossed it back to me saying, "We have no time for this!" They both left. I teleported to my Sister's rooms.

They were also alone. I walked in playing like I was trying to bounce the ball, but was having a difficult time. One Sister went behind me while the other was chewing out my eldest Sister for undermining the plan for a land grab. My oldest Sister was now good-aligned, but she was not weak. She stood her ground. They saw me. The youngest smiled, the oldest said, "Watch out, David."

My middle Sister snuck up and took the ball I was bouncing. She and my middle Sister played keep away as I pretended to try and get it back. The youngest tossed it out the fourth story window and I jumped after it. They looked out the window in shock and I was not there. I called the ball to me and teleported to the Queen's rooms.

She was with several maids that she was berating and blaming her failure on. I saw her at the same time she saw me. I called her a few words and threw the ball at her. She grabbed it in one hand while raising the other to cast. I dispelled the casting each time until she let go of the ball, then I called the ball to me as I teleported out. At the old castle, I was greeted by Kings and Queens. I quickly changed into my farming clothes.

Tabitha took my arm and said, "I like the hunter look better."

I changed; what else could I do?

Queen Linda asked, "Did all go as you planned?"

I smiled and pulled out the ball, "All are now goodly aligned. I expect changes to be made slowly, but they are coming. They will need to get their lands in order first."

The Elvin King said, "I recognized the Ball of Goodly Alignment the moment you brought it out. What will you do now?"

"Wait for the changes to take effect. See what happens."

The Dwarf King said, "That was a nasty thing to do to a royal family. However, thank you."

I said, "None of us can afford to have the largest army on the continent run by an evil King. The others will fall into place as they must to survive."

The Old Elf said, "You have food here. I cannot believe you are just going to give it away."

"Who said anything about giving it away! I plan on charging you greatly."

All of their faces screamed that I was in for it so I turned and started to walk down the path ticking off on my fingers, "First, I need a castle staff; second I need someone to decorate; third, I'm not taking charge of creatures, they need to watch over themselves, that will cost them; forth, someone's going to have to build cities, I'm not paying for that all by myself! Goodness sake, no. Fifth, Um, fifth. Well, I have no idea what the fifth should be."

Tabitha took my arm again and said, "Fifth, you need a Queen and I think I know who that will be."

I looked at her saying, "I don't know. She needs to be goodly of character, strong, capable of taking charge and running the kingdom, intelligent, compassionate, beautiful, loving of nature, fair to all creatures, wise, doesn't mind responsibility, and kind. Someone I am in love with who can teach me how to be a King. Where am I going to find someone just like you?"

She smiled, "I don't know. I'll check with Mother."

I chuckled, "You do that. If she says no, I'll put a spell on her and she won't even notice."

She hit my arm, "You will not."

We rounded the corner and there, floating high in the air, was my fairytale castle. I said, "Home."

The Dwarven King exclaimed in a whisper, "You found the floating Elvin city of Fen?!"

The Elvin King asked, "Was the tower intact?"

I knew what he wanted to know. The city was built to defend the tower, the tower was built to defend the Staff of Dolon. I answered, "Yes, King Falor. I own the Staff of Dolon. The greatest

Elvin Druid of all time. I happen to own all eight of the great staff; they came with the tower. How do you think I could become so powerful so quickly and build this paradise? Even still, it was hard work."

Tabitha asked, "Why did you hunt the Tower?"

I stopped and turned to her. "I talked to the Forest Druid. He told me the only way to rid myself of the nightmares of my childhood is to seek the Staff of Forgiveness. He let me know it resides with the Staff of Dolon in the Tower of Dolon, in the fabled City of Fen. I found the staff. I no longer wake up screaming. I can finally sleep. However, he did not tell me that touching the staves contacts the Gods and pours power, knowledge, and experience into me. The Gods told me that you are to be my Queen. They promised me I would never regret it. Now that I have found you, I know they were true."

She kissed my cheek and said, "I have prayed many times for a hero to marry. I have found my hero."

The End

Printed in the United States
By Bookmasters